Bene

CU00855585

Visible

Elizabeth Sheehan

978-1-912328-58-1

Orla Kelly Publishing
Kilbrody,
Mount Oval,
Rochestown,
Cork,
Ireland

To Aisling,

Hope you enjoy,

Liz xx .

To Theo and Olivia…

CONTENTS

TIGERS, TEENS AND AFROS

At 14 years of age, Duke didn't feel particularly special; he was an ordinary boy, living an ordinary life. Nothing unusual ever happened to him…well, until now. He felt weird. Not quite sure what was going on, his mum put it down to his age. But Duke knew that she worried it might be because he was adopted.

That had never bothered him; he loved his mum and his big sister. Recently he had begun to feel strange and he couldn't shake it. Butterflies did a jig in his stomach, feelings rumbled about his belly like a wandering gypsy unable to settle. He had hunches about people and knew when something was going to happen, long before anyone else.

He chose to shove these notions to the back of his mind, not prepared to deal with what they meant. He preferred to go about his business, ignoring the tingling in his hands whenever his sister was scared or the knot in his stomach when trouble was brewing. Ignore, ignore, ignore and it will all go away. That's what's best, and so for right now, he'd just get on with his life. But

1

this plan only worked well up to a point. It was becoming increasingly difficult to ignore the eight-foot-tall tiger that began appearing beside his bed on a daily basis. It was a Wednesday morning, he remembered, when he just couldn't ignore the creature anymore. Duke sat up in his bed, took a mental moment and offered a rather pedestrian, 'Hello.' Then he followed it with, 'Okay dude, I'm not going to ignore the elephant in the room any longer. Like, what's the dealio here, why have you been stalking me and why have you been sitting on my bed for the last week?'

'Well my dear boy, much as I love my pachyderm friends, I am a Tiger in case you hadn't noticed. In fact, I am the personification of the Tigers Eye crystal. We are found quite a bit in South Afrika, but because ah look like ah do, ah have been named the Tigers eye.'

Duke studied the luminous creature now and was rather impressed by his magnificence. He wondered momentarily if he was hallucinating. He looked around his small, messy bedroom as if the answer would suddenly appear; somewhere in the vicinity of the empty laundry basket he never seemed to get his clothes into it, and the old wooden wardrobe, door ajar, as if inviting the said garments in - they never made it. His mum, in a permanent state of exasperation, referred to the space in his room between the door and bed as the 'floordrobe'. Duke just never saw the point of putting anything away, simply to get it out again the next day. It was all way too much effort. As you may have gathered by now, he wasn't a highly-strung individual. Any more chilled and he would need anti-freeze to get going in the mornings.

The perplexed boy sat up straight and looked deep into the tiger's eyes. 'Okay Frosty, let's start this again. Who might you be and what might you be doing here?' he asked directly but with a heavy emphasis on good manners, as if that would make any more sense of this bizarre situation.

'Well my dear boy, as I have said I am the personification of the rather beautiful Tigers Eye Crystal that you have been carrying around with you for weeks now. Don't you recognise me? Can't you feel my vibration? Is it not the same as when you hold that crystal?' asked the rather magnificently self-assured creature.

Duke reached under his pillow and pulled out a striped amber and brown rock, about the size of his palm. It was silky smooth and had the striations and colours of a tiger's coat, which presumably was where the name came from. 'Eh you may have to run that one by me again dude. You are saying that you are this crystal, and somehow I can see you as this giant slightly menacing, in a scary old lady kind of way, tiger?' he asked.

'Well, ah think ah may have to take exception to the 'old lady' reference but essentially that is exactly what I am saying, yes,' the tiger stood, as if there was no more to say.

'Hold up, dude, so like, what are you doing here and why can I see you. Can my sister see you, like if she came in here now, or is it just me?' Questions began flooding into Duke's brain, was he dreaming? What is this really all about? He knew instinctively that this was real on some level, maybe not on a go to the shops and buy a loaf of bread kind of way, but more a 'Star Wars', outer space, other dimensional scenario, 'Okay, so I can see you but others can't, is that what you are saying?'

'Yes,' replied his new roommate.

'And so, what are you doing here?' Duke finally got to the point after the initial confusion.

The tiger leaned in closely now, his magnificent whiskers tickling Dukes face and smiled a Cheshire cat smile, replying, 'Well, that is for you to tell me, don't you think.' The large beast then sat down, slowly and precisely, in the way only a cat can; haunches first, then tail whipping around the front paws, carefully placing them one after the other in front of his heaving furry torso. He turned his magnificent head and began, 'Dearest boy, you have summoned me to your reality and I am here to help in whatever way ah can.'

This explanation, although clear, left the boy even more confused. 'But that rock was just something I found on my way home from school last week. It was just an accident that I came across it. I just liked the colours and thought I'd keep it. It's not as if belonged to anybody now is it?' Duke was speaking more to himself than the Tiger at this point.

'Well, ah like to think there are no accidents, or perhaps maybe we can call them 'happy' accidents, yes? Now, what do you think you need from me? I am very good at helping you focus or giving you confidence. After all, who would not feel confident with me walking by their side?' The large beast offered this last part rather proudly. I can help you feel strong, centred, and grounded.' And with that he held up his fur covered giant right arm and flexed his bicep. Black claws jutted out from the ends of the paws and Duke felt happy he wasn't on the receiving end of them. They looked like they could rip into iron.

Duke looked at the tiger properly now and for the first time really took in his size and might. It's true, there's no way he would feel afraid or intimidated by anyone or anything with this dude around. The tiger's face was broad, with whiskers sprouting out from the top of his eyes and mouth. It was as if his bright orange, black and white fur had been groomed to swirl around, starting at the centre of his forehead and running straight back in thick black lines then out along his brows, trailing down the side of his face and tapering around his chin where his bone structure narrowed; the lines, a secret hieroglyphic map to some mystical crystal energy. He was quite a fabulous creature with his broad glistening pink topped nose, panting in and out as he spoke.

His face had a kind quality, Duke thought to himself, an honest openness to it. It was his eyes that were the most captivating though. There were flecks of hazel and brown, swimming in pools of green and were really quite beautiful, more rounded, big and open than the usual almond shape of most cat's eyes. Duke stared into them and knew this was a friend. They were warm with a subtle glint of mischief, which Duke took to immediately. If he was to say what he thought of the Tigers Eye, at that moment, it would be that he recognised a kindred spirit. However as this would be way too much 'Ann of Green Gables' for his liking so he simply thought that the tiger was one cool dude.

The tiger appeared daily to Duke and regaled him with details of his adventures and travels. Apparently, crystals had the ability to appear wherever and whenever they were needed and could vanish just as quickly, once their work was done. Duke had been interested in the power of crystals for a long time, but never in a million years thought would he begin to have actual conversations with real live rocks!

Duke discovered that this crystal had in fact been of great assistance to President Theodore Roosevelt. With an air of authority, the tiger went on to explain that President Roosevelt was a war hero, a conservationist, and once gave a 90-minute speech after being shot in the chest. This was where the crystal apparently had aided the great leader, helping him stay focused and attending to the task at hand even in the face of great adversity. After hearing this story Duke decided to call the tiger 'Ted' or 'Teddy' after the president. The tiger didn't object and Duke thought there was a certain humour in it, a massive, scary, predator like this having such a cute and cuddly name. He enjoyed the irony.

Then one morning Ted enquired about Duke's name and where it came from, noting that Duke was a rather unusual title for a young boy; a ranch-hand out in the wild west or a rodeo cowboy perhaps, but a fourteen-year-old living in a small town in Ireland, was rather unusual.

'So', Duke began, 'it's apparently because of an actor called John Wayne. He was my mum's favourite and his nickname was 'The Duke', so when I arrived from the orphanage as a baby she got to name me and that's what she choose. Believe me dude, I have wished she was more into run of the mill actors, like, good old George Clooney, or Matt Damon, and even with her love of John Wayne, I have wondered loads over the years why she didn't go for the obvious, 'John', but oh no, not my mum, she had to go full throttle. She really didn't think it through. I have had my fair share of slagging and it doesn't help that I look different to everyone else; I have a cowboy's name but look like a Native American! Seriously, kids in school went to town, name calling, jeering, and making me the general butt of the joke fodder. It doesn't bother me anymore. I have got used to it, and they got tired of the jeering. Everything gets jaded eventually. As a kid I dressed up every year as a cowboy. I thought it was hilarious. No one else seemed to think it was as funny as I did.'

Ted looked over at the dark-skinned boy, with his long shining black hair, angular features and deep set, brown, brooding eyes. He was on the cusp of becoming a man and had the sinewy limbs of a youth but the attitude and fierceness of a budding adult. His hair shoulder length was a sign of him finally embracing his differences. Duke had grown tired of trying to fit in and stopped keeping it short and shaved. The kids in his local school learned to accept him for who he was and as more kids from other countries enrolled, he stood out less. It was fabulous now; there were kids from Africa, Poland, and Lithuania. There were traveller children, Muslim kids, the list was endless. Duke loved it because not only did he love not being the odd ball anymore, he enjoyed chatting with them and finding out about their culture and what made them tick.

He had come to terms with his physical differences but the other side to him, his sense, his intuition, this was a challenge still. Thankfully with the appearance of his new buddy, Teddy, he was coming to terms with this aspect of himself. However, he hadn't actually told anyone about his visions, but it was time…Duke decided to approach his sister, Willow. She was four years older, and at eighteen, she was technically an adult. They had grown apart in the last few years but there was still an underlying closeness. Duke knew she would listen and take him seriously. She was into crystals, yoga, meditation, the whole 'ugga bugga' bag as he called it, so he felt if he were to tell anyone what had been going on, it would be her. She could help him figure out if he was actually seeing visions, or was hallucinating, and therefore in serious need of medication.

'Morning turd,' Willow quipped affectionately one bright, but rather cold day.

'Morning mole face' he jauntily threw back. The insult sparring was something of a tradition now between the two siblings. Willow had a beauty spot on her left upper lip, and had been rather self-conscious of it growing up. This fact, Duke obviously took great advantage of. He mocked her at every opportunity and over the

8

years they had amassed a rather healthy collection of endearing nick names for each other: 'turd' and 'mole face' being the chosen monikers for this day. 'So, well… like… thing is….' Duke started rather sheepishly.

'Duke what's the story?' Willow had no patience for his hesitation.

'Okay listen Wills, I need you to hear what I have to say and then tell me if I am going nuts. Seriously, I think I may be losing it, like for totes real, major bonkers like,' Duke was more serious now.

This got Willow's attention. Any admission of madness on the behalf of her younger brother was something she would listen to. 'Dearest darling drongohead, I could have told you that years ago,' she tried to make a light of the situation.

'Willow, I have been seeing an eight-foot tiger at the end of my bed for weeks now and having some very interesting conversations with him. His name is Ted and he's a giant crystal.' Willow just stared at her younger brother. There was silence. It did occur to her that he had been sipping their mum's wine, although this was not really his style. Duke was sitting back in the chair; hands on his lap, just letting this information permeate her brain, a look of quiet defiance on his face, one that said *See, I told you, its nuts!*

Willow placed the box of cereal back on the table and slowly put the cap back on her carton of almond milk, as if imposing order on her surroundings would help with her thoughts, 'Okay, lets back up,' she instructed, 'start at the beginning.' And with a deep breath he began to tell the story of his new crystal buddy…Willow listened to her brother with growing fascination. This really excited her. She had long been a believer in the power of crystals but to actually see a living crystal, well that was awesome. She wanted to know more but they had to shelve their conversation with the arrival of their mother down to breakfast. They were conscious of what they were saying and how it sounded. They didn't want to give their mum any cause for alarm and a conversation about holographic crystals appearing out of nowhere may raise an eyebrow or two.

Willow decided that she would spend some time meditating on it with some of her own crystals. She was a bit jealous of Duke as she had been the one to introduce him to rocks in the first place. It would have to wait though, she was late for yoga.

Once in class Willow settled down on her mat. Calming her mind, she thought she saw a shimmer of something pink flash at the corner of her eye. She looked over but just saw an extremely flexible pair of legs draped over a prostrate head. In and out, long and slow, in and out… breathing became the focus. Something sparkling caught her eye again. The lights are playing tricks on me, she thought. She tried to calm her mind, which was now racing as she sensed something was amiss. Turning to stand at the front of her mat she was immediately and almost violently shocked into looking at the rear end of a giant glittering pink bottom.

'Sugar, how on God's Earth do y'all do this downward dog. I'm feeling more upside-down clown, ya get me?' And with that this beauty stood, all eight foot of her and turned to Willow with a smile so wide and welcoming that Willow momentarily forgot to be shocked.

'Honey, y'all need to close that big ol' open mouth you got goin' on there, your tonsils will catch a cold,' again the huge smile. 'Ahhh, apple blossom, don't you recognise your old friend, Rosie, Rosie Quartz? But y'all can call me Fro'Ro on account of my stupendous do,' she offered with a pat of her hair, other hand on her hip. Willow noted the rather marvellous pink afro that this creature was sporting. Coming back into her body and becoming aware of her surroundings again she tentatively looked about the room but everyone else seemed engaged with their own warm up practice and no one was taking a blind bit of notice to what she was doing; it was as if she was invisible.

Fro'Ro commented, 'Chilli pepper, you are the only one who can see me. Now, what say we skip this popsicle and get better acquainted, huh?'

Feeling like she had gone temporarily insane, an immediate exit from the room was required. Furtively Willow rolled up her mat and quietly stepped out into the hallway. There waiting at the bottom of the stairs was Fro'Ro. It was only now that Willow was able to take in the full extent of her incredible appearance. Her super tall frame was leaning against the wall, her right leg bent, hands in the pockets of her pink hoody, aviator shades perched on the tip of her nose, as she peered over them. Her massive explosion of arresting pink afro hair was captivating. Willow clocked the shocking pink, jewel encrusted cowboy boots and instantly fell in love. This chic was quite possibly the coolest creature she had ever clapped eyes on.

Willow rushed down the stairs, past Fro'Ro, straight outside. She needed air and to gather her thoughts. Her head was swimming and she had no idea how to react in this situation.

'Now look apple juice, y'all need a minute to take this in, I get that, but am I really such a surprise? Y'all have been meditating with me forever you know.'

It was true; Willow used her rose quartz crystal a lot. She sat with it in meditation, holding it in her hand. She had an antique rose quartz silver ring that she found in a thrift shop and frequently wore bracelets and ear rings made of the pretty crystal. She was used to its loving vibration. It helped her a lot when she was suffering a serious bout of self-doubt and loathing, a few years back.

It had been a particularly hard time for her; she was bullied and teased because of her hair. Willow was one of those fortunate people who had a mane of auburn curls, rolling down her back. Many people paid a small fortune to have hair like that, but Willow went through a period of hating it. She was called all sorts of names, like Curly Kale, Ronald McDonald, and her particular 'favourite', Ginger Nut. It wasn't easy looking different and she often confided in her younger brother. He was used to it himself. No two people could look more different, and yet they were brother and sister, not biologically but in every other way, and in all the ways that mattered.

Willow really felt the power of her crystals during

that time. Rose Quartz was a loving vibration and it helped Willow develop an appreciation of, not only her appearance, but also her uniqueness. Through the use of her crystals, she slowly began to see things differently. She could understand that the teasing was nothing more than their jealousy or boredom, or both. Whatever it was, she began not to care anymore. And after a while, always with her crystals to hand, in her pocket, or as jewellery, she changed her mind about how she looked.

More importantly she changed her mind about how she felt inside. She literally let her hair down and embraced all of her wonderful beauty. It became apparent to everyone around that there was no point in taunting her as it really had no effect. Or rather it had the opposite effect than what was hoped for. Willow began to love the attention, and thanked the other kids for noticing how amazing she was. This totally worked and the teasing stopped. And her self-esteem never dipped again.

From then on, Willow valued and appreciated everything about herself. Remembering how she felt holding the crystals in her hands she took a moment to feel Fro'Ro's energy. It really was a gentle, loving vibration, and Willow, taking a deep breath, began her curious interrogation of her new best friend, 'Okay. So, like, what's the deal here? Am I, and my brother for that matter going mad, or like, do you actually exist? And if so, what do you want with us? Where have you come from? Are you connected with the giant tiger that's been stalking Duke?'

'Girlfriend's gonna chill, yeah?' Fro'Ro had her arms

raised and was inciting Willow to calm down, 'Peanut brittle, we need to get you home and we need to have a chat, you, me, that great big gorgeous tiger and your kid bro, yo. Y'all ready to split?'

Willow nodded, dumbly. Her mind was in over drive and she had no defences other than to simply acquiesce to whatever the crystal suggested, got into her adored little mini and drove home.Extremely conscious of her new BFF sitting in the passenger seat, she kept looking around to see if other drivers were looking at her during the trip, but not one of them seemed to. She phoned Duke on her hands-free phone and simply said, 'Hey skuz-bucket, meet me at home in like, half an hour. We need to talk.' 'Whoa, yes Herr Commandant, your wish is my command obvs,' Duke said sarcastically but picked up on something in her voice and immediately changed his tone, 'Okay, cool bananas man, see you soon.'

Bursting in the door and racing to her room Willow sat down and began to rock back and forth. This was overwhelming and in a barely audible whisper she said, 'Either I'm going mad, or its very, very, very early onset Alzheimer's. There must be a reasonable explanation for this.' Panic began setting in and she instinctively picked up her malachite stones and began twirling them in her hands. Luckily, she was unaware of a very large green, Egyptian looking gentleman, wearing a floor length cloak, standing outside her bedroom. This would, in all possibility, have totally sent her over the edge...

Fro'Ro appeared beside her and laid a gentle hand on the freaked girl's shoulder. Again, in her confusion

Willow was unaware of Fro'Ro silently shooing the green giant away. Then gently and softly she spoke, 'Willow doll, y'all got to calm down now, ya feel me? You know who I am and you know I am a friend.' The bewildered girl looked up into the beautiful brown face of her beloved crystal and immediately felt her heart steady, it's pounding halting. The shot of adrenaline that had sent her into nervous overdrive was abating with the calming presence of Fro'Ro. *Right so, breathe, just focus on your breath,* she thought.

Duke arrived home, bounded up the stairs two at a time and burst into his sister's room. He ducked from an invisible shoe that he expected to be thrown, but when no missile came, he saw a serene girl sitting cross legged chatting to what looked like a holographic, giant, shimmering pink clad, black chick with the most amazing hair he had ever seen, after his sisters of course, 'Whoa dude, what's going on here?' he exclaimed.

Duke was still hanging on the handle of the door when Willow jumped up, a little annoyed, grabbed him and pulled him onto the bed. 'Shhh, Mum might hear and that's the last thing we need,' Willow was back in big sis mode.

Standing right behind Duke, as if vaporising from thin air, appeared Teddy, 'Greetings old friend.' He brushed past Duke and embraced Fro'Ro'.

'Well looks like the gangs all here,' Duke quipped. Willow was still trying to take all this in and didn't know which was more astounding, the fact that there were two giant personified crystals in her bedroom or that her kid brother seemed to be taking this all in his stride. She sat down suddenly exhausted.

'So, what's the plan Stan?' Duke asked of his new buddy. 'Well, my dear boy, there must be a reason why we have been summoned by you,' Teddy replied.

'Wait a minute; I didn't summon anything, no black magic, no spells, no incantations. I never asked for this to be happening. I'm not sure....' Willow broke off, at a loss what to say next.

Teddy looked at Fro'Ro who sat down beside her charge. 'Sweet cheeks, y'all don't know it yet but you did summon us.' Fro'Ro began working her magic on Willow.

The girl began to feel calmer, soothed. Fro'Ro's energy wafted over Willow and her palpitations stopped. The troubled girl was now being bathed in an intense flow of maternal soothing energy. Slowly, her mind stopped racing and she came back to herself. She began feeling the energy of the crystal just as she would have done if she sat quietly with the rock in her hand, or close to her heart. This was a very familiar feeling to Willow and she was at ease again. She looked up smiling at Duke, 'Okay folks, sorry I was just having a bit of a panic there, I'm feeling much better now.' She smiled her appreciation over to her crystal friend, who winked and smiled back.

Teddy, the ever-practical crystal of focus and action, piped up, 'Now, dear humans, we must try to figure out what is going on here and why you so badly need our help.'

ROYAL REVELATIONS

Teddy was, first and foremost, a stone of practical action and focus so it generally fell to him to make the decisions and he thought a walk outside was just the ticket. The elements always seemed to provide the answers and right now he needed the wind and the air to advise him. After all, he was made up of crystalline rock so returning to his natural environment simply made sense.

Duke and Willow grabbed their coats, slammed the door and headed off out the back, towards the caravan park behind their house. They were in the enviable position of living very close to the beach, a fact not lost on Willow. She roamed the dunes and shore daily and especially loved the winter time when there was no one about. She loved the feeling of aloneness she got when she sauntered along the shoreline. The expansive sea breaking at her feet never ceased to leave her with a sense of wonder.

Trudging through the marshy rain-soaked grass they made their way to the fence, a demarcation line between the park and the wasteland they were now in. Their heavy boots squelched and Duke zipped his hoody up to his neck and stuffed his hands in his pockets, wrapping himself up tightly for protection. 'Willow, maybe we are both experiencing a joint hallucination,' Duke was beginning to have doubts, 'You think we should maybe tell Mam what's going on? I mean she's quite open to other worldly stuff. I know she went to a psychic after Dad died...'

'Duke, seriously?' Willow cut him off, 'I don't think we should tell anyone anything. Anyway, what are you really going to say, you have been having visions, and you are seeing giant beings in your bedroom? I mean, come on, no one would believe you, it's just too mad. No, we need to go with this for a while till we see how it plays out.' Not entirely believing what she was saying, Willow hoped her brother would be pacified enough for now. Jumping the fence, they made their way through the deserted holiday village, past empty caravans, tennis courts and BBQ areas; all sitting, dormant, waiting for life to inhabit them once again. A caravan door swung creakily on its hinges, forced open by the wind, now banging impatiently and angrily as if calling on its owner to return. Willow always felt an eerie sensation here, like the ghosts of summers past roaming about. This was the shadow side of the sun village, it's dark needy alter ego. It was the people that brought the light to these places she thought, not necessarily the sun. A plastic bag floated by in the air, dancing to the tune of the winter breeze.

The walls of the playground were silent, like good little children, sitting with their fingers on their lips, in hushed quiet, waiting on the return of life, noise and laughter. The metal chains of the swings groaned with the weight of wind instead of bodies swooshing through the air. Rabbits darted in front of them, running madly from an invisible predator as they made their way to the wooden steps that led up and over the dune, guiding them to the beach below. Their thigh muscles were beginning to burn from the climb. The wind was whipping up the sand and Willow pulled her scarf around her face to protect it.

Teddy and Fro'Ro were now in sight, striding purposefully along the water's edge. Then suddenly stopping and appearing to sniff the air, they turned abruptly and moved towards the dunes. Willow and Duke exchanged glances and silently followed. They were each lost in their own thoughts. Willow anxiously wondering what they would find, and Duke just confused as to what this all meant.

They trekked over the sandy hills. 'Man, this place looks like Mars,' Duke remarked through panting breath. It was sand and hills and small walking tracks all around. Little tufts of dry grasses sprouted up here and there. The misty rain obscured their view of anything beyond a few feet in front and they had lost sight of the water, but they could still hear the rolling noise of the ocean breaking in the background.

'Okay I'm beginning to feel as if I'm in a sci-fi movie; Star Wars, or Alien. I wouldn't be surprised if a huge green man with big googly eyes appeared over the dune and said he was taking us back in his space ship,' Duke began chatting nervously.

The wind was blowing Willow's hair all over the place and she pulled it back with her arm holding it in place with her hand. She wanted to see clearly but was failing miserably. Muttering behind her scarf she chastised he brother again.

'Eh, so who died and made you lord and leader of all she surveys?' Duke was not impressed with her bossiness. 'May I remind you that you had these visions first and that maybe this is all about you? I'm not the one who's psychic or whatever it is you are. I'm not the one who had the first visitation by a huge tiger crystal thingy. I'm not the weird one here, buster,' Willow retorted and immediately regretted every word. Taking a deep breath, she turned to Duke and said, 'Ah buddy, I really didn't mean that. I'm just a bit out of my depth here, and I'm taking it out on you. Forgives?' She put on her best 'hang dog' face and began poking him in the ribs.

Not one to ever hang on to a grudge and always wanting everyone to get on he was immediately back to his nonchalant self, 'Yer grand sis, I totes get it, this is not like a usual day down at the beach. No Mr Whippy here,' and with that he lovingly punched her arm.

Gulls circled overhead with shrill squawks announcing their arrival. The salty smell of the ocean mixed with the misty rain filled their lungs with wet pungent air. In the distance they could see their crystal guides shimmer in the muted light and they made after them. Willow's hair was dancing in the wind and Duke thought she looked like a beacon, illuminating the way. Slightly sweating now, the two adventurers followed their crystal quarry over the dune and arrived at a valley below. The wind immediately died down and Willow unzipped her coat, suddenly feeling hot and sweaty.

'Yo, yo, yo, sis and bro, have a go and see how we roll,' Fro'Ro appeared, apparently trying her hand at a bit of rapping. She stood with her hands crossed in front, lips pursed and was, it seemed, channelling her inner Snoop Dog. 'Too much y'all?' she queried as if the look on their faces was not enough to tell her all she needed to know, 'Okay I guess I'll work on my delivery. Now, honeysuckle and beach ball, you need to come over here to Ted. We got to tell y'all something.'

'Hey Ted, what's the dealio here?' Duke asked.

'Patience my dear boy, patience,' came the cryptic reply.

Willow inhaled deeply to steady her nerves. They were very isolated now, with the dunes closing in on them. Walking tracks weaved their way around the top of the hills like snail's slimy trails and spiky little flowers sprouted from tufts of coarse grass. The green brown and yellow grass mixed with the sand forming a very autumnal palette and the dark grey sky hung heavy all around them. Evidence of late night teenage activity dotted the landscape, with empty coke cans and burnt out fires the only remains of their illicit meetings. The waves crashed in the distance, the sound muted by the high dunes and Willow began to feel safe surrounded by the sandy enclave.

'Okay magic muffin, you sit close by me', Fro'Ro told Willow. Duke was growing fonder by the minute of this crazy black chic, and her nuts little ways. 'String bean' she looked at him.

'That would be me I presume,' he answered smiling, 'Yes, you come beside Ted,' beamed Fro'Ro.

'Yes, siree, Mam,' Duke saluted and did as he was told. The little group sat crossed legged in a circle. Feeling a bit self-conscious now, Willow looked around the tops of the dunes for hardy joggers or random dog walkers. However, the imposing mountain of sand at her back stood like a sentinel and she felt her heart calm. This had something to do in part with her beloved crystal beside her.

'Okeydokey folks what kind of magic are we gonna pull off here,' Duke was getting into the spirit of the adventure and was expecting fireworks, maybe some fierce dragons to appear over the horizon, he could stretch to an alien or two appearing over the top of the dune, providing they were of the friendly variety. 'Now, we must sit,' Teddy instructed.

'Yeah dude, I got that part, what happens next?' Duke began rubbing his hands expectantly.

'And breathe...' Teddy continued ignoring Duke's comment. 'Eh, like yeah man, I think I got that part nailed, I do that all the time, it's called stayin' alive yeah?' Duke really wasn't catching on to the vibe.

'Duke, you need to calm down and relax. I think we're going to do a bit of meditating,' Willow instructed her brother. Crestfallen Duke sat back and did as he was told. Meditating was not something he counted in his top ten things to do of a rainy afternoon, sitting in the middle of a valley of dunes, freezing his butt off. However, also not one to rock the boat unduly he complied with the instruction.

Suddenly Teddy began to sway, and hum, and with his eyes closed he seemed to be going into some sort of trance. Fro'Ro followed suit and feeling like an intruder watching them he automatically closed his own eyes, not wanting to invade their privacy in their moment of contemplation.

Duke sat listening to the gentle rhythms of Teddy's humming chant and began to lose himself in its lilting melody. Unable to resist he creaked open his right eye just to check quickly on Willow and immediately snapped it shut again. She was sitting holding the hands of the crystals on either side of her and was moving slowly to the rhythm also.

Duke could feel the soft sand under his bum and was feeling very relaxed. There was a split in the clouds and he could feel the bright rays of the sun warm up his whole body. He was happy. Swaying, chanting, swaying, he couldn't feel the hands of the others any more. It was as if he had left his body and was flying, lighter and lighter, he soared up over the dunes and suddenly was looking down on the party of four, sitting in a small circle below him. Bright sparks flew in his vision and he was momentarily blinded. Everything was illuminated, radiating, glowing and he was slammed back into his body but not behind the dune. He fell back and looked in wonder around him. He was somehow in the centre of a glistening purple shining cave. He rubbed his eyes and turned to see his partners in crime right beside him. 'Whoa, dude, what the...? Willow, you alright?' he asked looking at Willow who seemed as confused as he was.

'Duke, where are we? Are you here, seeing this too?' she asked a little nervously.

'Easy now my little flying saucers, it's all gonna be just fine and dandy. Take a mo now, and breathe. Y'all just did your first journey to the other realm. It can be very disorientating, now just chill,' Fro'Ro was emanating her calming vibes.

Taking a deep breath, Willow stood up, 'Fro'Ro where are we?' 'We, my beautiful buttercup, are in the Amethyst Cave,' the crystal replied as if this answered all questions.

'Far out,' Duke was totally digging these shenanigans.

Walking over to the sides of the caves, Willow rubbed her hand along the glistening jagged purple wall. It was cold and shiny, consisting of clusters of crystals, all pointy and sharp. The myriad of colours danced in front of her eyes; from soft pinks and lavender to the darkest violets, plump and ripe like bursting summer berries. She was dumbfounded. She stared at her brother, looking for confirmation.

But Duke was just as baffled and turned to Ted to see if he could help him make sense of it all, 'Okay dude, what is going on? A minute ago, I was sitting behind the dunes, channelling my inner yogi bear then wallop, suddenly we're here. I remember feeling dizzy then it all went Fourth of July on me and now this. Ted, where are we?'

'Everything is as it should be. Now, come here and I shall explain. We are in the Caves of Amethyst. Now tell me, how do you feel?' Ted replied with quiet authority.

'Well, now that you mention it, I feel okay considering we seem to be travelling through space and time and I have no idea when we return to the dunes, if we ever do, that I won't be a ninety-year-old man, with warts on my face and a hump on my back,' Duke answered glibly.

'You need to come closer to these walls and just let the vibes wash over you,' Ted gestured, his gaze fixed of Duke.

Duke looked at his sister. She was very calm and instructed, 'Duke, you need to chill and let the crystals do their thing.' Breathing heavily and deeply Duke approached the walls to get a better feel of the spikey rock. It was beautiful. He took a deep breath in, dropped his shoulders and immediately felt relaxed. 'Yes, I brought you here to seek the council of the Lord and Lady Lapis Lazuli. Ah thought it best to approach them after you guys had time to calm down and there is no better place to feel calm than inside one of these caves. They are my happy place, don't you know,' Ted explained to the now rather more relaxed humans, who looked like they had just swallowed a vial of Valium, stretched out on the floor of the cave.

'Ah hem, don't you guys think that we should find out what it is we are supposed to be doing here and why we were sent to you. What if it is you who need to do something to save humanity? Teddy attempted to stir the youngsters into action.

'Dude, you have been reading waaaay too many fantasy novels. I mean, serio, fo'schizzle, like, you think that me and my dumb-ass sister here, are like, sent to do some major superhero antics and save mankind from baddies? Come on, Ted, I know this is a bit nuts, but that's totes bonkers man,' and with that he gave Ted an affectionate dig in his very large and furry arm.Fro'Ro spoke, 'Now you listen to me. Serious stuff is going on here and we need to figure this out. We don't just appear out of nowhere to anyone. We have been summoned, by you, I may add, to help you. Now y'all may not be too familiar with your gifts yet, or, have used them much but let me assure you, you do have some, shall we say, special abilities, and we're here to help. Now, before y'all get too cosy soaking in the peaceful vibes of the amethyst crystal, we should get going and do as Ted says.'

With that little speech out of the way Duke and Willow felt compelled to comply with whatever either of the crystal guides demanded. 'Ted, what's the next step? Duke questioned.

'Well we must seek the council of the elders. Let's walk,' he said commandingly. The intrepid group gathered themselves together and strode down the large rock corridor. The purple hues, swirling all around them created a rainbow of colours, changing with them, as they moved. The air was cold, but they were calm. The amethyst was doing its thing, keeping them relaxed while they began to tune into the higher vibrations of the other crystals.

Teddy stopped, raising his hand to halt the others. There appeared to be a small room ahead. He approached delicately, and Willow noted how graceful he was considering he was so large. Willow and Duke stopped where they were, and the two crystal guides continued into the small chamber. 'Well this is rather unusual to say the least, but I don't feel scared at all. How 'bout you?' Willow enquired of her brother.

'Nah, I'm sweet man, this is cool. What do you think is going on in there?' Duke asked.

'Search me,' came her simple reply.

Fro'Ro appeared and gestured for the two to join them. Treading cautiously Willow led the way into a larger than expected round chamber. It was made of the same amethyst crystal as the rest of the cave but with two huge shining gold thrones in the centre and perched very regally on these thrones were what looked like Egyptian royalty.

'Far out,' Duke was loving this adventure now.

Teddy bowed to the royal couple and Fro'Ro followed. Standing mutely behind them was Willow. Duke was calmly taking it all in with a huge smile on his face.

'My children, why have you come?' The Lady spoke first. She looked down at them one by one and Willow felt her heart skip a beat. It was as if she was looking directly into her soul. Feeling naked, exposed and vulnerable Willow moved beside Fro'Ro for comfort. The lady moved her gaze to Duke, 'Ah, the chosen one, come closer my child.'

Dukes face fell, he looked pale and as though he was going to vomit. 'Duke, you okay? Willow was worried.

'I think I just did a little puke in my mouth.' Duke whispered. 'Ah, Duke, TMI' Willow was now simply grossed out.'It's okay my dear boy, we are here with you and you are among friends,' Ted comforted him.

'Yeah, man, that's not the problem, it's this chosen one thing. Not sure I signed up for this. Where's the escape exit Ted? I'm done. Like, over and out Smokey. I really NOT interested in any "chosen one" thing,' this last bit he emphasised with air quotes.'Dear child' the Lady interjected, 'there is no need for anxiety. Come closer. You need to know that you are safe from all harm and we are with you. You must relax now and hear us. You cannot avoid what awaits you, for it is your destiny. It is written in the stars above. You must activate the skulls, the crystal skulls. They lie dormant and are ready, waiting for you to call upon them.' She was now looking into the distance as if in a trance.

'Listen, I read my horoscope this morning and it never mentioned anything about destinies or skulls,' Duke responded, resorting to humour when in difficulty. But this time it was falling on deaf ears. 'Okay, note to self, crystals don't seem to have a sense of humour,' he said to no one in particular.

Willow was transfixed by the beautiful woman/crystal/entity in front of her. She actually had no idea what it was she was looking at but whatever it was, whatever she was, she was magnificent. Her skin was light brown like Dukes. She had piercing deep green eyes. They were al-

28

mond shape slanting backwards up her head; they made her razor-sharp cheekbones protrude even more. Her eyes were rimmed with thick black eyeliner and she had a turban on, made of dark navy silk fabric encrusted with jewels of all colours, jade, emerald, and ruby projecting their dazzling light off the walls of the amethyst cave. Her robes were of the deepest navy also and had swirling flecks of gold swimming through them. Her partner in crime, so to speak, was equally as mind blowing. Although he hadn't spoken yet, he had such a commanding presence, he communicated through the tractor beam of his eyes. His torso was bare, but his head covered in similar fabric to his lady's but with navy and gold stripes and it fell down his back. He also had bejewelled arms and his tunic covering the lower half of his body was also glistening with precious gems.

Teddy moved closer to Duke and put his arm around him. Duke dropped his head as if in defeat and stepped nearer to the impressive couple. He took a deep breath in and knelt down. He knew this day was coming. All his life he felt different, weird, an outsider. He learnt to deal with this by being funny, being the joker. He began to appreciate his quirks and didn't need the approval of the other kids so much. He could handle being an oddball and began to think of himself as pretty cool.

But now, this was being laid on him, he initially wanted to run. He didn't want to know. This wasn't what he envisioned was going to happen when Ted first appeared in his little bedroom. He just thought this would be a bit of an adventure, a laugh even. But now he knew, deep down in the bowels of his body that what was happening was unavoidable. And so, he knew instinctively that resistance was futile. And as he thought these thoughts he smirked silently to himself. He could see himself in his mind's eye, doing a robotic dance, shouting 'Resistance Is Futile. Resistance Is Futile.' He restrained himself and simply asked, 'What is it I need to know?'

'You need to believe you are as regal as we are. You need to reach down deep inside yourself and feel your Inner Divinity. You humans all have this inside of you. Simply feel our presence when you are in doubt and we will raise your frequency to that of ours. We help you see the truth in the situation. It is our mission to help clear the fog of confusion and uncertainty that hangs over your eye,' the Lady spoke kindly to him.

Duke stood silent for a moment. Willow was desperately trying to make sense of it all. It was happening too quick for her to process. Her brother was a chosen one, her disgusting little runt of a brother who had smelly feet and drove her mad. Her brain scrambled to catch up with her eyes and ears. And what was all this about a skull? She looked over at her beloved Fro'Ro and she was smiling benignly back at her.

As if reading the minds of their guests, the Lady continued, 'The skulls are buried deep within Gaia, your Mother earth. She has protected them well for thousands of years but now it is time. She must give birth to these oracles of ancient wisdom for it is within these skulls that the vibration for a new humanity resides. They must be activated, and it must happen soon. We are running out of time. The dark forces are waking up too and they will stop at nothing to prevent this activation. This is the Ascension of humanity. This is the new dawn for you humans and we all will guide you to your destiny and will travel the journey with you. Evil resides dormant near you and it has the face of power and prestige. It does not look as you would expect it to. It is a malevolent force and it is searching for you. It does not know who you are yet, but that is only a matter of time.'

Duke swallowed, hard. He was also trying to process what the Lady was saying. This all sounded very dodgy to him, and dangerous. What if something were to happen to him? Worse, what if something happened to Willow, he couldn't bear it. Plucking up all his courage he asked, 'So your saying I don't really have any other option here than to go look for these skulls? I mean if I don't then we all die? Yeah? Like all the humans on the planet, everything, the world will, what? Explode?'

'My dear child' the Lady went on, 'it is not that the world will die as you know it. Rather humanity will not reach its higher vibration. Gaia is ascending, and she wants all of her beloved humans, animals, plants and stone people to ascend with her. She is heading to a world of peace and harmony. It is the destiny of all to ascend with her and it is your destiny to help that process. You must become warriors of the Rainbow and together with the Stone people you will be victorious.' She stared straight at Duke who just swallowed, hard...again.

'The Awakening will begin with the turning on of the heart of humanity. This will happen with the first skull and it will happen within your own land. It is the heart chakra of the world, the vortex of love. This is your beginning. You must go to where the ancient stone mounds stand outside the ancient burial mound at Newgrange. They have their treasure buried deep within them. They are silent, waiting, expectant,' the Lady closed her eyes to emphasise the gravity of what she was saying.

There was a long silence. 'But what if I don't want to?' came the quiet sound from Dukes mouth.

'Boy,' suddenly there was a booming voice from the Lord, they all jumped. 'We all have free will. You will not be forced to do anything that you do not want to do or choose to do. This is the lot of the human on earth. But be warned, you must choose wisely' and with that his gaze drifted back to the end of the cave as if he was visibly tuning out.

'Jeez, who rattled your cage' again Duke was earnestly trying to keep it light but failing miserably.

'My dear boy, you must digest what the Lord and Lady Lapis Lazuli are saying. They are the crystals to help you see clearly,' Teddy said, trying to help Duke make sense of it all. Duke stared at Ted in silence.

The Lady spoke again, 'Once the planet's heart is awakened, the people will move from their heads and into their hearts. This is vital for the vibration to rise. There will be a loss of power for those corrupt and in governance now and they will stop at nothing to see you fail.'

'But why me?' Duke asked. Silence fell on the whole group. The air was electric. They all remained still, taking in what was unfolding and the question hung in the air like a bomb about to explode.

The Lord once more turned his head, awaking from his apparent slumber and replied, 'Why not you?'

Duke and Willow sat down on the cold hard floor of the cave. Willow had no words of comfort or advise. She put her arm around her brother lovingly and squeezed him tight. Duke sat hunched over, his arms around his legs and his head hung low. He was overpowered by the weight of what had been said.

Sensing his turmoil, the Queen looked down benevolently and beamed her radiant smile on him, 'Do not be afraid my child. This is your destiny. When we follow our true path, the Universe aligns with our course and aids our journey. You are on your true path therefore all is well. You must trust the Stone People and what they say. They are your allies and friends. The Tigers Eye and The Rose Quartz Crystals are wise, and you must listen to them, both with your ears and your heart. There will be others along the way but these trusted friends will be with you to the end.' Duke felt comforted somehow. It was all a bit much and his brains were scrambled but when she spoke now he relaxed a little. 'Well, I suppose if we meet other cool crystals like these two nutters then it could be a fun time,' Duke was speaking to himself as much as the group.

'Yeah Duke, that's the spirit. I think this could be an adventure of a lifetime. I mean think about it, who else gets to do stuff like this? I mean this is really way cool,' Willow was appealing to his sense of adventure.

'True sis, you're not wrong there, I mean, this is way cool, totes rad man. Yes, I think I could see myself as the saviour of the world, I could be that guy, so long as you bow to my superior knowledge and do as you are bid,' he said smirking.

'Eh like, that a negatory, dumbass I will never bow to your high and mightiness, just sayin,' she replied.

Duke addressed the group, 'Hmmm, it was worth a try. I'll tell you all one thing here and now, I don't care what happens or what I have to do, I am not, and I repeat not, wearing pants over tights, and no capes, I won't do a cape, or large letters on my chest. That's a deal breaker. '

And with that a roar of laughter erupted form Fro'Ro followed by Ted, then Willow and finally Duke, looking sheepish broke into a big smile and joined the infectious hilarity.

BEST LAID PLANS

E veryone regrouped back at bedroom H.Q. 'So, what do you think all this means Ted?' Willow asked hoping for an answer she can wrap her head around.

'Well my thoughts are quite clear on this dear Willow. We have to devise a way for you guys to get to Newgrange, activate the hidden buried crystal skull, then figure out where the next three skulls are hidden, somewhere around the world, go there, and do the same,' Ted outlined the facts as he saw them.

'Simples', was Duke's glib reply. He was sitting on the floor of his bedroom, staring at the swirling pattern on the carpet, knees bunched in under his chest. He ran his hands through his hair and sat with his back to the bed. He pushed the clothes on the floor out of his way with his feet and stretched out his legs. Duke looked almost too big for his tiny bedroom now, with his bunk bed at his back, the duvet hanging on the floor. The posters on the wall seemed tatty and redundant. It was as if something had shifted in him and the old familiar things he knew, and clung to for comfort; his books, music, clothes, now all felt alien.

Duke looked at them with different eyes, eyes that were not his anymore. He was squatting in his own body, wearing it as a skin that needed to be shed. He wanted to be alone and he never wanted to be alone again in his life. It was possible to feel two opposing emotions at the same time he realised. The magnitude of what had happened began to dawn on him. He could look at this as a simple moment of delusion. He could ignore the huge crystal beings sitting in front of him. He could talk Willow around, convince her that it was all one big mistake, a dream, a nightmare, but somehow these feelings were falling on unfertile soil. As much as he threw water on the allotment of his mind it failed to produce any thoughts of abandonment. When he stopped trying to figure all this out with his head and listened to the rumbling, groaning, churning feeling in his stomach, he knew there was no getting away from what happened.

His body was reacting to the events in a very visceral way. It was beyond his control. He felt a sense of urgency brewing in his belly and there was an unseen power, an invisible force pushing him from behind. It was bigger than him and it had a will of its own. Free will my eye… he reflected on the words he heard on the beach, in the cave from the Lord Lapis Lazuli, he really didn't feel like he had a choice in any of this.

Sensing his struggle Teddy sat quietly beside him. Often the best comfort is given in silence and Ted knew this. But it was Willow that spoke first, 'Well my little special one what do you make of all that?' It was a loaded question she knew but she also knew that Duke was worried, and she was trying her best to normalise the situation.

'I mean, sis, like, I dunno...' Duke trailed off. He struggled to think cohesively; his thoughts banged together in his head like the lotto balls in the big plastic container and an invisible hand was churning them around and around.

'Well, I think it's clear that we need to pay a visit, an educational trip shall we say, for a school project perhaps to Newgrange. God only knows what we are supposed to do when we get there, but I guess we'll just wing it. These guys will probably suss out some weirdy beardy, ugga bugga, beings for us to hook up with. You're probably going to get possessed by some dodgy entity and turn all green and slimy, and I'll have to go full blown exorcist on you and be all 'go to the light Duke, go to the light,' Willow offered.

Duke looked at her, his eyes held questions that she had absolutely no ability to answer. She knew he was worried. He was usually so quick to quip back at her. It wasn't like him to be moody and pensive. She was anxious; it was her job to keep him safe. She promised to protect him as soon as he arrived in their home all those years ago. Feelings of helplessness and fear rose up in her. Fro'Ro gave Willow a warm embrace, silently sat beside her and allowed her sweet, comforting vibration wash over her young charge, calming the soul like a soothing balm. Willow felt her confidence return. She was a strong, capable, intelligent female and she wasn't going to let her younger brother flail around in the dregs of self-doubt. She was his older sister, his protector, and she was going to get this show on the road.

Fro'Ro always had the ability to let Willow get in tune with her inner Goddess. Her beautiful crystal shone the light of love on her best qualities and expanded her heart, so that she knew instinctively how amazing she was. Fro'Ro guided her down the path of confidence and self-assurance.'We need a plan Stan, what do you suggest', Willow said at last, prodding Duke with her questions whilst doing the same with her fingers. She was hoping to rouse him from his funk.

'Dude, leave me alone' he snapped back at her.'

'Euuuu', she made a high-pitched squealing noise and began taunting, 'Ah da lickle girlie is gone all quiet. Feeling a bit scardey wardey?' She poked him in the arm, giggling. He looked at her and burst out laughing. She always had the ability to get him to laugh. Breaking into a snorting roar he sat up and promptly punched his sister firmly in the arm. 'Hey, what did you do that for?' Willow had a hurt expression on her face but really didn't care. Duke was responding and beginning to be mildly abusive in a friendly sort of way which was good. This was normal transmission resuming.

'Dude, you are literally the most annoying person on the planet,' Duke was coming back to himself, 'I mean seriously, Willow, act your age not your shoe size.'

'Listen Superboy I'm not the one who is all Flash Gordon, saviour of the Universe. So, like what is your superpower, flight? Invisibility? Being mega annoying?

I'm sure I can find some tights you can borrow,' she offered.

'Oh, hardy ha-ha, Willow cracked a funny,' Duke shot back at her with a wry smile. He was the cooler kid; Willow's taunts were amateur at best. 'Willow, dude, you are never going to get me riled up with your pitiful jabs. I mean come on, is that the best you got, seriously. I think I have established that there will be no tight wearing, and no superhero nonsense. If I were to have a super power it would be the elimination of all annoying siblings from planet Earth, or at least make them my subservient slaves.''Oh, would you now Mister High and Mighty; one little session with a holographic set of royal crystals and it has gone to your head,' Willow was getting mildly annoyed now which was the actual aim of the taunts by her brother.

'Chillax sis, I'm only messing. Now what do you suggest? I bow to your superior knowledge' this last bit he said with a flourish and a bow.

'Well, that's more like it. You may be the chosen one, but it's not all about you, you know. Now, sorting a trip to Newgrange, thirty miles away is no hassle, yeah, but, I mean, like, how are we going to suss out where the other skulls are and when we do, how will we know what to do. And then,' this bit she really emphasised, 'how do we know where to go next?'

'Listen my little cupcakes; you are getting' your panties in a bunch, yeah. One thing at a time, Newgrange first then we figure the rest out as we go along,' Fro'Ro added.

'Okay folks let's go,' Duke was feeling his confidence grow along with his sense of purpose and urgency.

'Right, there's no time like the present. We'd better get there early so I suggest we all get some sleep, well us humans that is, I'm not really sure what you crystals get up to. Do you sleep? Wow, like there's a good pub trivia question. Do rocks sleep? Do crystals have feelings?' Duke began to ramble.

'Duke, focus,' Willow rebuked him.

'Sorry, okay like I was saying, we get an early night and meet here at zero five hundred hours,' Duke finished off.

At this Willow threw her eyes up to heaven, gave him a mild slap around the head, 'Okay, I'll set my alarm.'

Across the 'pond,' a few thousand miles away in New York, Senator Wayne Johnson sat at his prized 'Parnian' desk, twirling a piece of fossilised amber in his hands. It was a gift from his sister whom he adored; she was probably the only person who he actually had any feelings for. This beloved piece of amber was helping to keep him calm just this minute.

Despite being a powerful, influential man, not to be underestimated, he had just lost a bidding war to a rival. Wayne didn't like to lose, he wasn't any good at it. He expected to get what he wanted, at all costs. Something was up, and he couldn't put his finger on it. The more power he got the more he craved. He was building his empire, and not getting what he wanted didn't work well with his plan.

Wayne had built his fortune on instinct. He could read people; he knew exactly what they were thinking. He found it fascinating that people believed thoughts were invisible. He could look into your eyes and 'see' what you were thinking as if he were looking up at the large screens in Times Square and reading the writing at the bottom. But his sharp instincts came at a price it seemed.

His heart had been hardened from years of bullying as a child and he swore as he grew and became a man, that no one would be able to intimidate him again. His father died when he was a boy and his mother had raised him and his sister alone. She was a loving and kind woman who had done her best, but Wayne grew up with a profound sense of lack and inadequacy. So, when he finally found his inner strength, in his early teens he used his confidence and self-belief to go after whatever it was that he desired.

He excelled at sports, no longer a weakling, he gained weight and muscle. He bulked up, physically and mentally and he liked how he felt. Even when he began losing his hair early, he shaved it all off and now was a man in his mid-forties, at the peak of physical fitness, imposing with his muscular frame wrapped in designer suits and slightly menacing with his bald head. But along the way he somehow lost a sense of himself. They say we all have shade and light within us and it is a constant battle of one over the other. Well, in Wayne the shade was definitely winning.

When Wayne entered politics, he had done it for the right reasons; helping others, the greater good, to become someone. But along the way he had changed; greed, malice, and avarice took over. These things happen by degrees, invisible and insidious, the melting away of principles. He sat here now fuming, and not being accustomed to losing, he began plotting his revenge. But there was something else. What was going on in the world? The energies have shifted, he could sense it. He was a gifted intuitive, he knew something was moving and he didn't like it. Change was not good for someone like him or his business…

PALACE OF THE BOYNE

Willow woke early after a fitful few hours. She pulled on skinny dark tartan jeans (a nod to her punk sensibilities), black docs and a hoody. She didn't go in for trends, or bright colours. Her wardrobe lent itself very nicely to a cat burglar, night-time assassin or someone who was about to go traipsing through a 5000-year-old burial mound in search of a hidden crystal skull. She crept towards Duke's room, taking care not to wake her mother. The last thing Willow needed was her mother making inquiries about why they were up so early, where they were going, or what they were doing. 'Duke, Duke, wake up,' Willow said as she shook him gently. He turned to the wall, pulled the covers back over his head and grunted. Willow punched his arm. 'Duke, get up, come on, we have to go,' more urgency in her voice now. Duke sat up and rubbed his eyes. Willow was losing patience, 'Duke, get your skinny ass into your oversized jeans and let's go,' she commanded, 'we don't have time to waste.' She loomed over him like a drill sergeant.

'Okay, okay, jeez, I'm coming,' Duke mumbled as he rolled out of bed, and pulled on his jeans, bright orange trainers and t-shirt, blindly following orders; he'd had years of practice. Willow stood back in horror staring at her brother's choice of footwear, 'Duke, your trainers! For goodness sake, we're supposed to be keeping a low profile. There'll be loads of people up there for the Winter solstice. We don't need unnecessary attention.'

'Good call Watson,' he quipped back, a bit more alive now than before, and with that he pulled on his own Docs, standard footwear for any self-respecting, anti-establishment 14-year-old. The two of them stealthily headed out to Willow's battered old rust covered, red 1970's mini cooper. She had saved up her wages from her weekend job to get it and loved it more than life itself. She liked to think it was 'vintage' and that she was making a statement about her values of recycling and non-materialism, rather than it was all she could afford, having only cost a few hundred quid. Getting into the car the two front passengers were suddenly aware of a presence in the back. Looking around slowly they were pleased to see Fro'Ro and Ted sitting there.

'How's you bro?' enquired Ted.

'Yo sweet cheeks, how you doin'?' added Fro'Ro.

'Guys we can see you clear as day, what's going on?' Willow was perplexed.

'Oh, don't worry, no one else can see us. You have tuned into our frequency and because you have the gift, you are able to see between worlds. You know, shimmy shammy, here and there, in and out, above and below, ya dig? You are using your sixth sense now to see us. Shhh, listen, Duke, you got some more crystals in your pocket?' asked Fro'Ro.

'Eh yup, I never go anywhere now without my turquoise stone and my malachite crystal,' he answered. With that they turned and peered out the window, shining the torch to see Mahpee and Mala-Kai standing beside the car.

Mahpee was completely turquoise in colour, strong, muscular; he looked like an Avatar creature on steroids. His long, jet black hair was held in place by a leather headband with a white feather sprouting from the side. He had face markings along his cheek, under his eyes, which Duke assumed to be tribal, or perhaps the marks of a warrior. His bare torso was home to a bow and arrow; he wore dark suede loose fitting trousers and moccasins on his rather large feet. Dude be impressive, thought Duke.

Mala-Kai was also big; both crystals were at least 8ft tall. Mala-Kai was a beautiful rich green colour with swirling striations all over his body. He wore what looked like a skirt, Roman style, and also had a bare torso. His dark hair was tied in a ponytail. He wore what looked like thick black eyeliner; similar to the ancient Egyptians and his feet were bare. But his stand out feature was a luxurious, floor length, deep forest green cape tied at the neck with what looked like a tiger's eye crystal. He also carried a large round shimmery metallic shield, slightly darker in colour than himself. 'Holy golden bikini Batman, we're not in Kansas now Toto,' Duke was fond of mis-quoting movies.

45

The turquoise crystal did the introductions; communicating was one of his strengths, 'Greetings humans, we are your guides as you have called on our powers and we are here to assist in your mission. You have tuned into our frequency and so now, we will aid you whenever and wherever possible,' he smiled, eyes twinkling and with a subtle shake of the head continued, '…my name is 'Mahpee', it means 'Sky' in Sioux. This is my ally Mala-Kai, the malachite crystal.

Duke was in awe. Willow complimented Mala-Kai on his fabulous cloak. He informed them that, if need, be his cloak could hide them from psychic attacks and his shield would protect them from negativity. 'Wowsers, you don't have a light sabre under there as well do you?' Duke joked, but the reference was lost on all present so he shut up.

Teddy appeared beside Mala-Kai and the two bent their heads together and wrapped their arms around each other. The air was charged with electricity. Apparently when crystals worked together their energies can be heightened. 'It would appear these two know each other' Duke said.

Mahpee spoke, it seemed, offering instructions, Teddy appeared in the back of the car again, just as the turquoise and the malachite crystals sprinted off. 'I guess that's our cue to get a move on,' said Willow.

Hands on the steering wheel, eyes ahead, Willow thought out loud, 'Okay, it's less than an hour drive from here to Newgrange, so we should be there by 6am. We know that the solstice happens around 9am so we have a few hours to figure out what were supposed to do.'

'Cool,' was all Duke could muster. He folded his arms against the cold, sat back into the seat and pulled his hood over his head. He was having difficulty with the early hour and wasn't used to being up, conscious and having to communicate at this time. It has to be said, he was also finding it slightly difficult to wrap his brain around all these giant personified crystals.

'So, we know that Brú na Bóinne has three main sites, Newgrange, Knowth and Dowth. We will have to be very careful to sneak in without being noticed. I reckon that we head to Knowth first as everyone will be gathered at Newgrange to witness the solstice,' Willow articulated her plan aloud.'So, what exactly is Brú na Bóinne?' Duke was waking up and wondering what was in store for him. He knew that it had something to do with burials, and rituals and he thought that was pretty cool but other than that he really wasn't sure.

'Well, Brú na Bóinne means 'Palace of the Boyne'. It's the name given to the area in the Boyne Valley where there are burial mounds and passage tombs, you know, those large hills that we visited a few years ago with the school. The most famous is Newgrange, obvs, everyone knows about that one, I think it was built around 3200 BC, which make them way cool in my book,' Willow informed her brother with a smile.

'Wow, holy shizola Batman, that's old,' Duke remarked.'They were used as burial chambers, ancient temples, places of astronomical, spiritual, and ceremonial importance,' Willow continued rather impressively, 'what we're going to have to do is find out where we are supposed to go, and what we are supposed to do when we get there.'

'Simples,' said Duke, somewhat sarcastically.

The drive went quickly. The air of anticipation in the car was palpable, aided by the fact that the two intrepid adventurers knew this trip involved trespassing on sacred land, a fact that Willow was rather uncomfortable with. Not a rule breaker.

Willow had been reading up on her Newgrange history and continued to explain to Duke that every year there was a lottery for entrance to the main tomb in Newgrange. Fifty people were selected from over 30,000 applicants from all over the world and of that fifty, only around twenty gained access inside the tomb to witness the solstice shining through the roof box at the entrance to the mound, shining down the length of the nineteen-meter passage and hitting the back wall of the chamber at exactly 9.09am. Willow knew there would visitors gathered outside to celebrate the event. She figured they should head to the other chamber of Knowth; no people there and it was as good a starting point as any.

Stopping the car on a dark country lane Willow and Duke looked at each other and nodded as if to say, 'let's do this', whatever 'this' might be. Getting out of the car, they braced themselves against the biting wind. Their breath let out spirals of steam as they walked in the icy morning air. Duke was glad he took the time to layer up. Willow pulled her coat tighter around her, shivering. Why didn't she put on the thermals? She just couldn't bring herself to don the ugly granny-like underwear but now she regretted the decision. Damned vanity!

They both unconsciously shoved their hands into their pockets and held the crystals. Willow immediately felt the presence of her now beloved Fro'Ro. How could anyone love a rock she thought, but she did for sure. 'Sweetness, I sense your anticipation. You know y'all be just fine. You have been chosen for a reason and the universe wants to help you, the elementals will be on your side, I have spoken to them and I have considerable charm when needed. Have faith in you and have faith in me.' Fro'Ro offered.

Duke also had his fears. He always knew he could sense the other world; the space between what he could see with his eyes and what he could feel with his heart. He could almost feel the world that lay beneath his reality; the mystical, the magical, and the unknown. This was the world of the elementals, the angels and the devil; the imaginal world. The smell of the ether was his to taste but he didn't like it. He was afraid of it and what it meant. He didn't know if it was a gift or a curse, or perhaps both.

He had long since learned to ignore the feelings he would get when he walked into a room, or shook hands with someone, or simply felt something in his bones. He thought everyone had these feelings, but he gradually realised that this was not the case. And as he got older he learned to mask these intuitions, but when he ignored his gut feelings it resulted in bad stomach aches. He was too young yet to connect the dots. He didn't want to be an outsider.

He was odd enough, being a different race in a school of all Irish nationals. Thankfully the Polish kids who arrived in the last few years took some of the attention away from him. There were some Africans too, so he blended in a bit better recently but as a younger kid, it was hard. He felt so out of place and self-conscious that he dreaded going to school. But his mum was strict and there was no getting out of it. Gradually he made a few friends and morphed into the background. But with these more powerful insights, and premonitions, he was in fear of standing out again, for all the wrong reasons. It was only a few hundred years ago that they burned witches at the stake. What would they do to him if anyone found out about all this malarkey?

He rubbed his tigers' eye and heard, 'It's okay big man, I am right here with you. Remember you are far more powerful than you think, and you have Mahpee and Mala-Kai for protection,' Ted gave as confidence boosting advice. Mahpee and Mala-Kai took that as a cue to run on ahead and scout out the way.

Willow and Duke walked down the dark country lane, their heavy boots crunching the stones under foot. They could hear the distant murmur of people already gathering over the hill at Newgrange, their voices being carried on the wind. They heard the low mooing of cows in a nearby field; this was rich agricultural land after all. The smell of cow dung was dense and heavy, like an air freshener for the underworld. Breathing in was difficult as the cold air burned their nostrils. The grass in the field glistened from the dew catching the light of the moon.

Willow looked up to see a sky filled with sparkling stars, unusual for this time of year where the cloud cover meant usually there were no stars visible at all. The chill of the morning was impossible to avoid, and Willow was freezing to her bones. Her red nose began to run, and her eyes were watering. This was not pleasant, she thought. Mahpee and Mala-Kai stopped abruptly and gestured for the youngsters to join them. They stood beside a stile in a bush, small, unnoticeable but useful. They looked at each other and climbed over.

In the distance they could see the silhouette of the most westerly of the mounds, Knowth. The area covered about 5 square kilometres and even in the dark they could see how impressive it was. They didn't break their stride and continued, heads down, pounding through the field with determination and purpose. The dew on the grass making their boots glisten and the ends of their jeans wet. They trudged through the field and as they came closer to the hill they were halted by Mala-Kai. He seemed to assume the role of leader and they heeded his instruction immediately. Crouching down low they all took a moment. Mala-Kai appeared to be listening for something and holding his hand in a halt gesture he said simply, 'We have company, the Tuatha De Danann are here.'

Duke heard the snapping of a twig underfoot, and suddenly the rustling of the leaves sent shivers down his spine. Willow knew from her Irish history that the 'Tuatha De Danann' were an ancient race of God-like beings gifted with supernatural powers. It is thought they originated from four mythical Northern cities Murias, Gorias, Falias and Finias, possibly located in Lochlann (modern day Norway). They are known as the people of the Goddess Danu, and ruled Ireland before the coming of the Celts and afterwards retreated to the fairy mounds and forts and became 'Aos Si' or 'Otherworld'.

'That is good' said Mala-Kai, 'however, wherever the Tuatha De Danann are then the Fomorians are never far behind.''Don't tell me' Duke offered, 'That's not so good' in his pragmatic, flat, slightly sarcastic tone.

'They are harmful beings of destruction, chaos, darkness and death,' answered Mala-Kai.

'Oh, is that all, nothing to worry 'bout so,' said Duke at which point Willow punched him to shut him up.

'Well then, let's go,' she said unable to mask her anxiety.

The group arrived at the formidable mound, used once as a burial chamber, for ceremonies, and for rituals of all kinds. It spread over a 2.5acre piece of land with nineteen smaller satellite mounds radiating off the larger one. On closer inspection they could see it was a circular structure covered all over by grass. All along the edge of the mound was what was known as kerbstones, 127 in total. Each kerbstone was covered in intricate megalithic art. They shone their light on them as they walked around the perimeter of the mound. They could make out spirals, lozenges, triangles, zigzags, ovals and concentric circles.

'Wow, that's pretty cool,' remarked Duke, 'I wonder what they all mean.'

'I don't think anyone really knows although there are many theories. Some people think they are maps of the landscape. Others believe that they are related to the night sky. For sure they were excellent astronomers, able to calculate the exact moment that the sun will rise and shine in through the roof box and hit the back of the chamber of the Newgrange mound,' said Willow. They walked silently around the tomb, stopping to take in the enormity of the structure and examine more closely the art on each stone. They came to a halt in front of the entrance.

'Should we go in?' asked Duke.

Willow looked over at Ted, and Mahpee. They nodded and the gang went in. Shining their torches, they were blown away by the huge standing stones called 'orthostats' that lined the entrance of the passage all covered in the same Megalithic art as the kerbstones outside. They found two passage tombs back to back, one facing eastwards and one facing westwards. It had the musty dry smell of a stone enclosure in winter. The beehive looking corbelled roof kept these chambers dry as bone. Looking around at the artwork on the wall Duke noticed some graffiti. He wondered who did it. He was a hip hop fan and so he tuned into graffiti art as well. He got a real kick out of what looked like Neolithic graffiti. Shining his torch on the shapes and letters and tracing his fingers over each of the words he made out the names of Snedges, Conan, Teimtennac and Garbltar.

'They are cool, no?' said Ted, 'These are markings of the people from the Kingdom of the Northern Brega.

Just goes to show you Neolithic kids liked to graffiti too. Nothing new nowadays, eh?'

Wondering who these people were, who would leave these markings and musing, that things haven't changed much in a few thousand years, Duke was suddenly jolted form his reverie by a deep booming voice coming from the end of the passage. He jumped, which made Willow jump and in unison they both looked to Mahpee and Mala-Kai for instruction. Mahpee went first and gestured for them to follow. Duke stayed beside Ted, knowing when he was near he was okay. Fro'Ro led Willow up the long dark passage and Mala- Kai brought up the rear. Willow's heart was pounding and she broke out in a cold sweat. What the hell was she doing here? If this was a horror movie on TV, she would be screaming at the screen to run.

They shone their torches on the back wall of the tomb and began to make out the figure of a very tall man. But he wasn't as clear as their crystal guides. He looked like a hologram. He was a shadow figure, tall again, but dressed in translucent white flowing robes. He had grey hair tied at the back of his neck and a very long beard, down to his waist. He looked like a typical wizard. With his arms stretched out, crucifixion style and his head tilted back slightly, he shimmered as he spoke, 'Dia duit mo chairde, ná bíodh eagla ort. Tá mé White Beard, an personification an Bán Grianchloch Crystal a sheasann garda thar na Nemeta naofa.'

He was speaking Irish. Willow understood what he was saying so she began to translate for Duke, who never took to the language. 'Hello, my friends, do not be afraid. I am White Beard, the personification of the White Quartz Crystal that stands guard over these sacred Nemeta,' she said.

Suddenly it was as if Duke could understand what he was saying and needed no translating. He instinctively looked over at Mahpee, who smiled knowingly at him and understood that his energy was working here. White Beard continued, 'I am also the guardian of the quartz crystal skull that lies buried deep within this place. I am here to guide you, for it is foretold that two of the chosen ones would enter this tomb on this date. They will be led and aided by the spirits of the Crystal Kingdom. Welcome my fellow spirits for I recognise you as my brethren.'

White Beard now addressed individuals, 'Turquoise you have come to help the chosen ones stay calm, and balanced. Allow them to see through the lens of compassion and aid them in their communication along the way.' Mahpee knelt down in reverence to this crystal spirit.

'And Malachite, you will work with Tigers Eye to guard and protect these humans. You will help them develop their psychic radar in order to sense danger. You can use your cloak of invisibility when emotional or psychic danger approaches. You are the stone of the enlightened leader, welcome dear one,' White Beard said as Mala-Kai approached him and knelt down in reverence.

'Tigers Eye, you have a profound connection with the young one. You are a solar stone of vitality, practicality and physical action. You are the stone of mental clarity, sharpening the spear of logic and you are vital to his confidence and well-being. He has been blessed with the gift of 'seeing' and you will aid him in working with his powers and balancing both sides of his polarities,' White Beard continued as Teddy bowed in respect. Then White Beard's attention moved to Fro'Ro as she now knelt before him, 'My dear beloved sister, it is wonderful to greet my fellow quartz crystal, especially one who embraces all that is love. You too have bonded magically with our young Goddess. You have helped her so much already to believe in herself and to love herself. She will need your strength as this mission progresses and she will need your loving energy around her at all times. Welcome to the circle of protection, trust and hope.' 'Fro'Ro bowed her head in respect.

Casting his gaze across the tomb to address them all White Beard made one more announcement, 'Now you must listen close dear friends, we have much work to do and the crystal skull is waiting...'

Duke and Willow looked at each other, excitement, confusion and incredulity in their eyes.

Travelling outside to the wooden henge that lies to the east of the entrance to the tomb, the group followed White Beard to the centre where there was a small fire burning. The twigs crackled, and sparks flew up into the night time sky. Their frosted breath mixed with the smoke from the fire and threw up shadows that made the circle in the wooden henge all the more supernatural. Duke looked at the wooden structure illuminated by the light of the moon. It was a circle of Neolithic timber which could be described as an inward-looking amphitheatre.

'Behold dear friends; this is the ceremonial circle where we will contact the 'Saol Eile' or other world. We must call on the Tuatha De Danann to guide and aid us in our mission and give praise to the elements,' White Beard spoke with real purpose and passion. Willow and Duke stood in the centre of the circle with their crystal guides around them all holding hands.

White Beard walked to the west of the circle and said, 'May there be peace in the West.' He then continued to the East and repeated 'May there be peace in the East.' To the South he did the same, 'May there be peace in the South.' And finally walking to the North of the circle he said, 'May there be peace in the North. May there be peace in this circle,' and with this he bowed his head. He then lifted up some earth and said, 'May the stability and grounding of the earth be with us.'

Just then a gust of wind rose as he proclaimed, 'May the life-giving breath of the air cleanse and inspire us.' Looking at the fire he spoke, 'May the passion, power and warmth of the fire sustain us on our way.' The flames rose high up to the sky, sparkling, twisting, and writhing as if exalting in his words. Then suddenly it started to rain, just light drops, and the words, 'May the cleansing power of the water refresh us and balance our emotions as we travel' were uttered. 'We enter this sacred Nemeton and ask for your protection,' White Beard finished speaking.

Duke could feel a palpable change in the atmosphere, like it had suddenly become electrically charged with excitement. He could hear a rumble in the distance. He looked over at Willow, but she seemed oblivious. He suppressed an urge to laugh out loud, the situation was so bizarre that he couldn't help but switch to humour mode as it was almost too overwhelming for him. If he stayed in humour mode, then he wouldn't have to deal with the reality of the situation. He calmed himself, but still had a rumbling knot of anxiety. He knew he could feel things happening here that Willow couldn't. This was an altering of the regular sense of order. Willow was usually in charge and he took his cues from her. He sensed that something was different now and he really didn't like it.

White Beard could be seen more easily now, and it looked like he was wearing a massive cloak of rainbow colours, made from feathers of all kinds. Similar feathers adorned his huge headdress and there lay a sword by his side. He spoke again, 'They are here, welcome Tuatha, the tribal people of Danu, mother Goddess of Ireland, enter our sacred circle, our temenos ground oh shining ones and grant your protection.'

The flame which had been dulled by the light drizzle rose up in the centre and Duke got scared. He held Willow's hand tighter and she looked reassuringly at him. Duke glanced behind him and felt the comforting presence of the guides. He felt encircled and protected and relaxed slightly. Suddenly the presence of a thousand warriors surrounding the henge could be felt by Duke and the crystals. He squinted to see but couldn't make out anything tangible through the drizzle and blackness all around. He tried to connect to the landscape, he felt as if he had become one with everything that was organic, of clay and soil. His heart throbbed to the beat of the earth. The dark imposing silhouette of the mountains rose in the distance like contemplative guardians. He could sense the running water from the rivers like the tears of the earth. The silence of the stones deep within the ground began to reveal their secrets. The noise of their silence was palpable. It didn't make sense. He flew with the birds of the air, ran with the animals of the ground and splashed in the seas with the fish. He had become one with the soul of Gaia. His body swayed and his head swam.

Mala-Kai and Mahpee rose and walked to the outside of the circle and stood guard. They had an aura of yellow luminosity and it stretched for miles around the sacred circle. 'The Fomorians are coming, we must hurry,' announced Mahpee. Duke was now back to feeling scared, more scared than ever.

White Beard instructed him now, 'Take up this sword of Nuada, king of the Tuatha De Danann and don the crown of the ancestors, the bones of which are in the chamber you will shortly enter.' With that a small water hole appeared beside White Beard. Duke gazed down into its dark swirling liquid. 'Now you must drink. For it is said that knowledge is bestowed on he who drinks from the well of eternity,' White Beard said looking straight at Duke, piercing his very being with every word.

Teddy appeared beside Duke, swished his hand

through the water, brought it to his mouth and sipped, showing Duke what to do and reassuring him it was safe. Duke knelt down and ran his fingers through the holy water. It was the most beautiful water he had ever drunk, crystalline, fresh and clear.

White Beard looked down at Duke, 'Your spirit body will now travel to the main tomb. You cannot do this physically as there are too many humans there. You must do this astrally. Do not be afraid for you are surrounded by the benevolent beings of this ancient land. You will be safe but first you must ground yourself. This is why you are afraid. You must connect with Mother Earth. Your soul has joined hers, but your spirit is wandering. Stand still and feel you have roots growing from your feet into the soil. Imagine they are growing deep down into the bowels of the earth and connecting with a pulsating giant green crystal that resides deep within the earth's centre.'

Duke took three deep breaths. He felt himself stand strong and solid, with light flowing from him down through the earth wrapping tendrils around the crystal and coming back up to his body. Teddy stood behind the boy and his aura surrounded him. His energy seeped into Duke's and allowed Duke to begin to feel safe, strong and centred. Duke knew what he must do. He wanted to take action.

'Now you are ready,' White Beard announced and instructed Duke to lie down in the centre of the circle. White Beard then beat a drum. Duke wondered where the drum came from but then thought to himself that this was not the most unusual thing to happen here so far. There was a mad wizard looking type of guy, instructing him on how to travel into an ancient burial tomb, not physically but somehow energetically, to connect with a magical crystal skull hidden deep in the earth somewhere. And there were baddies on the horizon...

To his surprise Duke felt himself get in synch with the drum beat, and his very being began to pulsate, slow rhythmical movements. He could hear a bird call in the distance and laughed to himself at all the random thoughts that were floating through his head. He breathed and sighed.

Willow was sitting at his head and Fro'Ro was on his left, Teddy was on his right and White Beard was at his feet. They held hands and encircled Duke. He looked like he simply went to sleep. Mahpee and Mala-Kai walked further out from the circle. Willow instinctively knew that there was danger approaching. She also knew that the ritual must happen now as the sun was about to rise and everything had to be connected with the solstice.

Duke felt himself stand up. He walked slowly and steadily over to the well, peered into it and then jumped. He swished and swirled down through crystal waters of the well. He felt electricity spark from him through the crust of the earth, connecting him to the crystalline grid that ran around the planet. He was no longer a singular individual but one with everything. He was the water, he was the rock, he was the earth. He was weightless and free. It was as if time stood still and he was suspended in space.

There was a bump and he landed at the entrance to Newgrange. He had the sword of Nuada by his side. He was empowered and excited. There was a connection happening between him and the ancients of the land. The armies of the Tuatha were standing beside him. He looked at the kerbstone to this tomb, different to that of Knowth. It was more impressive. It had three spirals to the left, the interlocking spirals of the triskelion and two on the right with lozenge shapes and waves. It kind of reminded him of Vincent van Gogh and his 'Starry Night' painting. He was outside his body and everything had a supernatural feel, intensified and heightened.

The structure was made from different types of stone, mainly greywacke, but dolerite, sandstone, limestone and granite were also used in the construction. He looked around at the surface of this mound and noted that the walls were completely covered in white quartz crystal. White Beard made sense now. There were also small round stones about the size of a man's head interspaced in the white quartz crystal.

Duke calmly entered the mouth of the tomb and walked the length of the nineteen-metre passage way. The orthostats, upright stone slabs, on either side were covered in art just like the ones at Knowth. The air was cold and reverberated with the essence of the souls of all who were buried there. He arrived at the end of the passage to see a circular chamber with three recesses, one at the end and one at each side, in cruciform shape. He looked into the recess on the right and saw what looked like a large bowl. He knew this was where the burned remains of the dead had been left. Outside Willow was growing increasingly nervous. The wind blew harder. She was aware that Duke was in a deep sleep or trance like state. She held tight to her guides and began to recite the 'Om' chant; she didn't know why but she had to do something. If nothing else, it kept her calm. She sensed a dark shadow coming over the horizon. At first, she thought it was low lying cloud, but she could see it taking shape as it moved closer. Willow instinctively grounded herself; planting her feet firmly in the soil and stretching herself down deep into the earth and connect with her earth star. She was not afraid. The energy of Fro'Ro kept her on the right side of self-belief. With Fro'Ro there Willow could handle whatever came her way.

White Beard was chanting now, but Willow couldn't really understand what he was saying apart from a few audible words; Cygnus constellation, swan, Northern Cross. It made no sense to her but like Duke she retired her logical thought processes to the darkest recesses of her brain and suspended disbelief. She had seen photos of the passage in Newgrange and knew it was in the shape of a cross. Was this connected with the Northern Cross in the sky? Before she could wonder any more there was a loud bang and she was jolted from her thoughts. They were encircled by a dark black mass all around the henge. She could feel at the same time almost a magnetic pull and what could be describes as a force field around them.

White Beard chanted louder now, 'Tuatha stand strong, let the light of the Sun shine into the chamber!' The sun began to peep over the horizon. Suddenly an army of the most grotesque looking grey creatures appeared just outside the sacred wooden henge. They were huge, ten feet tall at least, each one more terrible than the next. Mostly they had bulging muscles, welts and boils all over their bodies. Their heads were covered in what looked like round metal helmets that covered half their face and had a long nose protector. They were without eyes and therefore seemed soulless. Their mouths were like the shrunken mouths of the dead, and the gnarled crooked teeth were protruding through the wrinkled purple lips where sickly drool seeped out. They were marching with conviction, howling and screaming. The ground shook under foot. Weaponry of all types were being brandished, spears, daggers, giant balls with nails on the end of chains.

Duke was in the darkness of the chamber and suddenly there was a shaft of light just appearing at the roof box over the door at the entrance. He knew he had progressed in an uphill direction, walking up the passage as the light, now beginning to peer in the chamber, was at his feet. It crawled across the chamber floor as far as the first edge of the recess at the back of the tomb. As the thin line widened it illuminated the entire back chamber and he began to feel the earth shake. He had no idea what was happening, but he lifted his sword and waited.

Without warning the chamber was saturated in the brightest light he had ever seen, like the floodlights of a stadium in this one tiny space. He couldn't make out sound but felt like his head was filled with white noise. He felt the energy of the ancients all around him. Four white doves flew in the chamber, the flapping of their wings beside his ears made him jump and he felt like the light of the whole universe was streaming up from the ground, through his body filling every cell and shooting out through his head. His spirit was being stretched out through the cosmos. He was connecting with the furthest star in the solar system, while at the same time reaching deep down into the belly of the earth. His physical body was but a mere fulcrum for the energetic body that shot from the centre of the earth to the farthest star.

The Fomorians outside were charging and soon reached the group in the wooden henge. Willow could see the Tuatha De Danann appear; tall, Nordic looking beings with wild red and blond hair, green and blue eyes, wearing metal looking armour and wielding massive swords.

Willow felt a surge of panic that turned to hilarity. Thor vs. the ugly zombies, who will win, she suddenly wondered to herself, somewhat disassociated from the current events. Self-preservation was kicking in and her brain was reaching overload capacity. She was also petrified and needed to make it not real in some sense. Then it was on - a battle of epic proportions. Willow could make out daggers flying, the glint of metal in the morning sun, the crash of bodies falling to the ground, roaring, howling, and chaos. The world was ending, and it wasn't a pretty sight.

The crystals were holding fast with their force field around the henge. The air was menacing. The rainbow colours on White Beard's cape began to shine like beacons, flashing too. Suddenly there was a magical bright light that encompassed the entire sky. It looked like a laser had been turned on over the entire horizon and it reached high up to the heavens. It was blinding, its brightness too harsh to look at directly. There was a humming sound all around them drowning out the noise of the battle, and it began to grow louder.

White Beard was silent. He looked up and shouted, 'Crystalline Grid that covers Gaia, behold the activation of the first crystal skull, ancient keeper of all knowledge and freer of souls! We connect with the power of all that is good! We implore you to accept this activation as the start of the Ascension! We spread this white light through the universe for the good of Gaia and her inhabitants. We offer gratitude to Elcmar, Aengus and the Dagda!' The world seemed to swirl, Willow was faint and nauseous. What was happening? She began to cry, and then sob; her emotions couldn't handle it anymore. She was breaking down. Mala-Kai was beside her, 'Willow you are okay. The battle is over. We are here for you and you are safe.' His benevolent presence immediately calmed the crumbling girl. He wrapped his cloak around her and she felt protected.

There was a thunderous crash, a fork of lightning and the light was gone. Willow looked at her beloved brother. Afraid to speak but unable to stop herself, 'Duke, Duke, wake up,' she implored. She looked around and White Beard was gone. Fro'Ro, and Teddy were there and Mahpee was walking back to the centre of the circle. The danger had subsided and the terrifying Fomorians were nowhere to be seen.

It was first light and the new day was dawning over the distant mountains. Duke slowly opened his eyes and looked at her, exactly as he had done that morning. Time stood still, the group waited, the air was charged. 'Wow, what a trip man' he said eventually. Willow sat back drained, and exhausted but relief washed over her like a soothing balm. Duke sat up and rubbed his eyes. 'Like, OMG, that was epic! I remember a sword, and a flash of light and I dunno, what happened,' he told his sister as he became more conscious.

Willow began to laugh, and laugh, and tremble. Her nerves were all but shot to pieces. Her brain was running at full speed to process the events of the last few moments. She knelt beside her kid brother and wrapped him in an embrace that was so strong he was nearly smothered. 'Duke I have no idea what just happened but we're in the middle of a wooden henge in Knowth and there are hundreds of people over at the other tomb and we are not supposed to be here so what do you say we just blow this popsicle and vamoose?' she suggested as a smile of relief washed over her face.

'Aye, aye, captain,' and with that he made a salute. She helped him to his feet. He was unsteady and needed to hold on to her for a few moments, feeling light headed and dizzy. Willow exhausted and Duke 'buzzing', they headed for the car as quickly as they could. They ran over the wet, slippery grass, warming up under the gentle gaze of the morning sun, towards the little red mini that was still exactly where she was had parked it. Hopping in

Duke turned to Willow and said, 'Yo sis, I have no idea what went on back there, but I sure am glad you were watching over me, much love oh old one.'

Willow turned to him smiling but with nothing but utter love in her eyes for him. She immediately gave him a punch in the arm saying, 'Yer grand, ya big girls blouse. Now let's get home before Mam notices we're gone.'

Willow and Duke eventually schlepped their exhausted bodies' home. Ted, Fro'Ro, Mahpee and Mala-Kai all stayed in close vigil to mitigate any aftershocks from their experience at Newgrange. Dodging their mother's questions, brother and sister dragged their feet up the stairs and into Duke's tiny bedroom. Sitting crossed legged on his bed he just stared at Willow. 'Well, like, where do we go from here? I mean, I can't even process what just happened back there,' Duke thought aloud. He was trying fervently to make sense of it all but was failing miserably.

'Listen, I know it's all a bit overwhelming Duke...' Willow started.

'Eh, like, ya think?' he cut her off.

'Look, I know I can't get my brain around it either, but I think we need to stay calm and figure out our next step, yeah?' Willow was trying to be the voice of reason.

'Ha, yeah, like let's get T-Shirts printed... Keep Calm, and Activate a Crystal Skull,' Duke replied.

'Duke stop being facetious, this is blowing my mind as much as it is yours,' Willow retorted.

'Yeah but apparently, you're not the 'Chosen One', this last bit he did in air quotes. He was getting fond of using air quotes to emphasize his point. 'Like, what am I even supposed to do with that. What does that mean Willow? It's kinda freaking me out man,' he put his head in his hands and began to silently cry. Willow simply went over to him and sitting beside him on the bed, put her arm on his back and allowed him to weep, all the tears that had been clogged up inside him. She didn't tut him or implore him to stop. She knew this was badly needed. She graciously allowed him to weep out all his frustration and fear. Duke rolled over in his tiny bunk, pulled the duvet over him and promptly fell into the deepest blackest sleep of his life. Willow looked to the crystal guides now for some answers.

'Apple blossom, I know you are scared witless right now and are so confused that your brains feel like they will implode but y'all need to hang on in there. Have faith, we are here with you, and we will see you right, ya dig?' Fro'Ro was soothing her frayed nerves and restoring her belief in herself.

'Fro'Ro speaks the truth Willow. You need to stay strong now, especially for your brother. He will look to you now for guidance and answers. None of us have any but the process has begun now and we will be directed. We know there are more skulls. We know they will be in the four corners of the globe. Trust that the universe will guide our actions and provide what is needed. For now, you must rest,' Teds words resonated in Willow's head as she lay down on the other bunk, a bed normally reserved for sleepovers and visiting guests. She was not going to abandon Duke now. She simply needed to be near her kid bro and make sure he was safe.

Sleeping fitfully throughout the day Willow rose late that evening; the memory of bad dreams hanging in the ether between her conscious and unconscious mind. Ghouls, ghosts and demons seemed to rampage through her brain. Rubbing her eyes, she noticed the four crystals standing guard over them like sentinels, forming a protective barrier around the room. Nothing was getting in here that was not invited.

Night had fallen, and Willow was groggy and disorientated. She hopped down and checked on Duke. Out cold he looked like he hadn't moved a muscle since he went to sleep hours earlier. She looked at Ted.

'Greetings female human,' he said with a smile. Willow looked at him with a blank expression. His attempt at levity was lost on her half-awake brain.

Fro'Ro was lounging along the floor, 'Yo Sista, so heads up, your Mama is in the kitchen and I think she may be wondering why y'all be sleepin' the day away. You may want to get your story straight before you go down for a 7pm breakfast.'

Willow took in this information and went to the bathroom. She splashed cold water on her face and stared into the mirror. She still looked the same, but inside, well that was a different matter. She knew everything had changed and there was no going back. The world was calm now, here in their little house. She could hear the tv downstairs and the soap her mum was fond of watching. She realised this was what it must be like for anyone who has gone through a great change in their life, a major event, or the death of a loved one. The world keeps turning as usual, dinners are eaten, tv is watched, babies cry. But her world had just changed irrevocably. The events of the morning were less than twelve hours ago but seemed like a lifetime. She even wondered momentarily if she dreamed it all but with Fro'Ro bursting through the bathroom door she was jolted back into her new bizarre fantasy reality.

'Honey, you ok?' the crystal asked of her.

'Actually, I really don't know, but I guess I'll have to be, right?' Willow offered with a smile.

'Lovely jubbly' came Fro'Ro's retort in a cockney accent.

Willow laughed. She guessed that hanging out with Duke was rubbing off on them, they seemed to be developing a rather good sense of humour or trying at least. Willow collected her thoughts and decided to tell her mum absolutely nothing about what had taken place. She knew she was open to this stuff but really didn't have any answers and didn't want to worry her unduly. Willow could do that enough for them both. Forming a tummy bug scenario, she knew she could get away with that as an explanation of Duke sleeping the day away.

When Duke woke early the next morning, after his mammoth sleep he was greeted with the four crystals and Willow sitting in a circle, humming, cross legged, and apparently meditating. 'Woah, sup guys?' he was still half conscious.

'Ah our young warrior arouses from his slumber. How goes it with you dear boy,' now Ted was doing a weird posh English accents and Willow looked askance at him. What is going on with these guys, she thought.

'Eh, Ted' Duke enquired, 'like, you have gone all la dee dah, I'm very confused.com.'

'I am simply trying to add some levity to your morning but I seem to be failing, never mind. How are you feeling?' he replied. Duke sighed, 'Like I have been hit by a ten-tonne truck. How long have I been asleep?'

'Ages,' came Willow's simple answer.

Duke stretched out his legs and lay back on the bed, 'So what's going on folks, I can tell something is cookin'. Spill.'

'Well, my dear little brother, it seems that our Uncle Brownie in New Zealand was on to Mum last night. They got chatting and he suggested we go visit him as we have never been, and he thinks it will be good for us. Like, can you honestly believe this?' Willow could barely contain herself.

'What, wait, back up, like, we're going on a holiday, the three of us, to Kiwi land, are you serious?' Duke was very awake now.'Deadly' Willow replied, 'but not the three of us, just us two. Mum can't take time off work and I've convinced her that it will be hugely beneficial if she lets you take time off school. I can postpone college for a while so it's all systems go, but I am totally and one hundred percent in charge, like, I am the total boss. I am the boss of you.'

Duke roared laughing, 'In yer dreams, ya numpty,' and with that he threw a pillow at her head, hitting her dead on.Mahpee, a crystal of few words, piped up, 'It seems that the universe has aligned for us and we have been guided to our next destination. Isn't it marvellous how everything works in perfect order?' All those gathered just stared at Mahpee, surprised at his sudden input.

'Yeh man, I guess it is,' smiled Duke.

TURNING TIDES

Senator Wayne Johnson woke early. Jumping out of his silk sheets, he pulled on his sweats, grabbed his kit bag and headed to the very exclusive, very expensive, members only gym. Arriving disgruntled after a bad night's sleep, he threw himself into his workout. Taking time to glance sideways in the mirror as he sat on the bench, wiping his neck dry, he admired his physique. His muscles were bulging, and he was stacked better than most of the guys half his age. The tattoo on his upper right arm, a serpent circling his biceps, was more becoming of a dodgy downtown nightclub bouncer than a respected politician. Vanity was evident in the form of neon white teeth, thanks to much cosmetic dental work and together with his amazing bone structure and sallow skin he cut quite a striking image.

His daily routine was important to him and he kept it no matter what: gym, protein shake, and after showering he dressed in a bespoke designer suit. Today it was Italian linen, pale blue, starched white shirt and pastel striped tie, with flecks of pink and dark purple. There was a nod to glitz in the form of twenty-four carat gold cuff links with spirals on them. He tailored his attire according to who he was meeting. Today it was a journalist, a female journalist. He liked to wear softer colours when dealing with women. Budget meetings with the city council, old cronies required something more sombre, and severe; dark navy or black, emphasizing his authority, but today was about schmooze. He went into wooing mode, being an excellent communicator and knowing the effect he had on women, he was confident of a win. This was a PR exercise, but it was an important one – he needed to turn public opinion around.

The Senator got into the back seat of his limousine and his driver took off. In the car he looked over the file he had on Abigail Dent. She was in her late twenties, bleeding heart liberal, cute, intelligent, and graduating with top honours in investigative journalism and social science, he smirked. He would have her eating out of his hands. Thank God for social media. He had everything he needed to know about her. He was going to hit her with the good old-fashioned nugget of 'jobs'. Who could argue with job creation? Think of all the local jobs that would be created from this proposed pipeline. Thousands of people would benefit from this project, mechanics, electricians, pipe fitters, welders, heavy equipment op-erators. God the list is endless. How could she in good conscience argue with that?

Sitting back on the expensive leather seats of his car, lost in thought, he twirled the piece of amber through his fingers. Outside the landscape was a gentrified city scene of apartment blocks, art galleries, restaurants and bars. Gone now were the slums and homeless. Good riddance to bad rubbish, the Senator smiled to himself. Who needs to be looking at all that poverty anyway, much better to move all those 'less fortunate' to the outskirts of the city, or further. He almost believed himself that he was doing a great service to the people of the city, providing them with fabulous housing and cultural outlets. Never mind that the problem of overcrowding and not enough housing was simply moved to another borough. Not his problem anymore.

Once in his office his elderly secretary brought him in his green tea. Mrs Winters had been with him since he began in politics. She was now in her late sixties, conservative, in her appearance and in her attitudes to life. She believed in hard work and loyalty. She dressed in a dark navy two-piece skirt suit, white blouse buttoned to the neck with a single strand of pearls at the collar. Her plump legs were covered in thick brown tights and her smart sensible black shoes sported a small kitten heel, her nod to fashion. Her hair was grey, she never dyed it, knotted at the back in a small bun, and she wore thick black glasses, having never got around to trying contact lenses.

She'd seen Wayne rise through the ranks, standing by his side through thick and thin. He was like a son to her. In a town where most high-profile politicians would have pretty young secretaries, she felt more like his right-hand woman, his aide-de-camp, his trusted advisor. He had helped her out when her Ronnie got into trouble and she'd never forget that. She was the first to defend him and simply ignored any rumours when they cropped up about his dirty tactics and corrupt dealings. She didn't believe it, not completely anyway. She knew there was another side to him and that's what she chose to focus on, 'Good Morning Senator, your nine o'clock is in reception.'

'Thank you, Doris. And make sure that my 9.30 will be ready,' he instructed.

'But Senator, you don't have a 9.30... oh I see, yes of course,' and with that she exited the office.

Within moments the door to his office opened and Doris Winters showed Ms Abigail Dent in.

'Good Morning Senator, thank you for taking the time to meet with me,' Abigail began, shaking hands with the Senator.

'Not at all, it's a pleasure. Please do sit down. Can I get you anything, coffee?' he asked, playing the gracious host.

'No thank you I'm fine, if we could just get straight down to business...' she asked, sitting down opposite him and taking out reports from her briefcase.

'But of course, Ms Dent, how may I help you today? You have some questions regarding the pipeline project?' he smiled at her flashing his pearly whites.

Continuing to focus on her reports, she took little notice of his subtle attempts at winning her over, 'Call me Abigail please, well Senator I do have some grave concerns about the land through which this pipeline is to be routed. There are a lot of unhappy people in this region and...'

'Let me just stop you there Ms Dent… apologies, Abigail, I can assure you no one is more concerned for these people than I am. I think you will find my track record speaks for itself in this area,' the untruth just slipping off his tongue with the ease of a professional liar. He stood up and walked around to the front of his desk casually perching on its edge, hands under him in a manner that was informal and disarming. He wanted to let her know he was friendly, on her side, affable. He was an excellent communicator and body language was his weapon of choice. He was aware that his huge frame could be intimidating, and he used this fact to his advantage.

'Indeed, Senator, but there are statistics that I believe you have not been made aware of concerning the river through which this proposed pipeline is to run and also the land is believed to be sacred to some of the indigenous people living there and I don't think that these…' her brave outburst thwarted in midsentence again.

'Abigail, Abigail, let me assure you that every person affected by this has been fully consulted and as for the river, well nothing but the latest technology will be employed here. I can emphatically support the project and its safety one hundred percent,' Wayne Johnson was not letting her get on top of this conversation.

'Senator, this really is not a trivial matter. It has massive consequences for these people. I have studies here of pipelines similar to this one bursting and the crude oil spillages have had devastating consequences for the environment and as for the land being sacred, well this is just something that cannot be ignored,' this time Abigail made deliberate eye contact as she tried once more to pin him down to a proper discussion rather than just being fobbed off.

The intercom rang, 'Senator, your next appointment is waiting,' Doris' voice announced to the room.

Sensing she was being shown the door, Abigail lowered her voice a little, calmly and collectively said, 'Senator, we really need to discuss this matter in more depth. I believe the people have a right to know what's going on here.'

'Abigail let me assure you, I will do everything in my power to ensure the welfare of these people is a top priority. Now if you will excuse me, I really do have other pressing matters I must attend to,' the senator lied through his smile, offering a hand to help her off her seat and to the door.

Abigail was stumped. She was being given the heave ho. She suspected some resistance but so soon, this was a surprise. As she got up from her seat, declining his assistance she said, 'Senator, I appreciate you seeing me on such short notice but rest assured, this matter must be discussed at length. I assume you will have more time for me on our next meeting.' She let the statement, hang in the air for him to digest and beat a hasty retreat out of his office.Abigail Dent was fuming. She knew he was a slippery fish but she hadn't expected him to be so smooth. He was charming alright, but she knew he had something to hide. She could sniff out foul play a mile away and as for the games he was playing, she had his number, she hadn't grown up with four older brothers and not learnt a thing or two about the male of the species and their tactics. She wasn't in the least bit intimidated by this guy and if he thought for one minute she could be shoved aside then he was sadly mistaken.

Back at her tiny office she went over what she knew. The Senator was a high ranking official so she would have to be careful. But she was fed up with ordinary, decent people getting pushed around by corporate industries, politicians and government institutions and she was determined to find out what was going on.

The Sabre Oil pipeline development was a massive billion-dollar project to build a pipeline carrying crude oil through several states and also through the sacred land of the indigenous people who lived there. On paper it was all legal and above board. But that didn't make it right. All the information she had on this project was in favour of the Oil Company, tests done on the land, farmers compensated for land disruption, statistics proving how safe the technology is. This was all very nice and clean, but why were there hundreds of people camping out in the freezing weather to protest about this. What were their concerns? What was the report not telling her? She decided to pack a bag a see for herself.

This was her chance too to make a name for herself in journalism, for all the right reasons. She really was interested in social issues and the plight of the little man. She had grown up watching her father struggle all his life in low paying jobs. He was a good hard-working man who did his best to provide for his family. She admired her

Dad and loved him very much. Although he had never received any formal education and drove a truck most of his life, he was very well read, and she respected his opinion immensely. She decided to bounce a few ideas off him and called him, 'Dad, hey it's me, do you have time for a quick chat?' 'For you my darling, I always have time. So, what's going on?' his voice was comforting.

'Well, do you know Senator Wayne Johnson? He's campaigning for this pipeline that is to run through the sacred lands of the Native Americans who live there. Have you heard anything about it? What do you think?' she couldn't hide her desire to see what her Dad thought.

'Abi, it's a disgrace. How these people have been treated over the years and now, to have this monstrosity running through their ancient lands, with the potential to contaminate their water supply, well, I just can't express my rage enough. Abi, if you can do anything to help these people and shed some light on this, you would be looking at one mighty proud father, I can tell you that for nothing,' the smile clear for all to hear in his voice.

'But Dad, if I do take this story on, I am potentially making an enemy out of one of the most powerful men in the city,' Abi said looking for confirmation rather than permission.

'So, I didn't raise you to be afraid of any of these people Abigail Dent. I raised you to do what's right and just, and I believe you know what is right and just here,' her father replied. Just what she wanted to hear, 'Okay Dad, I hear ya.'

'That's my girl, now go get 'em tiger,' he encouraged.

'Dad?' Abi was the one now smiling.

'Yup?' her father asked now beaming with pride.

'Thanks' she said.

'I love you Abi,' his voice so smooth, deep and reassuring.

'Me too Dad, tell Mum we'll chat this weekend,' she said.

'Will do sweetheart,' her dad replied. And with that Abi hung up the phone with all her confidence and resolve back in place.

When Abigail was gone, the Senator returned to his seat, rather uneasily. There was more to this young lady than met the eye. He knew she had a steely reserve, a backbone; she was not one to be easily intimidated or brushed aside. He was going to have to keep a close eye on her. The bad feeling in the pit of his stomach was hanging around for too long now. Was it to do with this girl? Was it the pipeline? He stood to lose a lot of money if it didn't go ahead, but there was something else going on here and it made him uneasy.

Pressing the button on his intercom he instructed Mrs Winters to cancel all his meetings for the rest of the day and headed out into the frosty streets of the city. Shoving his hands into the pockets of his cashmere camel coloured coat and pulling his scarf tighter around his neck, he strode with purpose. Whenever he had this feeling he always needed to walk it off and think. The tide was turning on public sentiment. He could feel change in the air. Years ago, people didn't give a hoot about the environment. Aerosols were in, tanning booths ruled, and no one had heard of carbon footprint. What was going on with the world? Suddenly everyone was a bleeding-heart liberal, eating organic, doing yoga, and being mindful. He sneered to himself. Mindfulness, what the heck was that all about anyway? The world had become a playground for aging hippies and do-gooders.

He walked to his usual spot in a corner of the city park. It had a covered entrance to a small enclosure where there was one very large oak tree, sitting regally in the middle. There was never anyone here because of the overgrown path leading in to it. He considered it his sanctuary. He sat down on the bench beside the tree. He got great comfort sitting here. Perhaps it was the size of the tree or its cover and shade. Trees had a certain aura, a presence, like old grandfathers who sat and said nothing but knew everything. Trees didn't judge, and it was judgement he was trying to escape from, his own judgement of himself.

His buried demons really wanted to raise their ugly heads and breathe. He twirled his piece of amber in his pocket. He couldn't put his finger on why he was disgruntled but it was there plain as day. He looked down at the ground and became entranced by a raven, sitting beside him, pecking at the ground. It was a big bird, jet black with almost ruby coloured eyes. There was a strange ethereal feeling to it. Wayne bent down closer to the bird as if to say something. The bird looked up at him, squawked and flew off. Wayne sat back on the bench, hands in his pockets, his breath letting out streams like smoke into the frosted air. He was at a crossroads and for the first time since he became this all-powerful Senator, he felt stumped, unsure of himself, questioning. This had to stop. Gathering himself he stood up and strode purposefully back to the office.

Back at his desk he ordered Mrs Winters to get Kurt Gelder on the phone. Kurt was the Chief Executive Officer for Sabre Oil, and he was a close confidant. These two bed fellows had climbed the ranks of the political and corporate world almost side by side. They couldn't be described exactly as friends but had known each other in professional realms so long that they were at least very familiar with each other. 'Wayne, how are you? To what do I owe this pleasure?' Kurt answered the call.

'Kurt, this isn't a social call. We need to meet,' Wayne abandoned the small talk.

'Sounds ominous Senator, usual place, say 4pm?' Kurt suggested.

'Done,' Wayne replied and hung up abruptly.

The two men met in a seedy café as agreed. No one would notice them here. It wouldn't be good for either of them to be recognised and certainly not with each other. In public Wayne Johnson maintained an impartial stance on all things political and was seen to be pro the environment but of course he played to the highest bidder. Kurt Gelder was that bidder. He had lined the pockets of the Senator considerably in order to land the contract for the pipeline development. They had been vigilant in their research and in covering up whatever they needed to.

Ordering coffee Wayne got straight to the point,

85

'Kurt, I think we may have a small problem in the form of one Abigail Dent, a journo. She's been poking around and I don't like it. How well have you covered your tracks?'

'Relax, we're sweet. This is not my first rodeo, if you know what I mean,' Kurt was an experienced C.E.O. used to handling the press. He wasn't a politician, he was a businessman and his business was to make money, period. The pipeline was a development that both men needed to succeed. Kurt Gelder was heavily invested financially, and Wayne Johnson's public reputation was at stake. Neither man would let anything get in the way, especially a nosy journo like Abigail Dent.

The senator leaned in a little closer, 'Well, I'm doing a background check on this Dent chick, I'll see if I can dig up any dirt but, in the meantime I need you to expedite this as best you can. Any delays are costly delays. We need to get moving. I have done my best to force a media blackout on these damn protestors but with this Dent woman poking around, there may be some unnecessary coverage and that's not good for business. I've put pressure on the cops to get heavy handed if necessary, but this has to end. We can't have an exposé about the camp up there.''Okay, but we need to get the permits in place and get it finished. Who do you know in City Hall that you can lean on?' Kurt asked as a believer in the time-honoured traditions of backhanders and blackmail.

'Look, I have the cops in my back pocket, city officials; whoever I need to have on the payroll is on the payroll. You leave it with me; I'll stop her,' Wayne was feeling a little uncomfortable and didn't like his authority being questioned.

'Wayne, you better had. I don't need to tell you how much is at stake here,' and with that Kurt Gelder rose to his feet and left the premises.

Wayne sat staring out the window at the dull, wet day. He wished momentarily that he could go home, relax in front of the open fire with his 'significant other', indulge in a large glass of Merlot and read one of the many books that lined the shelves of his library. He collected these books with the intention of one day getting around to gleaning their wisdom, but it never happened, it was more about having them for show than actually reading them.

He looked down into his now cold coffee. The waitress sidled over. She had been eyeing the two men for a while now but didn't dare interrupt. She had been a waitress long enough to be an expert in body language and these bodies were clearly saying, 'do not disturb'. When one of the two men left, she waited a while before approaching. She was intrigued. He wasn't the usual type of customer that they got in here. This guy was very well dressed. She noted his solid gold cuff kinks, his bespoke leather brogues, his silk tie, and manicured nails. 'Anything else? 'More coffee? Piece of pie?' she asked while flashing him her grade A smile, swinging her hips around and holding her tray up high. She couldn't help herself.

'Just the cheque,' he answered without really noticing her. She walked off slightly deflated. She recognised this guy from somewhere but just couldn't place him.

Maybe he's a big-time crime lord, she thought to herself; if so, it was best to get him out. She didn't want any bullets flying. Her shift finished at three, and it would be a damn shame to be caught in a turf war before she got to clock out. 'Here ya go sugar,' she dropped the bill and moved on, already forgetting about this mysterious stranger.

Wayne just sat there taking in his surroundings; the fluorescent lighting, the chatter of the other diners, the steam rising off new arrivals as the heat of the cafe met their wet clothes. The rain was making the familiar pitter-patter on the roof, and against the glass. He felt hot and sweaty as he casually glanced out the window into a dismal looking alley. A scrawny, miserable, stray dog was rummaging in the bins for a morsel of food. His hair stuck to his back emphasizing his thin spine. He sniffed the ground fruitlessly. There was a time that this sight would trouble Wayne, not any more. He was self-aware enough to know that this poor emaciated animal, alone on the winds of the world, stirred absolutely nothing in him. His shields were permanently up.

Wayne wiped his brow with the paper serviettes that were housed in a tin container sitting on the table against the window frame. They dissolved in his hand. He felt disgusting, sticky and somehow unclean, his immaculate linen suit now creased and uncomfortable. Loosening his tie, he was almost in a trance as he sat transfixed on the last vestiges of the cold, tan liquid in his mug. Something was brewing in his head. He had to stop this girl. He didn't understand why he felt so threatened and he didn't like it. He was staring down into the cup, the liquid swimming round, he was mesmerised, she needed to be stopped and he suddenly he knew how to go about doing just that.

With renewed determination, he threw some cash on to the table and exited the building. Once in his car he instructed his driver to step on it. He phoned the office and informed Mrs Winters that he would be gone for the weekend and he took off for his country cottage up-state. They drove through the rain for what seemed like forever. Wayne couldn't relax. He needed to get there, wash the stench of the city from his skin and have a very large brandy. Finally arriving in the dark, he dismissed his driver back to the city with instructions to pick him up the following evening. Whenever Wayne felt like he needed to take stock he would retreat to this place. It was a small simple cottage. He didn't need to keep up appearances as no one ever came with him. It felt like home and for the first time in quite a while he felt like he could breathe easily. The floral patterned worn sofas still sat where they always did in front of a big open fire. The huge granite mantelpiece covered nearly half the ex-posed brick wall. Throwing his phone and briefcase on the large oak table by the door, flicking the switch on the ornate antique lamp, he scrambled together the makings of a fire and throwing a match on it, removed his tie, lay back on the sofa and fell into a weary sleep within minutes.

The crackle of a dying fire woke him in the middle of the night. He was stiff and groggy. Sitting up he tried to shake the anxiety that still lingered. Trundling into the kitchen he turned on the light and filled the kettle. There was nothing but blackness outside the window. But the demons weren't out there, they were inside. Was this madness? Was this depression? But Wayne was far too powerful to suffer from such things. Was it his conscience pricking him? Surely not, that was unthinkable. He would rather suffer from a debilitating mental and emotional illness than have a crisis of conscience. Resolving to sort out this bleakness he turned, grabbed a large overcoat from the stand in the hall, pulled on some old walking boots, and tore out the front door towards the lake.

It was pitch black but knowing dawn was rising he marched with conviction over the field and through the woods that were so familiar to him. No light was needed here; just answers… and the lake would provide them. Navigating like a tracker and ignoring the biting air inside his nostrils he pushed on. Ducking under branches and sloshing through wet muddy puddles he arrived in no time by the edge of a large black body of water.

The sun began to peep its fingers over the horizon. Wayne was looking for something in particular. He used to come here as a boy and stare through a large old wooden mirror. It lay like a portal to another world in the shallow depths at the edge of the lake. Invisible now, it needed to be coaxed into the light. The morning sun obliged as if doing his bidding. Something glistened to his left and he just caught it out of the corner of his eye. Manoeuvring himself through the muck and reeds and pulling back some long grass there it was; his mirror, his oracle, hidden, yet available as soon as he called, awaiting him like a still flat crystal ball.

Dawn was breaking and obligingly illuminated the scene. Wayne squatted down on his hunkers and grabbing a log, he pulled the edge of the wooden mirror nearer to him. It had old white cracked, flaking paint around the edge. It was arched at the top with straight sides and a flat bottom. There was a type of ornate decoration in the centre. He had never really looked closely at it before but now it screamed at him, like a beacon. A figure of some type of black bird sat perched on the top of the mirror. The water around it was dank and murky. There were dead leaves, pond scum, and long grasses floating around the prized object, as if masking its appearance to the outside world. Only those in the know could find it. The light of the rising sun shone over the water and began illuminating the glass of the mirror, unfolding a scene like the way photographs used to be developed, in a dark room, with the picture slowly, steadily revealing itself in front of the observer's eyes.

The water was icy on Wayne's hands, but he didn't notice, at once becoming transfixed on the image in front of him. He knew he was witnessing something of great significance; he just couldn't make sense of it. Then slowly but surely, he began to make out the image of a boy, a young teenager, dark skinned. He seemed to be spinning, arms outstretched, shining, rising. What the hell was he looking at? He strained to see more clearly. There were armies, battles, wars. Wayne saw a matrix, a geometric shape that he couldn't quite make out. Then there in front of him, as the sun shone full beam over the lake, like a spotlight on the mirror, was on object coming into view, round and rotating slowly to face him, boring a hole into his very soul, a giant, clear omniscient crystal skull.

Wayne flew back onto the bank as if punched in the stomach, hard. He sat stunned and shaken for a moment and then quickly gathered himself and ran back as fast as he could to the cottage, properly spooked. Slamming the front door, he tore off his crumpled, damp and smelly clothes, ran a shower and stepped in as if he was cleansing his soul. The water ran down his shaking body. He stood there under its spell, letting the hot steamy liquid melt his flesh. His skin began to burn under the pressure and temperature, but he didn't care. He needed it. What was it he had seen? Whatever it was, it frightened him.

Finally, when the water began to run cold, he forced himself to stand there even longer. It got very cold and still he stayed. The longer he stayed the stronger his resolve. He didn't realise but his hands were clenched into two tight fists and his jaw was set firm. Wayne came out of that shower a different person than the one who had gone in. The morning sun was beaming in through the steamed-up bathroom window. He wiped the condensation from the mirror and looked at himself, properly looked at himself and instead of hating what he saw, he was in awe of it.

He knew what he had become and there was no going back now. This thing that was happening must be stopped at all costs. He knew the skull was powerful. He knew this because he felt it in his bones. Its power must be stopped, or even better, harnessed for his own use. This skull held the key to everything. It and others like it, were the gateways to all knowledge on Earth. He knew the activation was the beginning. 'Ascension' had begun; the start of the humanity becoming more enlightened; people thinking for themselves; believing in themselves and not big corporations that had fed them lies for centuries; people rejecting the paradigms of society, the businesses, the governments, the religions.

It was the beginning of the dawn of a new consciousness on the Earth. Everything on the planet including the planet has a consciousness and this skull has just raised it. Wayne could feel the heart energy of the world rising as he stood in this tiny old cramped bathroom. If people really began to approach life from their hearts instead of their heads how could anyone manipulate them? This was the fundamental basis for his business and his success. He needed people to believe him when he fed them his version of the 'truth'. He couldn't have them becoming aware. He couldn't have them becoming awake. He would lose everything. Wayne knew he could not stop the activation of this skull, but he was dam sure he could do something about the next one. He knew instinctively there were more.

He strode into the small bedroom and rummaged in the closet where he always kept spare clothes. He pulled on a pair of jeans and a sweater. They smelled musty, he didn't care, he was on a mission now. He needed to use his instincts like he had never used them before. He had the ability to tune into the energies of the universe. He could sense things, feel them as if they were being played out on the T.V. in front of him.

Back in the living room, he stoked up the fire again, sat down and began to meditate. He calmed his breathing and tried to clear his mind. He focussed breathing in and then breathing out. Slowly his mind began to empty. Randomly thoughts crossed his mind, but he allowed them to float by as if they were clouds in the sky. His back was straight, and his legs were crossed.

Images began to flash before his eyes, ice, winds, fields. He felt cold. He thought he heard Uilleann pipes and flutes and the haunting lyrical melody of a woman. Then there were giants, huge, Celtic, and mythical. He knew immediately they were in Ireland. He could see the hill of Tara. He saw that young boy again; long hair, dark skinned, the familiar feeling came upon him. This unsettled him and he stopped with a fright. He had to come out of his trance. He felt fear. He took some deep long breaths and settled himself back down on the floor.

Closing his eyes, he went back to his breathing. He turned his attention to the point between his eyebrows, his third eye. Imagining himself to be travelling down a swirling vortex, he felt his head swim, down deeper and deeper. He was swimming in the ether of the other-world. His body felt light and breezy. This must be how a bird feels, floating on the currents of the air. Rainbow lights began to sparkle beside him. Out of the corner of his eye he could sense movement, people, human and not so human. He was drawn to the heart space of a girl. He was feeling her distress. She was afraid but not for herself. There was an apocalyptic bang, an explosion and there it was: the skull in all its glory and might. Radiantly it shone as if covering the entire earth with its magic beams. The laser like light blinded him and Wayne was slammed back into his body.

He sat, drained, overwhelmed and in awe. He was hunched on the floor, back bent, head hanging low. It was as if all the life force was drained from his body. When he did raise his head, his eyes had a menacing hue. He now knew that the crystal skull had been activated in the Northern hemisphere, in Ireland, in Newgrange. He'd have to stop the next one. He sensed four in all, one for each of the directions of the world. Which would be next? South? East? West? And where would these places be? How could he find out in time? He needed to speak with the Elementals.

Abigail Dent reached the camp where the protestors had set up. She inched her car slowly through the gates operated by aging Native Americans, tribe logos pinned to their leather waistcoats. She was instructed to park up on a ridge. She got out and tried to orientate herself in the pre-dawn darkness. As she was deciding on a game plan, the sun began to rise and exposed the protestor's camp right in front of her. There were tents, tipis, yurts, all making up a sprawling spread of a make shift settlement; all made quite beautiful by the morning sun.

Abi set off in the direction of the centre of the camp where there was a large canvas geodesic dome. She trawled through muck, past camp fires where people were singing, talking, strategizing. There were thousands of people here of all nationalities. She passed a series of flags representing the various nations of the indigenous people and flags with 'Black Lives Matter', 'Protect our Water', 'Save Mother Earth', 'People not Pipelines', 'Veterans for The Earth', 'Indigenous Lives Matter'. There were people of every colour, and age here. It really was quite incredible - it was peaceful but purposeful.

There were babies in scarves slung around the bodies of aging grandmothers. Young men with faces of conviction were driving trucks, chopping wood, building corals for horses. It was a hive of activity. Stopping in to the mess hall where it looked like they were preparing to serve the first meal of the day, she asked after the man or woman in charge and was directed to a man called Sam Wetherill, who usually hung out in the 'office' at this time of the morning. Right on cue she heard over the loud speaker, 'It's time to get up. This is not a vacation. We've got work to do, relatives.'

Finding her destination easily she was introduced to a man in his fifties who had, he informed her, lived on this land all his life, as had his family for many generations before him. Sitting over a very welcome hot cup of coffee, Sam filled Abi in on what was essentially going on in the camp, 'Basically we are protectors of the water, not protestors. If the proposed pipeline goes ahead then the potential danger for contamination of our water source is almost guaranteed. We simply can't let that happen. Not to mention, the land through which they are building it runs right through our sacred burial sites. We are used to camping in protest like this and we will be victorious. It is up to us to protect the water supply not just for ourselves but for future generations. Mother Earth needs our help and we are here for her. We don't just see this water as a resource to be used and abused. We believe in the living consciousness of it. That's why we have to protect it.'

'But what about the oil company,' Abi enquired, 'I know they have received all the appropriate documents needed and carried out various surveys to ensure the safety of this project.' Abi was playing Devil's Advocate.

'You really think just cause it's legal that it's right?' Sam seemed rather disappointed in her. Abi was quick to make her position clear and that she was very eager to help. Sam told her the best way to help was to get the story out there. They had set up face book pages, twitter feeds, a go fund me page but there still seemed to be some sort of media blackout. The news of their plight and struggle just wasn't reaching enough people. Sam believed that if enough people knew what was happening then they would get the support they badly needed, and they would have the influence to change policy.

Abi chatted with Sam for as long as she could then set off to explore the rest of the camp. She sat with the 'protectors' and got as much research as she could. She was enamoured by the singing and the drumming that could be heard in the background. The smell of the campfires in the morning air hung to her clothes like a potpourri of protest. This was quite something she decided, and she had to get the story out there. There had already been some news reports but only minor ones, and very brief. She wanted to do a full exposé on the cause, which she was behind one hundred percent. This was not going to be a simple human-interest story or social diary. The news of this struggle needed to be told and people needed to be informed. Once again big business and corporations were railroading over the indigenous people of this country and she was going to do everything in her power to stop it. She could make out a chant in the far distance 'Mni Wiconi' and bent down to ask an elderly gentleman what it meant; he looked her straight in the eye and said, 'Water is life'.

Abi resolved to set up camp up and stay. She sat down and phoned her editor. She told him what she was planning and requested a photographer to be sent up. Her editor, being a crumpled weary old news hound, but with a soft spot for Abigail, acquiesced to her requests. Good for her, he thought to himself when he got off the phone. She may actually make a difference here…

LAND OF THE LONG WHITE CLOUD

Willow and Duke got off the plane, their insides scrambled as if they had been through a blender. Duke had slept sporadically during the long-haul flight, but for Willow it had been a real struggle; her brain was spangled, and her body wasn't doing much better. Walking toward the baggage claim area, she moved as if under water, her muscles unfurling like octopus tentacles having been trapped so long in a compact aeroplane seat. She followed the crowd and arrived at the luggage belt. It was only now that she noticed the accents around her, higher pitched, with a drawling intonation.

Collecting their bags, they made their way out from the baggage carousel and emerged to the waiting crowds of people, all straining to see the first glimpse of their loved ones. It had a rather weird feeling, touching down on ground that is so very far from home. Willow was disorientated but knew it fell to her to get them sorted; Duke was not the most tuned in kid at the best of times, and a 'practical' nature was not something that could truthfully be said about him.

She wheeled the bag laden trolley out through the open doors and looked around but couldn't see their uncle anywhere. Duke was not in the least bit bothered. Willow was. Parking themselves by the wall they waited and scanned the large open space for any signs of a friendly face. People mobbed past them, there was noise and confusion. Willow had the sinking feeling of free falling through space. She had convinced her Mother to let them both do this trip, swearing madly that they would be okay, now here they were barely off the plane and already in a fix. Should they just sit there and wait? If so, for how long? They knew no one and were thousands of miles away from home. The unfamiliar sounds and sights were bombarding her senses. What if he doesn't show up? She could feel panic creeping in.

Duke on the other hand had the luxury of being younger and therefore really didn't need to worry. Not that his nature was to stress, he took everything in his stride, life is too short to worry, was his motto and he sure did live by it. 'Willow relax dude, he'll be here, take a chill pill, it's all good man,' he said channelling his inner Californian hippy.

Willow wanted to punch him. There was nothing worse than someone telling you to chill when you were freaking out. 'Duke, as usual, it's up to me to do all the adulating, yes? Okay then, please don't tell me not to stress, I am not stressed!' she retorted - all bark and no bite. Instructing Duke to mind the bags she searched for her phone. She had just begun to text a message of help to her uncle when suddenly a rather plump and frazzled, older man came trundling up to them, arms waving, all a bother. 'Willow, Duke, I am so sorry, traffic, madness, Auckland is a nightmare at this time of day. Hello, how yooz doin'? I'm here now, it's all good.' The man grabbed Duke's hand with both of his and shook madly. 'Come 'ere ya beauty,' he said while pulling Willow into a massive bear hug. 'I'm ya Uncle Brownie, but you guys can just call me plain ol' Brownie. No need to stand on ceremony with me, eh.'

I love this dude, Duke thought, *we're gonna get on just fine.*

Brownie was a big man, at least 6'6" with long unruly greying hair and a wide, warm weather-beaten face. For all his ramshackle appearance, Duke noticed he had intelligent and kind eyes. He wore his short-sleeved shirt rolled up even more, like he just needed to be extra prepared for work. His bulging muscles were on display, not in a vain way but simply there from years of hard work, a by-product of his life. Even his forearms were as big as Dukes legs! Both arms were covered in traditional tattoos or more specifically 'Tā moko' depicting what was sacred to the wearer. Duke noticed spirals, triangles, repeating patterns in fading black ink and wondered what the tattoos meant. Each arm looked more like a small tree trunk which had been engraved, rather than simply painted on. His jeans looked like they were in fashion in the seventies and he had been wearing them ever since. They were hanging low on his bum like the rappers Duke listened to but somehow, Duke thought, this was an accidental look. And there they were, the requisite funky, trendy sneaker that Duke noticed on other older people.

Duke always thought it bizarre to see the old guys in his town wearing old man clothes, faded jeans, tweed jackets, woolly jumpers, and boom, mad trendy trainers; the kind that he lusted after himself. It was a fashion anomaly. He marvelled at the farmers in their thread bare mud brown suits, yellowing shirts, and flat caps. The suits were bought aeons ago, worn as Sunday best for years and now relegated to daily clobber. And then they teamed them with up to the minute Nike or Adidas footwear. Perhaps old people saunter into sports shops looking for comfortable footwear and end up getting the latest trend in trainers sold to them, without them even thinking twice about it? Duke looked down and Brownie was no exception, the latest high tops peeking out from under the denim. They had a retro eighties look about them. Come to think of it, Duke thought, he probably had these since the eighties too.

'It's lovely to meet you Brownie,' Willow said managing a smile that showed all too clearly her immense relief at being 'found', collecting her thoughts and instructing her head to begin working, formulating sentences and communicating with this lovely man. Duke allowed the others to dispense with the pleasantries. It was one of the advantages of having an older, more sensible sister. She took care of the niceties for him. Anyway no one expected a fourteen-year-old boy to have the communication skills necessary for all this mannerly how-do-you-do nonsense. Usually a grunt and a nod would suffice.

Bundling them out through the doors of the airport,

into the blasting midday sun, Brownie hustled them along to the car park and got them safely ensconced into his truck, with the bags in the back. 'All righty now, it's a bit of a mongrel flight eh? Did yooz stop for long in Dubai or was it a quick connection? Ha, that flipping long flying, I bet your bums are gone to sleep. We'll be in need of a few bum transplants', he quipped and with that laughed a loud, belly laugh.

'Willow sat on the edge and Duke was in the middle of the front seat. She looked out the window at the Auckland motorways, trying to get a sense of the country she had just landed in. Cars looked much the same. They drove on the same side of the road as at home. The place names were unusual though, in Maori she guessed. Places like Whangaparaoa, Whangarei, and then some in more understandable English, North Shore, Northcote, Albany.It was hot too; they had left home in the middle of winter and landed in the middle of summer. Willow didn't like the sun. Her complexion said it all, alabaster skin, freckles, and a mane of fiery auburn hair, a walking cliché. She had always envied her brother's naturally dark, sallow skin. He just seemed to go a darker shade of gorgeous brown and could stay out forever without needing any sun screen. She sighed. She was going to have to watch herself here or it would be a major burn situation.

Hot, sticky and uncomfortable, Willow felt the fire behind her eyes. She wanted to chat to Brownie, get to know him, be friendly, but it was a struggle. There was a metal rod piercing her temple, skewering her eyeballs, with an electric current running through it. She regretted wearing her Black Docs and lamented the decision to leave her sandals behind. Her alternative, anti-fashion uniform of black clothing, heavy boots and a nose piercing were not so conducive to a New Zealand summer. It's all very well she thought, making a statement with your clothes, but what she wouldn't give for a pair of flip flops and a light summer dress. She made a mental note to go shopping as soon as; they are bound to have summer dresses in black.

Bending down to untie her laces she kicked off her heavy boots, peeled the sweaty socks from her melting feet, and sat back with a wonderful sense of relief. Her feet could breath, she felt the cool air con blow on the ground of the truck and she thought this must be the most pleasant feeling of free feet she had ever had. She drifted off into a reverie brought on by the exhaustion of the journey, the adrenaline rush of the arrival and the lolling of the truck. Squinting her eyes, she sat back pulled on her shades and let Duke take over.

'So, how far to your house Brownie?' Duke asked his uncle right on queue.

'Ah not long, 'bout two hours, depending...' Brownie answered, affording Duke a friendly sideways smile. Duke was getting a sense of the size of Auckland city, if two hours was not a long drive.

Willow observed how different the houses were here. Brownie explained that you bought a plot of land and pretty much built whatever style of house you liked. They were massive and all individual, built from weather board or brick or a mix of both. They had large windows, verandas, flat roofs; some had imposing columns at the front. Willow loved them, the size was impressive but mainly she loved the fact that each one was unique. What a wonderful idea. As they drove along the sea front she noticed how palatial they were; one had a balcony in the shape of a boat – that was pretty wild. They trundled along the coast road and Willow spotted a hammock. They stopped at traffic lights and she had time to take it in.

Willow imagined herself swinging joyfully in the shade, reading her book, or just sitting under the enormous palm tree, quietly meditating. There was a lovely energy here she thought. The house was art deco style; white washed, flat roof, three levels, with large glass windows all around. The light inside must be amazing. Willow could just glimpse the furniture through the shaded part of one of the windows. It was modern, clean lines, muted colours, creams, olive hues, and taupe. Colours she would normally think of as boring but here they really worked. It fitted in with the surroundings. Outside the front was blocked into rectangles by columns that ran along the whole front of the house. The property was separated from the next by a bush running down the garden. There were palm trees and exotic foliage of vibrant greens and yellows dotted everywhere.

The property next to this one was completely different. It looked like an American farm house. It was also three stories high, with pointed triangular arches, all around. It had windows on all aspects and a veranda running all around the middle floor. It was a wooden and brick build with bleached wood on all the balconies. The perimeter was demarcated by white washed wooden fences. There were little Buddhas, frog statues, a pond and twinkle lights hanging from a tree in the front garden. It appeared as it if sloped down to the sea at the back of the house and Willow could only imagine what it must be like chilling there at night looking up at the stars. She could live here she thought. The lights turned green and they took off again.

Her daydream was broken and she thought ruefully of the small council houses back home. They were a far cry from the palatial mansions of this place. Houses at home were small, council built, called two up two down. Her whole house would fit into one room here. She grew up sharing a room with her brother until she rebelled and her mum turned the small front room downstairs into a bedroom for her. She marvelled at how larger families' years ago all lived in those houses; families with five and six children, all sharing one bedroom sometimes, and one bathroom. Privacy was a luxury, an unknown myth. Even when someone did build their own house, it was still a square bungalow box, unimaginative, uninspiring and dull. They certainly wouldn't win any architectural competitions.

They travelled through the Auckland traffic and came to a place called Takapuna, a bustling suburb with bars, shops and restaurants. Turning down a side street they arrived at Brownies house. It wasn't as palatial as the houses they had been seeing but it was cute and cosy. 'Alrighty folks, let's get ya inside,' he smiled at them both, so pleased to have them home safe.

The two weary travellers almost fell out of the truck, but somehow managed to get themselves into Brownie's place. It was lovely. Duke felt at home immediately. He noticed the paua shells, Maori art, and photos of family all around. Brownie indicated to Duke that he would be sleeping on the pull-out bed in the living room and then settled Willow in his spare room. It was small but charming. The bed was made up with white linen, fluffy pillows to match and there was a small vase of yellow and orange gerbera daisies on the bedside table. Willow's heart melted to see them. They were one of her favourite flowers, the simplicity of them appealed to her. She never liked anything ostentatious. There was a large window facing out onto the road, with plain cream curtains pulled slightly closed to keep the sun out. Dropping her bag on the bed she joined Duke and Brownie in the kitchen.

Brownie explained that he had cooked up a paua feast and was eager for the two of them to try it. Duke squirmed and made a face at Willow. She being an ardent vegetarian was all a fluster, not wanting to insult Brownie but not in the slightest bit enticed to try this delicacy. Brownie explained that he had caught these paua that morning especially for them and fried them up in butter for their arrival. Willow made a face back to Duke which told him in no uncertain terms not to insult this lovely man by refusing to try his food...or else!

Surprisingly Duke thought them not half bad. Willow ate simply to be polite. Luckily Brownie had a fantastic spread of all sorts of delicious food for them to feast on and after eating their fill, taking hot rejuvenating showers, a phone call home to let their mum know all was well, they both decided to put their heads down. Duke trundled into the living room, oblivious to anything except the bed in front of him. He kicked off his jeans and lay his head down on the cool cotton pillow. He immediately felt his entire body melt into the mattress and was unconscious in seconds.

Duke woke first. He looked around the sitting room, rubbing his eyes, and taking in his surroundings. It was a small room, warm with a slight breeze blowing in from an open window. The camp bed was surprisingly comfortable. He sat up. There was little light save for a street light outside. There wasn't a sound. It must be a quiet neighbourhood, he thought. It was then he remembered that it was the middle of the night. He glanced at his watch - ten past four in the morning! Wow, he had slept since their arrival that afternoon. His body clock was shot. He was now wide awake and it was the middle of the night. If he was at home he would probably be just coming in from school, grabbing a snack and heading out to football.

He examined the photos on the shelf. There was one of a younger Brownie, darker hair, less weathered face, big smile as usual, with Aunty Pam, Dad's sister. They looked happy and carefree. It caused a stir at the time, he remembered his mum telling him, the fact that Pam had decided to stay in New Zealand and marry Brownie. He knew that her death hit his Dad hard, and then thought how much it must have hit Brownie. He was now in his sixties and his kids were grown. They lived on the South Island and Duke was looking forward to getting to know his Kiwi cousins. Duke wondered what kind of man Brownie was. He struck him as pretty sound. He wondered how much they would be able to tell their uncle about the real reason they were there, besides a gap year for Willow and an educational trip for him. He had a sense that there was more than met the eye with this quirky but loveable man.

Duke was young but had a wisdom that belied his age. He felt in him a kindred spirit. Duke knew that Maori tradition and culture was very spiritual so he hoped that if they did tell Brownie some of what was going on, he would understand and not think they were nuts. Time would tell, he thought taking in the rest of the room. It was slightly old fashioned. There was a floral-patterned couch and chair, an old wooden coffee table in the middle of the room and floral print worn carpet under foot. He was very comfortable here. Sitting up he began to feel like something was missing. Turning slowly around he realised that his beloved companion, Teddy, was laying full length on the sofa bed beside him. 'Well, bout time, my boy, I thought you would never wake up. I have been sitting here, twiddling my thumbs, patiently waiting on your consciousness to emerge. I even tried to connect with you in your sleep, but I'm afraid there's not much going on in there at the moment,' he sniggered.

'Ha, ha, hilarious,' Duke quipped, but couldn't mask his relief at seeing his guardian, 'actually it's good to see you.'

'Sugar, you are not the only one who is patiently waiting on these kids to wake up. Willow is still snoring her pretty little head off in there, hashtag inacoma,' Fro'Ro was sitting with her long limbs draped over the chair, nonchalantly twirling her curly hair between her fingers.

'I'll go wake her, her body clock will be all messed up if she doesn't get up soon,' Duke offered.

'Nah ah honey, I'll make sure she comes right, but for now she needs all the rest she can get. You guys have a long road ahead of you and we have some serious planning to do,' advised Fro'Ro.Brownie emerged from the back room, 'What's all this noise?' And with that he stood dead in his tracks, mouth hanging open, in total shock.

There was a pregnant pause, Duke looked at Teddy, Teddy looked at Fro'Ro, Fro'Ro looked at Brownie. She took charge as any self-respecting, six-foot African American, bedazzling in pink, with a wicked afro, rose quartz crystal would do. She stood up holding out her hand, and clearing her throat she introduced herself, 'Hello Brownie, I am Fro'Ro the rose quartz guardian of your beautiful niece and this is Teddy the tiger's eye guardian of your spiritual and powerful nephew.'

'Yes, very spiritual and powerful,' echoed Duke with a little fist pump. Teddy thumped him reminding him that it would appear that his uncle could in fact see them. 'Oh shivers, yeah, eh Brownie, there are a few things that we need to fill you in on,' responded Duke, somewhat after the fact. 'Guess we're going to find out how open minded you are Brownie a little sooner than we thought', Duke said with a rather tentative smile, hoping that it would all be okay.

Brownie took a minute to evaluate the situation. He sat down then looked around at the human/crystal gathering, rubbed his chin and said, 'Well then, you better start at the beginning, eh.' So, by the time Willow had emerged from her mammoth slumber Brownie had been filled in on the real reason for their visit; the crystal skulls, Newgrange, the crystal guardians and so on. She walked into the sitting room to see the unlikely four sitting with a map out and chatting about their next move.

'What's going on, you guys?' groggy and not yet fully awake, she saw her beloved crystal and went to hug her adding, 'Fro'Ro, hello, I missed you. I was afraid to pack you in my hand luggage, because of customs. I packed you along with Mahpee and Mala-Kai. Speaking of which, where are those guys?' And sure enough, appearing in the door way were the impressive duo.

'Willow, we were sending you healing energy while you slept. We know you will need all your strength for the journey ahead,' said Mahpee.

Realising that Brownie was in the middle of this unusual scene Willow asked, 'Brownie, oh my God, can you see all this?' 'Sweetie, I been communicating with the crystal world way before you were a twinkle in your mother's eye, 'course I can see these folks clear as day. It's choice, eh' and he chuckled, a deep rich sound that put them all at ease.

And with that Fro'Ro gave a flick of her hair, always one to accept a compliment graciously. After all, she was all about the love...'Wow, that's pretty wild, I had no idea. It's kind of lucky that we ended up coming here don't you think?' asked Willow.'No luck involved Willow, everything happens for a reason,' answered Brownie, '...and looks like you kids have a bit of a job to do here, eh? I reckon yooz might need a bit of help. But first things first, any idea were the bloomin' skulls are buried, mate?' Brownie looked straight at Duke now.

'Err, not a clue Brownie,' Duke's heart sank a little.

'Righto, thinkin' caps on,' Brownie flattened out the map that they had been looking at. 'Nah, let's see, you say that the skulls are buried deep within the earth somewhere in New Zealand. It's a rather big place you know, we're talking 'bout a country that's 1600 kilometres long and bout 400 k wide. '

'No pressure then,' Duke remarked dryly.

'Look we obviously have to do some research on this. It just so happens I have a bit of practice in this area and I have some back up to call on too,' said Brownie a glint in his eye. And with that he disappeared into the back room then re-appeared with his 'hei-tiki'.

'What's this?' questioned Willow.

'Well Willow doll, this is a valuable family heirloom. It has been passed down to me through the generations from as far back as my great, great, great grandmother,' informed her uncle with pride.

Duke looked closely at the object. It was made of greenstone. It was a figure of a squatted man, head bent to the side, tongue sticking out rather provocatively, his eyes had the iridescent hue of paua shells. Brownie explained that its power grew as it was worn by each successive generation. He doesn't wear his as it's sacred to him but will call on its power to help him in times of crisis or decision making.

Then without warning, a large green man appeared, darker in colour than Mala-Kai, resembling the figure of the hei-tiki squatting over the map beside them. He spoke in Maori to Brownie but the crystal characters all seemed to understand what he was saying. Duke looked at Willow in astonishment, 'This is wild Willow, are you seeing what I am seeing?'

'Yes, I am but can I ask after all that we have seen why you find this so surprising? After all your best friend right now is an eight-foot-tall talking tiger made out of crystal.' Willow was beginning to adopt a very pragmatic approach to all that she witnessed.

Brownie now formerly greeted the hei-tiki and introduced him to Willow and Duke and explaining that the hei-tiki could help them close in on where to look for the crystal skulls. Brownie suggested a few places that he felt were sacred to the Maori people and might be the place of burial for the skull. 'Okay so off the top of my heed,' began Brownie,' I can suggest that Rotorua may be a place of interest. It's at the centre of the North Island, and is one of the most concentrated geothermal areas in the world. The air there smells a bit, because of the sulphur coming off the geysers and hot springs. I'm thinking it could have potential as it brings together the elements of fire and water which is an indication of a highly energetic place.

Again, the hei-tiki spoke in Maori to the group. Brownie translated. He was suggesting an alternative venue. It was in the Tongariro National Park. This area contained three active volcanoes, Tongariro, Ruapehu, and Ngauruhoe. 'Ah yeah, my spidey senses are picking that up as a key location,' said Brownie and then again, laughed aloud. He had such a cool sense of humour, thought Willow.

It was then that Duke spoke, 'Um, I think I may be able to help. As soon as I knew we were coming here, I started having dreams; images would flash through my mind of a wild sea. I am standing at the end of the world and I'm looking out over the horizon. There is a large tree with red berries on it and I am beside a man and a woman. I feel scared. I feel like I am going to jump into the water. I look behind me and there is a large crowd gathered. And then I wake up. No idea what it means, but maybe you guys do? Do you think this has any bearing on what we are doing here? I didn't want to mention anything as I was really petrified. It was a bit freaky.'

'Duke, you should have said something. I would never think you're crazy,' offered a sympathetic Willow. If there is one thing she had learned since beginning this journey, nothing is as it seems and there is so much more to everything than what is obvious and if Duke is crazy then so is she.

'Okay Mystic Meg, any idea where this place is?' Duke asked.Brownie and hei-tiki exchanged glances. Brownie stood up and declared that they need look no further, 'Ladies and gentlemen, boys and girls get yourselves ready for a road trip. We're going to Cape Reinga.' Brownie then suggested they chill that day. They would plan their trip for the next morning. In the meantime, he thought it would be nice for them to head out into Auckland and show them a few sights and sounds of his city.

They took in the National Art Gallery as Willow loved rambling around these big old buildings, taking in the exhibits. Duke went along reluctantly as he thought it would be boring. He was pleasantly surprised. He noticed the Kauri columns and a large canopy overhead as they approached the entrance. Once inside the light filled atrium was impressive with papier mache giant coloured flowers hanging down from the ceiling. He thought the view out over Queen Street was wicked.

They roamed around the gallery for a while and when they came across the portraits of Maori chiefs by Gottfried Lindauer, Duke really became interested. They screamed at him. He couldn't take his eyes off their faces, examining the 'ta moko' (face tattoos) on each one. He was particularly taken with one portrait of a lady called Pere Watene.

Her dark brown hair fell to her knees. She had smooth radiant skin and a bright complexion. She wore an elaborately designed cloak and sported two feathers in her hair signifying her tribal rank and superiority. Her eyes were deep brown, penetrating and beautiful. But the most striking feature was her 'moko kauae', her chin tattoo. There were spirals coming from the bottom of her chin and a line tattooed above her top lip. She held a large 'poumanu' or greenstone in her hand. This was the most prized of all handheld weapons due to the scarcity and durability of the rock. It was the ultimate statement of the 'rangatira' or chief. She wore a greenstone hei-tiki around her neck symbolising fertility and 'whakapapa', or lineage. Duke was transfixed, she fascinated him, but he didn't know why. The other portraits of chiefs and leaders were just as impressive, but she was magical. He had the feeling that she was following him with her eyes, but then decided that he had simply seen too many episodes of Scooby doo as a kid.

After the gallery Brownie took them to Albert Park which was right next door. He explained how the 'papakainga' or village that occupied the site prior to the European settlement was called Rangipuke. He pointed out massive trees where the Maori tribesmen would hang the bodies of their victims after cutting off their head, feet and hands and let the blood drain away. Then they would begin the process of shrinking the heads. This was an ancient tradition and the English settlers then began to steal the heads and ship them back to England.

Willow began to feel nauseous and decided to walk on. She never had much of a stomach for gory stories. She stopped at a massive tree, at least six-foot-wide which had the centre hollowed out. Brownie approached, concern on his face. Willow took out her phone and took a photo but just then her phone died. 'Ah ye found it then?' enquired Brownie as he got close.

'Found what Brownie? My phone has just died and I'm sure I had a full battery,' Willow replied a little pre-occupied.

'Ah yeh that'd be bout right,' he answered, 'see the park was turned into a barracks in 1845 and after an influenza outbreak in 1918 they used to throw the dead bodies into this tree. It was presumed that the tree would eventually die but nah, it's still growing. The tree holds the spirits of all who ended up in there.' It gave Willow the chills and she moved a step back nearly colliding with Duke who had made his way over.

Duke, having a stronger constitution for such matters, went up close to get a better look. Taking his phone out for a picture, he aimed the lens and the same thing happened. 'I definitely had battery, I'm sure of it,' he said.

Brownie, put his meaty hands on the shoulders of his young charges to comfort and add a little gravitas to his point. 'See kids, some things simply have their own power and the spirits of this tree obviously isn't so keen on the 'paparazzi' eh', and with that he promptly cracked up at his own joke. Willow smiled then turned to follow her uncle who was now heading off.

Duke hung back, slightly fascinated by its story. He could definitely sense something eerie here. Peering into its centre he wanted to get a feel for what it must have been like back in those times, soldiers piling dead bodies up on carts for mass burial, throwing corpses into this unlikely grave. The wind whipped up and it suddenly felt very cold. The rustle of the leaves got louder, and the birds stopped singing.

It was a hot summer's day, yet Duke was freezing. This didn't feel good. He stood on the massive roots growing out from the ground and peered into the middle of the tree. How many bodies had ended up in here? Then without warning he spotted a pair of legs on the ground. His heart leapt, he nearly vomited with fright, frozen to the spot. He thought he was going to be sucked into this macabre world of ghosts and demons.

Then the body moved, sat up and looked him straight in the eye and said, 'Spare change bro?' It was a homeless person taking shelter from the world in the belly of this burial mound. Relief flooded through Duke and he rummaged in his pockets for whatever he could find. He stumbled backwards, happy to be away from this place but melancholic also. It wasn't lost on him how awful it must be for this person, to seek refuge in a place that seemed to be a portal into the underworld of death and disease. Without noticing, Mahpee, Mala-kai and Teddy had formed a circle around him and were actively deflecting any negativity that was emanating from the tree. It was only as he walked away that he felt their energy.

'That was not a nice place, eh?' stated Teddy, 'Boy, be very careful where you go. We are here to protect you, but you must become more aware. You could feel the change in the atmosphere? Did you feel it in the pit of your stomach? Well you must learn to listen to this. It is your instinct, and it is warning you. It will be your best advisor in life, let me tell you. We may not always be around to shield you.'

'Man, that was far out. Sure Ted, thanks for the back-up guys,' Duke was most grateful. Catching up with his uncle and sister, he calmed himself, and happily trotted through the rest of the day, taking in the sights of the sky tower and the city, having a nice lunch and staying away from any topic that was scary or uncomfortable. He'd had enough excitement for one afternoon.

Willow and Duke woke before dawn the next morning, excited and apprehensive. Brownie had estimated a five-and-a-half-hour drive and suggested they stop for lunch along the way, so he set an 8am start time. It was 4am when Willow got up and crept quietly into the sitting room, not wanting to rouse her brother, but found him sitting at the kitchen table eating a bowl of cornflakes. There was a low lamp on and he had his mandatory headphones on his head. It's amazing, she thought, how some things are so unfamiliar in another country; sights, sounds, smells, and yet some things are always the same. Cornflakes are cornflakes no matter where you go, just different packaging. There's a life lesson in there somewhere…

She stopped for a moment looking at her younger brother. She really did love him dearly. She remembered the day he arrived in the house. She was about four. Her parents didn't go into the details then about where he came from or how he was going to live with them, they just said he was her new little brother and she welcomed him with open arms. He often accused her of being a bully, of trying to control his life, of being over protective. He could be heard yelling 'You're not my Mother!' to which she would retort 'Thank God for that, I could never spawn a monster like you' but he knew deep down that she was only looking out for him, and he secretly loved it.

Willow was worried for Duke. She knew that he was somehow intricately tied up in all this. She had her part to play, she was in tune with the crystals and she was there to guide him in some sense but the big picture, well, that was all centred on him and she didn't know what was going to happen. An anxious feeling grew in the pit of her stomach, but she brushed it aside and slapped him on the back as she entered the kitchen. 'Yo dude, sup,' holding index and pinkie fingers up with middle two folded down, she mimicked his rapper idols.

He choked on his cereal and in a whisper, 'Willow, don't do that, and please don't try get down with your 'bad self' you look like a total lamo.'

Pouring herself a bowl she sat down, 'Brownie still asleep?' 'Yup, listen, that's not a kango hammer Willow, that's our delightful uncle snoring his little brains out', Duke raised his eyebrows, and with that the two burst into a fit of giggles. 'You know it's a full moon out there, so we should put the crystals out to cleanse them,' suggested Willow.

'Dude, I'm way ahead of you. I left them all out there before I went to sleep,' replied Duke, rather proud of himself.

They looked out on the deck surrounding the house.

There were the four crystal buddies, soaking up the moonlight and a fifth, Duke noticed, the hei-tiki lying among his new pals at the end. His contorted green body, bulging green eyes and twisted head looked rather scary, and he had a tendency to stick out his tongue which made him look even more frightening. However, Duke was happy to have him as part of their little team. He knew instinctively that the hei-tiki or Poumanu, as he asked to be called, would a be good guide for them on their travels here. Native crystals were always a welcome addition.

Mahpee was sitting cross-legged, eyes closed. Mala-Kai and Teddy were deep in conversation - they worked very well together. Fro'Ro was laying down soaking up the vibration of the moon and seemed to be in a rapturous world all of her own.

'Okay my little beauties, how we all doin? Brownie appeared and seemed in fine fettle.

'Ah sorry Brownie, did we wake you?' asked Willow.

'Nah, darlin, I am a light sleeper. Did you guys manage to get some sleep or have ya been awake all-night?' Brownie beamed at the two of them, his attachment to them growing ever stronger. 'No, I slept like a log. The room is lovely. I guess my body clock is still adjusting,' Willow replied with a little smile.

'Okay then you two, ready for a big adventure? Got ya big boy pants on Duke, 'cos it will be one hell of a ride, I can tell ya,' and with that Brownie gave Duke a hefty slap on the back. 'Why do you say that Brownie?' asked Willow nervously, 'and why do you say we're going to Cape Reinga? Where is it, what's the vibe with it?'

Brownie began, 'Well, Cape Reinga is where the souls of the Maori people go to depart this world. They leap off the headland, where they climb the roots of the 800 year old Pohutukawa tree, to descend into the underworld and return to their spiritual homeland of Hawaiki. They turn left briefly at the Three Kings Island for one last look at their homeland and then continue on their way. Now having consulted with my Poumanu, I feel this is where we need to concentrate our efforts. You mentioned a man and a woman in your dream Duke; well my guess is this is the meeting of the two waters. Te Maona-a-Rehua, the sea of Rehua, and Te Tai-o-Whitirea, the sea of Whitires. Rehua is a female entity and Whitirea is a male. That's why I believe the cape is the place, eh. It's sacred in Maori tradition and culture, and if anything was to be buried for the advancement of the human race, well, I reckon it would be there.'

'I see,' said Willow slightly daunted.

'But, this won't be easy. No freebies for us, eh. If someone hid this skull of yours, well they did it for a reason, and in my extensive experience, no one hides anything valuable without protection,' Brownie was quite serious now.

'What kind of protection?' asked Duke, no longer finding it all quite so 'cool'.

Brownie looked them both in the eyes and replied slowly and deliberately, 'I reckon we gonna run into a Taniwha.' And just as this foreign sounding name slipped from his full brown lips, the Pounamu appeared beside him, jumping up and down, his head shaking back and forth startling Willow and Duke, who blurted out, 'Crikey, what's up rubber duck? Is this a bad sign?' Duke was getting increasingly worried. He wanted to know more about the hei-tiki and what he knew, 'Brownie, what's going on?'

'Ya see kiddo, Poumanu is connected with the spirits of the dead. It carries the energy of all who wore it in the past and it can communicate with them and ask for help. If need be we can invoke their help to shield us, to put a protective wall of energy around us, but we must be careful, this wall can amplify our thoughts and our intentions. We must clear our minds and more importantly our hearts before we invoke this kind of help. It is very strong and powerful and can very easily go wrong,' Brownie explained, in the hopes it would provide some comfort to his niece and nephew. 'Oh, is that all,' quipped Duke, trying to make light of what seemed like rather a desperate situation.

'You'll be right mate,' reassured Brownie, patting his back.

'But Brownie, what the hell is a Tani... what's-it,' Duke was far from feeling reassured.

'Argh yeah, the Taniwha have long been part of the myth and lore of ancient Aotearoa,' Brownie sensed this was not going to be an easy sell, but before he could get any further Duke was waving his hands in protests.

'Okay hold up, now what is A...O...E?' Duke was beginning to find it all a bit much.

'That's the land of the long white cloud, Aotearoa, it's

the name us Maoris gave to this beautiful land,' Brownie replied, going on to say, 'And the Taniwha, 'wh' is pronounced as an 'f' sound, so it sounds Ta-ni-fa,' he paused looking at the clock on the wall, 'well, let's get on the road, and I'll tell ya all about it on the way.'

They packed a lunch, gathered their crystals and set off into the Auckland morning traffic heading for the north western most tip of the Aupouri Peninsula, on the North Island, destination the cape. The mood was now lighter and rather fun. They told stories, jokes, ate sandwiches and got to know each other better. Willow really liked Uncle Brownie, he had soul. Duke felt like he had known him all his life; he couldn't put his finger on it but there was something very comforting about him.

Duke broached the 'Taniwha' subject again, 'So come on Brownie, what's this Taniwha all about?

'Well, ancient lore states it's a mythical creature that can be either dangerous or very protective. It can take the shape of a large sea monster, or a dragon - think the Loch Ness Monster meets Jurassic Park,' Brownie explained as best he could.

'And if we get on the wrong side of this dinosaur dragon sea beast thing?' Duke asked.

'Well let's cross that can of worms when we get to the woods, yeah? Brownie tried to brush it off and Willow laughed at his mix mash of metaphors.

However, Duke was not letting it go, 'But you said it could be protective. Why would it be dangerous to us? Our intentions are good. We're not setting out to do harm to anyone, just a light bit of world saving.'

Brownie knew he couldn't just brush this under the carpet and so explained that the Taniwha could be influenced by other forces. He felt there may be something else at play here. He wasn't sure what, but it was a powerful feeling nonetheless. It didn't inspire confidence in either his niece or nephew. Everyone fell silent for a little while and it wasn't long before they pulled into the small town of Kaitaia, just a few miles shy of the Cape.

Brownie guided them away from the tourist area and into the thick of the abundant nature that surrounded them. He did his best thinking in that environment. He didn't want to come across to the kids as an aging hippy, but he knew they needed to be still and silent and connect with the ancestors. 'Right so, this is my plan, kids. I think we need to get away from all the people here in town, they will ruin our buzz, eh? We need help here, and Poumanu is going to help us. '

'Sound man, let's go', Duke was now more eager to get the show on the road. He knew that he had no choice and besides he also had utter faith in his comrades in arms. He held his Tigers Eye crystal in his hand and immediately felt the comforting arm of Teddy around him.

Gathering themselves; their back packs, and crystals, they set off on foot, having no clue what to expect. 'Brownie, I have to say, you seem to be taking this all in your stride. I can't believe that you are so quick to accept what we are here for, and are so ready to help us,' Willow began as they walked.

'Look sweetie, I know there is a lot more to this fine land of ours than meets the eye. I have been around a long time now and the longer I live the more I feel that I haven't actually got a clue about anything. So, if you kids come to me and tell me there's a bunch of buried crystals, or treasure, or whatever, and it's up to us to free it, for the good of mankind, well, who am I not to lend a hand, eh?' Brownie said.

'Well…when you put it like that…', Willow felt a little silly for asking.

Brownie put a comforting arm around her shoulder, 'Listen, after losing my lovely Pam, I thought life wasn't worth living. I couldn't go on without her, what was the point? She was my life. After the kids were grown, it was just the two of us, ya know. We did everything together, went everywhere together. She even got me to salsa dancing classes. Imagine a big lug of a fella like me, salsa dancing, not a pretty sight let me tell ya. But she wanted to go so I went. After she got cancer, I thought my life would end. I fell apart. But my kids got me through it and I had to be strong for Pammy. In the end it was a relief for her to go. I couldn't see her in pain anymore. Ya know what, I understood then what heartbreak meant. I never felt pain like it in me life. '

'That must have been awful, Brownie, I'm so sorry to hear that. I didn't know Aunty Pam well, but I know my Dad loved her dearly,' Willow said.

'Yeah sweetie she loved him too. His death hit her hard. But she was a woman of faith. She believed in the power of love and she was adamant that her love for her brother, your Dad, was still there, and that never went away, and because of that, he was always with her. In some way that prepared me for when I had to say good bye to her. I still carry her here,' and with that he put his free fist to his heart.

Duke was listening intently and was moved by what Brownie had said. Brownie continued, 'It was after her death that I rediscovered my Poumanu. It was buried in a drawer. I found it when I was going through Pam's things. It spoke to me. I discovered, not for the first time, that I could see beyond the physical. I seemed to be able to sense what the hei-tiki was saying to me. I could feel its power. It had been in my family for a long time and as I told you, it carries the memory of all who wore it before. I know it will help us here.'

'So, you began to see things that weren't there? Feel things?' Duke was really interested now.

Yeah son, I did. I always had this ability but I was too scared. I didn't know what was going on. When I was a kid I would see people, ya know, people that no one else could. I could sense what was going on with people, what they were really feeling. As I got older, I pushed this to one side. Ya know, I took ta drinkin' a fair bit, tried anything that would take my mind away from what was going on in my head. But when Pammy passed, I felt it again. I knew she was with me. I knew her love for me was still there. I started to believe again, and I opened my heart up to all that was going on. The hei-tiki came to me and I knew that I had a job to do,' Brownie revealed. Spoken with such honesty and clarity, Willow and Duke had a lot to contemplate as they walked on in silence.

'Dukey boy, don't be scared big fella, you'll be sweet,'

Brownie beamed at him. Duke nodded to his uncle, deep in thought. Brownie then stopped and looked about, surveying the land and sky, 'Now let's see folks, we need to take a rest and gather ourselves. The weather is closing in. We're nearly at the coast, let's head for the dunes and take shelter there.'

The wind was blowing, and the sand was whirring around in the air, blowing into their faces. They sat down, and a palpable feeling of anticipation hung heavy around them. Duke could sense they were not alone. 'Others' were with them, closing in. He just couldn't tell if they were friend or foe. Brownie got Poumanu and placed him in the middle of a circle that they had formed; Brownie, Mala-kai on the left, Duke to his right with Teddy beside him, Willow, Fro'Ro, and Mahpee. Poumanu began to dance around, hopping from one foot to another, trancelike with his arms flailing, around and around.

Suddenly a woman appeared. It was the lady from the portrait in the Gallery, the tribal chief that had caught Duke's attention. 'I am Pere Watene. I have come to guide you. There is one among you who is of our lineage. He is descended from the great elders that have passed through here. His soul knows these lands as he has been here many times before. He is of your kin,' she looked in the direction of Brownie who looked slowly and with purpose towards Duke.

Duke swallowed hard and began to sweat. What does this mean? What am I supposed to do now? His thoughts raced, and Pere Watene responded, 'Do not be afraid, the ancestors are here to protect you but there is great danger. You must go to the cliff top before dusk. We will meet you there.' And with that she vanished.

The crystals manoeuvred into action. Duke glanced at Ted, he nodded a silent affirmation. Mahpee helped Duke to control his emotions and not get overwhelmed. He needed his energy. Mala-Kai scouted the area, he embodied the energy of an enlightened leader and he was the perfect ally now. The vibration of Mala-Kai and Teddy worked in tandem, they helped Duke focus, achieve mental clarity, and take decisive action. 'Right so, looks like I'm about to embark on some skulduggery, arrr,' Duke said trying to keep the mood light.

'Brownie, what's going to happen?' Willow asked nervously, worried for her brother.

Fro'Ro jumped in, 'Doll face, you shouldn't worry, you will only bring that energy to play for your brother. Remember Poumanu will amplify whatever you are feeling, so let's keep things nice and chilled? Keep the faith sista', your brother will be just fine.' Willow nodded in agreement but couldn't help having that familiar sick feeling in the pit of her stomach, like she had just been punched, hard.

'Okay, I'm going to do as Pere Watene said. I'll make my way over the dunes and up onto the cliff top,' announced Duke, determined not to let his nerves get the better of him.

'Then what?' asked Willow.

Duke threw her a withering look and replied, 'Dude, do you honestly think that I have the first clue about what the hell is going to happen next, hashtag noideaeither, duh!'

'Okay, keep your shirt on, I was only asking. It is all about you after all, as usual,' Willow said and instead of giving him a punch in the arm, she grabbed him close to her and hugged him. 'You're a massive pain in the bum but you better take care of yourself or I will kill you.'

'Yeah, yeah, ya love me really,' he said ran off over the dune. Mahpee, Mala-Kai and Teddy followed suit. Fro'Ro stayed with Willow. Something else was now stirring, only a lot further away…

MIRRORS, DRYADS & DRAGONS

Wayne Johnson gathered himself and sitting up, he made a plan. He phoned Will, his driver, instructing him to collect groceries and fresh clothes and deliver them to the cabin. He brewed up a pot of steaming hot coffee. It would be a few hours before Will arrived, so Wayne decided to head out into the woods and do some exploring. He always felt better when he walked in nature and now it was vital. He needed to connect with the Elementals and he needed to do it quick.

Knowing that the trees were protected by the dryads; mystical woodland entities, he would need to connect with them first. Without hesitation Wayne walked into the forest and stopped in the middle of a large copse of tree trunks, bent and writhing around in a circle like a snapshot of still snakes, their roots exposed, covering the floor like, a natural obstacle course.

Wayne then asked permission to enter before smelling the musky damp thicket and sitting down on a large branch. Sunlight dripped in through the small openings of the leafy roof. Squinting his eyes, the autumn colours of burnt sienna, yellow ochre, timber browns, moss green and olive all mingled together in the palette of his vision to become the canvas for his magic. The dank wet smell of the enclosure tingled in his nostrils, calming his nerves.Feeling the ground beneath him rise up to surround his body, engulfing him in an aura of earthly mist, he began to zone out in a trance. But almost immediately someone, or something, darted beside him. He only just caught sight of it out of the corner of his eye. He turned his head but saw nothing. Uncertainty started to creep in, but Wayne managed to get to his feet and mustering a modicum of bravery, called out, 'Mystical beings of the forest, dryad of the tree, keepers of the knowledge, please show yourself to me!'

He took the candy from his pocket, a sweet offering, and placed it around the enclosure to appease the fairy folk. Again, there was movement to his left and spinning around he noticed the tree sway. Then in unison all the trees began to move, slowly, in a gentle ballet of wood. Wayne felt a presence, many eyes were on him. Softening his gaze, he noticed beings moving within the trees. The knots in the trunks became eyes, deep set and piercing. Branches became arms waving in the air, leaves rustled, trunks morphed into bodies and he was suddenly surrounded by these beings of nature, the tree dryads.

'Greetings, I come in peace. I am here to ask for your help. I know of great danger and misfortune about to befall nature's guardians on the other side of the world. We need to warn them. There is grave evil descending on Gaia. There are two humans who mean the world and all her charge harm. But they are young and can be stopped. I implore you to come to my aid. Invoke the help of the fae, the undines, and the salamander. They are in the region of the Taniwha. I beseech you to awaken the Taniwha to stop them,' Wayne implored.

Movement happened all around him. The wind gusted through the area, harder and harder. He could barely see for the leaves were now swirling in a clockwise circle around his body. A sound growing louder and louder filled his head. It was the sound of the others arriving. Everything was pitch black. His heart was thumping out of his chest and he had never felt so alive as he did in this moment.

Wayne knew that it was a great risk to mess with these entities. Even if one were being true and honest of intention, it was dangerous. Especially the Fae, they had a reputation for being mischievous. Many a baby was born to be branded a changeling where the fairy had taken the baby and replaced it with one of their own. They were capable of acting with harmful intent if they were crossed.

Right now, Wayne was banking on the dryads to act as leaders. Wayne hoped he would convince them he was coming from place of integrity. He had years of practice in delusion and appearing to be something and someone that he was not but fooling humans and fooling these entities were two completely different things. Then Wayne heard a response in the manner of a resonating echo, 'Who are these humans who mean Gaia harm?'

Wayne held a mental picture in his mind of the young boy he had seen. Even now, to remember the image of him being held up turning around, gave him shivers. There was something about this kid that struck deep terror into his heart. He knew the tree guardian could read his mental image. He thought of the girl then and knew this was registered.

Again, the mysterious voice spoke, 'These are the folk who mean harm to the world? They are in the land of Aotearoa? Why do you come here to tell us this? What proof do you have that this is so?' the voice demanded.

Wayne replied, 'Gatekeepers of Nature, I am of your kind. I have the gift of sight. I have had a premonition of this. My inner eye has seen them and their intention for destruction. I come to ask for your aid and help before it's too late.'

Wayne was prostrate and humble. He was careful not to think of anything but what he was speaking of here and now. He knew his thoughts could be read. He fully believed what he was saying right there and then, in that moment. He knew that these kids must be stopped. He had never used such deception before and was hoping he could pull it off. Years of practice gave him that extra ounce of courage to embark on this in the first place. He knew to keep the screen of his mind clear and to cloak his heart. 'We will speak with the Elementals,' replied the voice. And with that silence descended; the wind stopped, the air became clearer and there was a large beam of sunlight streaming in through the top of the clearing. Wayne knew this was his cue to leave. He had been dismissed and so he walked back to the cabin with trepidation. Messing with such things was something he didn't do lightly; the consequences could be serious, fatal even. This was a new departure for him. He had never gone to this extreme before, but desperate times called for desperate measures. There is no denying that his ego had a part to play in these actions. He was so used to fooling everyone that he truly believed he could fool these beings.

They lived in the other world; existing in a realm not visible to the human eye, but that didn't make them any less real. The dryads were the gatekeepers of the knowledge on Earth. They were connected to her, communicating with each other via the root systems of the trees. Their whispers can be heard when leaves rustle, their voices carried on the breeze. They are mythical, ethereal beings and are most respected here in this other world. The animals of the woods were now on high alert. They had the ability to see and sense what mere humans could not. The rabbits twitched, the mice ran around, squirrels darted here and there. The birds convened on the tree tops and were waiting. Every insect was involved. The faeries arrived, but not the 'fairies' of the movies, nothing so twee or cute. They were forceful, powerful entities and were rightly enraged. Their lithe limbs and tall bodies belied a strength that should never be underestimated. They were the cause of much mischief and could cause harm should they need to. The Fae folk were here, and they meant business. One by one the Elementals converged on the circular copse of woodland that Wayne had been in earlier. This became ground zero. The pixies appeared, guardians of the animals, the air sylphs, those beings that rode the currents of the wind and helped clean the air. Elves, leprechauns, dwarves all came, knowing that there was some serious business for the planet going down.

The sky turned a deep, dark navy, a strong wind was blowing and the air sylphs were carousing around as if in an ethereal rodeo, riding the airwaves with mastery and ease; their long, lean bodies writhing in the sky as their hair flew behind them, flowing tresses of light. The tree branches were bending under the weight of all the animal life they were now supporting. The woodland floor teemed with insect activity. Leafy smells, pungent and damp, swirled around the nostrils of all gathered. Moisture hung in the air like tiny shimmering glass beads, covering everything in glistening refractive rainbow coloured mirrors.

As with everything in this realm communication happened not as in our world, but telepathically, though, impulses, thoughts, movement. The dryads conveyed what had happened with Wayne. All of the beings gathered were already fighting a losing battle to keep the Earth safe. The air sylphs were fighting pollution, the fairies were struggling against the destruction of the soil and its nutrients by fertilisers and modern industrial farming methods. Everyone gathered was already on high alert and were more than willing to help.

Now the trees began to sway in; their bows bent and their branches, like arms, were waving, imploring, pleading with all the life around them; with twig fingers at the end reaching skyward as if in supplication to the Gods. The tops of the branches splayed out into the gnarled and bony hands of old crones. It became a cosmic ballet of swaying and bending, the air their vehicle for expression, dancing to the tune of an invisible conductor.

The rounded trunk knots peered out imploringly. The roots drove deep into the earth and twitched with impulse after impulse, speaking to the soil and the rocks, signals connecting with the crystal grid of the Earth herself. Meanwhile the wind, like the orchestra boomed its message, crashing and pounding its sound of danger. Sporadically there was a bang, louder than the rest, as if the consciousness of the air element itself was becoming impatient, and began screaming to the ether, through the penumbral light that was permeating the sky. Everything in this space was alive and throbbing with the urgency that was felt by all present.

The air sylphs were instructed to take the news to the oceans and inform the undines, the merfolk, the water sprites and water nymphs. These creatures of the sea were to travel to New Zealand and wake the Taniwha, for it was only a creature like the Taniwha that could protect them now. The instructions were clear: protect the Earth, protect Gaia, and protect us.

Flying through the air with the speed of light, swimming on the undulations of the currents, the air sylphs whispered messages on their wings, conveying what was afoot. They did their job with ease and efficiency and within moments the underwater guardians of the planet were informed of the impending potential threat.

The undines swished through the rips and currents of the seas, tumbling and twisting with splashes of their bodies they flew through the waves, their hair like seaweed trailing behind them, an oceanic rudder. They were iridescent sparkling creatures who worked with the mermaids and mermen of this watery world. The ocean floor their playground, and their domain. The coral reefs flew by, under fin, and swish of tail. Sunlight illuminated the tiny microorganisms in the briny depths as they went about their business, unaware of the urgency with which these creatures were moving. Speeding through the ocean, scales shimmering, the mermaids protected the undines on their vital mission. Nothing was going to stop them. They were aided by the whales and dolphins, creatures of intelligence and knowing. Their echo location system paving the way ahead for the undines, spreading their mission and message to the coasts of New Zealand.

When Wayne got back to the cabin he saw that his driver had left the groceries as instructed and clean clothes had been left in the bedroom. Wayne sat down, again, exhausted from his experience. Hunger hit him hard. The last twenty-four hours had been physically, mentally, emotionally and spiritually the most demanding of his life. He slouched down at the kitchen table and looked around him. Everything looked the same. Same old cranky stove, lace yellowing curtains on the windows, the Formica table had seen better days. All this was old and familiar as he had seen them a hundred times before but somehow everything had also changed beyond recognition and he knew in his gut that nothing would ever be the same again.

The following morning Wayne was greeted by bright sunshine as he walked out into the back field, hugging a mug of coffee to his chest, as if to survey all he owned. The smell of the crisp day filled his lungs. He had eaten some breakfast and had his coffee. Feeling good, he meandered down again to the lake, deciding to consult with his oracle.

The mirror had never failed him and he had confidence that it would serve him well again. He needed to know what to do next. Pulling in his energy field, he made himself as small and insignificant as he possibly could. It was imperative that he was not smelt, felt, sensed, or seen by anyone or anything in this area. Wanting the information but not wanting to arouse suspicion, he stealthily crept to the lake's edge. Bending down on his hunkers he reached out and pulled his prized object closer and gazed into the murky surface of the mirror. Using his intuitive powers, he mused slowly over his plan. He needed to connect with the Protector of the South. His senses were alight and he knew that some magic was needed, and quickly.

The swirls of mist evaporated to reveal an image showing what he should do. Wayne understood. He stood up and strode purposefully back to his cabin. Gathering on the way some soil from the ground, a feather that he came across and once home returned to the garden with a glass jar to collect some rain water. He set his bounty down on the lounge floor and lit candles. He wanted representations of the elements; soil became the earth, the feather the air, the candle for fire and the rainwater became the living embodiment of the ocean.

He now needed something that would become the Taniwha. Anything could potentially become the object that he wanted to manipulate, once he put his intention to it, but he still wanted it to fit, to be appropriate. Glancing around the room he noticed an old faded picture on the wall. It had a thin gold frame and depicted a dragon, rearing up on his hind legs, fire coming from his nostrils. It was made of old black velvet with embroidered thread and was soft to touch. Wayne figured it must be there since the seventies. Walking over to it and staring at it closely, he decided that it was perfect for his needs.

Taking it gently off the wall, feeling like it was all going his way, he gingerly placed it on the ground. Carefully and with much concentration he surrounded the picture with the feather to the east of the frame, the candle to the south, the jar of rainwater to the west and the soil to the north. He needed to connect with the Taniwha on an energetic level and so he began an incantation... 'Taniwha, Taniwha, great beast of the sea. Hear my call and answer my plea. There is danger afoot, you must be brave. Those on the shore, you must not save. They are evil and vile and want your life to end. Your mind and will they need to bend. Your power to harness, your strength to kill. Listen to me and give me your will.'

Wayne held his hands around the candle and invoked the passion and power of the creature, '*Oh, great being, listen to my call, use your fire and do not fall*'. He continued to the west of the frame and immersed his hands in the water; this was the route to control his emotions, '*Great being of the sea, feel my words, and set us free.*' Moving to the north, he held the soil in his hands and then rubbed it over his face, smelling the earthy mustiness, inhaling it in, swallowing its scent, '*Taniwha, oh Taniwha smell this clay, feel the earth, your enemies to slay*'

Lastly to have full power over the beast he needed to connect with his intellect. Wayne was careful not to underestimate the Taniwha as that would be a grave error. He held the feather, the symbol of air and began his incantation, '*Brave beast, creature of sea and land, use your brain and see what's at hand. These humans on the shore have evil in mind, it's you they seek and you to find. How will this end, how will you go, kill this enemy and end your foe.*'

Wayne knew he had to possess the Taniwha fully. He had to connect with it on all levels and now he placed both hands over the picture of the dragon and sent all his energy to it.

Far, far away, nestled in a corner of a huge cave in the bowels of the Pacific Ocean, lay a creature so awesome and frightening, that few believed its existence. The Great Taniwha lay dormant. It was a creature of myth and legend. But this Taniwha was no myth. It existed in this luminous dimension, where all these creatures live, half way between what we would perceive as Heaven and Hell. Suddenly it lifted its head, waking to an air of doom, not for itself but for all it was sent to protect. It roused itself from its watery slumber and shaking off the shackles of stillness, began flexing its muscles in readiness. The cavernous nostrils flared, eyelids rose, and its massive tail shifted into gear. Its senses were heightened, listening to the rhythms of the sea, the echoes of the undines, it heard the message. It was alert and fully awake now and ready to take action.

The Taniwha understood there was trouble brewing. He propelled himself through the ocean depths with folded back wings. He was covered in scales that seemed to shimmer as he moved and using his powerful tail as a rudder, he moved with a grace and ease that belied his size. No creature was going to get in his way. His eyes were a shimmering green, and his scales had flecks of aqua blue. He was an amphibian dinosaur/dragon with claws and talons that could rip a whale in two.

But this was something he wouldn't do, not unless he had to. A sound began to hum in his head, his eyes glazed over, and he seemed to lose consciousness. He slowly went into a trance, and all he knew at that moment was he must kill.

His prey was in his mind's eye. He could instinctively see what his target was. His reptilian brain was in overdrive now and it didn't matter what else was happening, the world could come crashing down around him, but he would not stop, he would not falter in his mission.

In that moment Wayne suddenly felt himself riding through the waves of the ocean. It worked. He had entered the body of the beast and was in control of it. He had but one thought; kill the boy on the cliff edge. He raced through the waves, speeding as if his life were depending on it. There was a whirlwind beginning to circle him. All oceanic life disappeared, much like on land. Every sentient being around for miles knew to scarper. There was danger and all life knew it. The Taniwha was transfixed; a vehicle of destruction; Wayne could kill this boy now.

On the shore the wind in the dunes was picking up, causing the sand to fly in the air like tiny razor blades. It cut into Duke's eyes and he squinted to see. He ran as fast as he could. The water looked menacing. The waves crashed on the rocks shooting spray high up into the air. Duke was out of breath when he reached the cliff top. It was unusually cold and he could feel it on his skin. Then he noticed his arms were wet with sweat. He glanced back. Brownie and Willow were holding hands with Pounamu and Fro'Ro. He could hear chanting but couldn't make out what was being said.

Down below, Brownie began to invoke the spirits of the ancestors and the Tangaroa - the God of the Sea. He asked for protection. He could feel the heart of the earth pulse harder. The ground shook under foot. He could hear a rumbling sound and looked up to see Pere Watene standing beside Duke, her arms outstretched. She looked like a banshee; her hair billowing in the wind, and her cloak floating like a sail behind her, as her chanting carried on the wind.

Duke turned to the sea. It was jet black, merciless, unforgiving, and enraged. The waves were so high now that there was no hope for anyone who might be in the water. He began to tremble. He had never felt so vulnerable and exposed. It was as if he were a new born child, completely helpless.

It was now he noticed the Pohutukawa tree and the light radiating from it. He could hear Pere Watene invoke the spirits of the tree. She was asking for help. Suddenly he could see layers in the aura of the tree. There were at least four layers of different coloured light emanating from the trunk and it seemed there were three more inside. Human forms began to float out from its centre. Duke was distracted momentarily thinking of the tree in Albert Park that housed all the dead bodies of the influenza outbreak. Then one translucent body after another floated out into the ether, but these were no bedraggled visions of sickly humans, these were warriors, strong and fierce. They were dressed in traditional Maori costume.

Pere Watene was beside him speaking in her native tongue. Duke didn't know what she was saying but the floating bodies seemed to take notice. They formed a line of magnificent men; some had capes, and feathers in their hair, others were bare chested, with straw skirts and leg adornments. Their faces and bodies were covered in interweaving spiral tattoos. They started to take a more solid form now, spirits inhabiting flesh. The warriors began to chant, stamp their feet, and move their arms in a very threatening way. He could hear their voices growing louder and louder as the ground shuddered in unison with them… 'Ka Mate Ka Mate, Ka ora Ka ora'. Somehow Duke understood what they were saying; the profound meaning of this challenge, he didn't know how but didn't have time to question it. (*It is death, It is death, It is life It is life…*)

'Ka mate Ka mate, Ka ora Ka ora,' the calls carried out as the stomping grew, and their hands beat on their thighs and chest adding to the aggression. These dudes meant business. 'Ka mate Ka mate *(It is death, It is death),* Ka ora Ka ora *(It is life, It is life)* Tenei Te Tangata Puhuruhuru (*This is the one*), Nana i tiki mai whakawhiti te ra (*Who will cause the sun to shine again for me*), Upane Upane *(Rise, Rise)* Upane Kaupane *(Up to the top),* Whiti te ra *(See the sun shine!)*

Under Wayne's influence the Taniwha sensed bodies above him. He could see shadows on the approaching cliff top. His instinct was to rise and without hesitation he shot up and out of the depths like a rocket being launched from hell. Roaring and with nothing but viscous intention he stormed towards land, moving with speed, water spraying off his slimy scales. Eyes wide open, black and soulless, he spotted a boy, and began his charge; flames rising from his throat and smoke billowing from the large upturned horns on his head.

The sky was now so dark, even the moon was too afraid to show its silvery face. Duke was terrified. He didn't know what scared him more, the weather, the sea and what it contained, or the floating etheric warrior bodies bellowing their chants behind him. Pere Watene wailed - a shrill piercing sound. This was answered by an inhuman roar as the sea rose up hundreds of feet into the air. Duke fell to his knees; he actually thought he was going to vomit with terror. Against all common sense and reasoning he forced himself to look up just as the mountain of waves parted and there, in all its grotesque glory, was the almighty Taniwha!

Someway behind Duke, Willow was screaming, desperate to get to her brother, but Brownie restrained her. She could only hear the bone-shaking roaring sound. She didn't know if it was the sea, the thunder, or coming from herself. Then she saw it too; a creature so monstrous that she thought she might faint. It was dragon like in appearance, rising out of the depths of the ocean, the foam from the spray whipping through the night sky like sparks from a firecracker. The creature bared its knife-like teeth, red bleeding gums, and saliva dripping from the open cavity. Its eyes were wild but intelligent, and its skin appeared to be covered in barnacles. The size of this creature took her breath away. It was ferocious and malevolent. It seemed to be sniffing for something. Willow feared for her life but couldn't decide if a tsunami would drown them or the beast would swallow them. The rumbling ground began to shudder violently. She turned her soaked face to the tree and saw the ancestors forming their lines and engaging in their war dance – the Haka.

Willow had seen this in rugby when the New Zealand All Blacks prepared to play. They would start each game with this symbolic ritual, paying homage to their forefathers and inviting their opponents to take them on all at once. However here it was different, it was for real. She turned to Brownie but he was gone. 'Brownie!' she screamed over and over till her throat was raw at which point Fro'Ro grabbed her and she fortified her nerve. They could just about see Brownie now running towards the gathered collective of ancestors. He joined in with them and so it began. They were just as determined and threatening as the creature. They moved forward in unison, Brownie too, their low voices getting louder and louder. They smashed their feet on the ground and thumped their fists together. Their faces covered with their 'moku' (tribal tattoos). Chests pumped, tongues splayed, signifying they were going to eat their enemy. This was war, and nothing was going to stop them being victorious. They stomped the ground even harder, their eyes bulged, their voices growing louder and louder…

Brownie was in the middle of them. He knew every move. He was as terrifying as the rest. He was a different man. Gone was the mild mannered jovial uncle. He had been replaced by a fierce and brave warrior. Pere Watene screamed again. The Taniwha turned and faced them. They were made of ether, of spirit, of soul. They were the sum of the knowledge, heart and wisdom of all the elders that had gone before. They were almost invincible, almost. But Brownie wasn't. He was pure mortal, pure man.

The Taniwha spotted him and moved swiftly through the water. It swooped down and swiped for their beloved uncle. Duke saw this and ran, screaming. Brownie ducked. Mala-Kai appeared beside him and suddenly Brownie was invisible. The tree spirits grabbed Brownie and carried him off into the Pohutukawa tree. The ancestors charged at the creature. Spears flew through the air; the monster twisted and roared, its eyes darting back and forth as it searched for its intended prey.

Willow saw her baby brother standing trance like on the edge of the cliff. He was twirling around as if to invoke some ancient spirit, some unknown entity, some God. The Taniwha charged at him as the sky burst open and it poured not with rain but hail, huge thick hard balls of ice. It was raining cricket balls from the sky. And they were deadly.

Willow ran to save her brother, slipping often on the soggy ground, tripping over the carpet of hail stones. She struggled to see even where she was going, there was no light save for the fire spewing from the monster's savage mouth. Her heart was pounding so hard she could feel her rib cage move under the pressure, her lungs were burning now too, but she didn't stop. Pere Watene and the ancients formed a circle around the boy. He was protected by the spirits of every Maori who had ever departed from this land at this sacred spot. They were innumerable and invincible.

But the Taniwha was not intimidated and relentlessly came for Duke. There was a crash of thunder and lightning lit up the night sky. Suddenly it felt like the whole world was on fire. Willow realised it was coming from the mouth of the monster. She thought the world was ending. Why was the Taniwha here? Why was he an enemy? Surely someone or something was manipulating it? Her thoughts were broken by another crash in the ocean. The sea began to whirl, the monster caught in the chaos, made an attempt to get to shore.

The Maori elders were invincible now and whatever they were invoking it was working. With a third crash the sky turned completely black. The waves swirled again, this time in a circular motion, clockwise, around and around, trapping the Taniwha in their icy grip. He pulled against the current but this was bigger than even him.

Foam rose and spray filled the air, it sounded as if the sky was splitting open and the ocean was about to be swallowed. Suddenly a laser like illumination glowed over the surface of the sea. Terror filled the Taniwha for the first time, and as if a spell was broken he stopped and feared for his life. But it was too late. The power of the Skulls had been activated and one of these sacred conduits now rose up from the depths of the earth, smashing through the ocean floor, up through the water, gaining energy as it travelled, turning as if surveying all before it.

The crystal skull broke through the surface of sea, magnificent and glorious just as the Taniwha screamed for life and succumbed to the force of the currents, hands of mermaids and mermen pulling him back down to the bowels of a watery death. And as they did the Taniwha could see a light in the water. It shone like nothing Wayne had ever seen in his life. Terror flooded through every cell of Wayne's being. He was feeling what the Taniwha felt and it was almost too much to bear. Wayne caught a glimpse of the second skull, twirling and rising up like the birth of a new deity. It spun around, beams of light flashing throughout the sea, it stopped, tilted back and shone its beacon directly into the possessed eyes of the poor sea dragon, and it bored a hole right through the blackened soul of Wayne Johnson.

Miles away Wayne immediately removed his energy from the beast as it suffered. Back in the relative safety of his familiar environment he extinguished the candle flame and threw himself at the soil, dispersing it over the floor. He got the feather and threw it on the fire followed by the water. He had never been so spooked in his life. He had messed around with the dark arts before but not with such monumental consequences. He felt his very being exposed for the evil he was incarnating. This was too much even for him. He was totally drained of energy and could barely manage to pull himself up onto the couch. Lying down in a foetal position, wrapping himself in a blanket, he immediately fell into a black pit of depressed unconsciousness.

Back in New Zealand, at the cliff edge, Willow saw Duke rising up, horizontal as if on an invisible sacrificial alter, arms outstretched, head hanging down from his arched back. The earth groaned, flashes of fire pierced the blackness, blood red tracers shot through the air. The sea engulfed the Taniwha, whirlpools formed around him, sucking him down to the deadly depths from where he came. He gave up one last scream of a dying being. A tidal wave formed and began to roll menacingly towards the shore.

Willow panicked. She looked through the tsunami and saw a huge light form in the ocean. It was like a neon beam shining up from the sea bed through the violent waters and on up to the night sky. It was a fluorescent beautiful beam of light. She was transfixed, mesmerised by the sight before her. There was a hum. She thought it must be coming from the light. It seemed to crack open the sky just as minutes before the thunder was ripping it apart. It was something so other-worldly that Willow thought she was dreaming.

Below the waves a circular shape emerged from the depths of the sea. It began to turn as it was rising, slowly, methodically. Water spray was falling off the round structure as it rose up towards the sky. Mini tidal waves rippled from its base. It seemed to be orientating itself. It was then that Willow noticed two holes in the front of the mound. The holes then began to shine a beam of light straight out over the horizon. It spread across the entire surface of the water like a laser. Another crack of thunder and the neon vertical light connected with the horizontal beam creating a triangular arc of blinding light radiating from what Willow knew to be the eyes of the crystal skull.

Then a rainbow coloured pyramid formed where the beams of light met over the ocean. It was almost nuclear in luminosity, but so stunningly beautiful, the prismatic colours all swirling, mixing with the air and water, creating something utterly bewitching. She looked again as the wind whipped her face, water spraying everywhere. At first glance it appeared to be jet black but now with the illumination of the light she could see it was actually made from the same greenstone as the hei-tiki. It began to spin faster and faster. As it spun so did Duke. Willow called out to him. She tried to run to him but the wind was too strong. Gripping the reeds with her hands, ripping them as she fought against the force of the gale, till they bleed, her heart was pumping but she persevered. It felt like Armageddon. She got to Duke as he was thrown violently to the ground, flopping like a rag doll.

The ancients engulfed him and Pere Watene sang a haunting, chilling melody. The sea calmed. The rain stopped and the wind died down. The crystals were surrounding their boy. The sun appeared over the horizon. The trees that had been madly swaying were almost still again. Willow looked up to the sky and a flock of seagulls glided by. She felt her head swim. It was as if the last few moments never happened. The world began to correct itself. Willow reached Duke to find him unconscious.

'Duke!' she screamed, 'DUKE!' She was grabbing him, sobbing. She pulled him to her, wiping his face, his beautiful face. Her heart tore open. She couldn't breathe. The earth stopped turning. In desperation she slapped her brother's face hard.

Slowly but surely Duke's eyes opened and gazing at his sister he simply said, 'Dude, slap me again and you're dead!'

Just then Brownie appeared from over the hill. 'Yooz don't mess around when ya got somethin' to do, eh?'

Duke was too dazed and confused to quip back, but Willow squealed with delight, relieved to see her uncle, 'Brownie!' She ran over to him and threw her arms around his huge neck. 'Steady on girlie, I'm sweet. Now, how's Dukey boy, eh?' Brownie was extremely concerned for the welfare of his nephew and was anxious to check him over.

Sitting up, Duke rubbed his head and felt for his limbs - still all there and intact, score! 'Man, I thought Newgrange was rad but that takes the biscuit! So... what? like, I mean, em...' Duke was struggling to put his thoughts into words.

'Righto let's get you two off this cliff and back to civilisation, maybe a bit of grub, eh?' Brownie was pretty good in situations of crisis and took charge easily. His massive bulk helped a dazed Duke up to his feet and he nodded to his hei-tiki to scout out the route ahead of them. Brownie knew malevolent forces were at work here and something had controlled the Taniwha to rise up like it did. He was anxious to get them all back to a place of safety and decide what the next step would be.

'Duke, how are you feeling?' Willow was anxious.

'Peachy sis,' came Duke's reply thick with sarcasm, 'Brownie we may have one small problem,' Duke added,' I feel like I have just completed a triple iron man competition and have absolutely zero energy left in me to drag my sorry ass back to the truck.' However tired he felt after the Newgrange episode, he was now feeling a million times worse.

'Ah yeah, see what ya mean Duke. Now, I reckon if we put our heads together we can sort this out, eh. What say you fellas come over here and give this young'un a bit of a blast from your laser beams,' Brownie addressed the crystals.

'Brownie, I don't think the crystals have laser beams.

It's not Star Wars you know,' Willow felt obliged to set him straight here.'Ah yeah, haven't ya ever had a crystal treatment? I tell ya, it's 'choice' for the soul, and really blasts up ya energy. It's just what your little bro here needs eh,' Brownie replied.

Obligingly all crystal guides present stood around Duke and held hands. Their energies connected and there seemed to be a buzz around the circle. Duke sat up and let them do their thing. Magically he began to feel clearer headed and more himself again. Ted was at his feet helping him ground his energy in his body. Having had an experience such as he just did, all present knew how vital it was for Duke to settle down into his physicality rather than stay floating in the clouds.

Brownie placed the malachite crystal on his solar plexus and Duke could sense both Mala-Kai and Ted connecting and sending him their vital power. Fro'Ro worked on his heart and he began to have faith in himself again. Mahpee stood next to his throat. The turquoise crystal sent his soothing vibrations to the boy and Duke began to feel a sense of serenity and peace washed over him.

With the help of Mahpee, Duke began to talk, 'I'm not really sure what just happened here folks, but I think I am beginning to come 'round. I'm probably able to stand...' and with that he rose to his feet saying, 'See, good as new.' But without warning looked like he was about to fall again.

'Duke' Willow shouted, and suddenly they all laughed. 'Oh, hardy ha ha, you think you're so funny, well I'm not a bit impressed. Now, get your butt up and let's get out of here. This place is giving me the absolute creeps,' Willow had enough, she wanted to get going.

'Yes siree, Ma'am,' said Duke making for Brownies truck.

Brownie lagged back to talk to Willow, 'Willow, sweetheart, how you goin?'

Willow wasn't much into talking right now. She was still trying to get her head around what just happened and she knew she had to be strong for her brother. It was all swishing around in her head; the Taniwha, the lights, the danger, the floating bodies… It was too much for her and she just looked at her beloved uncle and began to weep, soft silent tears.

Brownie put his bear arms around her and just as she had done with her younger brother after Newgrange, he allowed her to let the tears flow. He knew she needed this release.

Gathering herself, and wiping her blood shot eyes, she took a few deep breaths and stopped sobbing to ask, 'Brownie, what was that thing back there. I mean I don't think Duke has any idea of what actually happened. I have never seen anything like that…that…monster.' She was shaking her head while rubbing the snots away from her nose with the back of her hand. 'Brownie, I'm frightened, really frightened. What are we messing with here, what have we got ourselves involved in?'

'Well girlie, this is bigger than all of us. I have never seen anything like that either, but I know what it means,' he replied. Willow turned her head to see her uncle's face, she could read worry and anxiety in his expression. He rubbed his chin and stopped in his tracks, 'Willow, there is no way I can leave you lot to carry on with this, this...' he struggled for the words.

'Fun? Adventure?' offered his niece, channelling her brother's sarcasm.

Brownie chuckled, 'Yeah, adventure; let's just call it that eh. Well, there is no way on Earth I can leave yooz two to sort this out all by ya selves.'

Willow felt a huge wave of love, relief, gratitude, and love again sweep through her body. She hadn't realised how scared she was till now. The thought that this burly hunk of a gorgeous man was going to stay the course with them was giving her so much comfort that the tears began to flow again.

'There ya go sweetheart, let em flow,' Brownie held her hand and gave it a big squeeze.

Duke halted as he heard his sister cry, 'Ahhh sis, come 'ere,' and he threw his arms around her which made her bawl her eyes out even more.

Laughing, crying and laughing again she burbled as she spoke, 'This is all, hic, your fault. If you didn't, hic, give me a hug, hic, I would be fine,' and they all burst into convulsions of laughter at the sight of the poor girl falling apart. Emotions were all over the place; happy was sad, sad was scared and scared was so frightening it was unbearable.

They trundled back to the hotel in silence, too wrecked to speak. Brownie ordered them food and they sat around in his room and ate in relative silence.

The crystal guardians were standing to attention, calmly sending the troubled humans their soothing, protective and grounding energy. The crystals were always working, sending their vibes, whether the humans were aware of it or not.

Brownie, also too exhausted to think straight, decided to turn in and gave them all an early call for the next morning. He felt it best to get them all back home and decide what the next step would be, right now he had absolutely no idea. Sleeping fitfully, he tossed and turned in the lumpy tiny bed. He was a big burly man and was used to beds being too small for his frame. He travelled a lot around New Zealand and Australia with Pam and it never bothered him. As long as he had his love beside him, it was all okay. He could put up with pretty much anything when she was around. He always had a feeling of contentment and peace when he was with her. He lay there now in this bed and rolled over on to his back. He pulled the covers up close to his neck, exposing his feet. Looking up to the ceiling light he wondered what was going to happen next.

Agitated and uneasy he got up and lobbed himself into the bathroom. Throwing water over his face he stared at himself in the mirror. Well Brownie old boy, looks like ya have got yaself into a right ol pickle, he thought. What are we supposed to do now? Scratching his beard, he went back and sat heavily on the side of the bed.

'Well my little torere ', he began to talk to his dead wife, 'I hope yooz watchin' over us cos I have a feelin' deep in this big old belly, we gonna' need all the help we can get.' He took out his hei-tiki and rubbed it in his hands. The Poumanu appeared beside him and simply sat at his feet. Already Brownie felt better. He knew his Pammy was watching, he could feel her presence. If asked to describe what he sensed he wouldn't be able to but that didn't matter to him. It made him ache for her all the more.

Looking out the window Brownie waited for the sun to rise over the ocean. A glimmer of light daintily peeked up over the horizon and made him wonder at the beauty of the world. The sun rose and set every day regardless of what was going on below. What was out there in the skies? What untold storied did the heavens have? He remembered watching an episode of 'Star Trek' years ago, a series about a space ship floating through the galaxy. Whenever anyone wanted to get away from their intergalactic duties and chill out they would go to the 'Holodeck'. They could walk into this room and key in any situation they wanted. Most of the crew, it appeared to Brownie, would go to a wonderfully serene beach, or woodland forest, or sit in meditation on top of a snow-capped mountain. It was always somewhere beautiful from their home back on planet Earth.

He looked out now, through the thin net curtains at the light of the new day dawning and felt for that moment, right there at the window that he was in his own hologram. This life was one he imagined somewhere in a far off distant time and space; this was his very own holodeck. He was feeling very Zen like and began to look closely at his hand. They were the hands of a gifted craftsman, gnarled and weathered but there was wisdom and skill in them too. He spent his life fashioning lumps of wood into the most exquisitely beautiful objects and his hands told the story of that journey.

Arthritis was gnawing at them now and he couldn't quite do what he used to but that didn't deter him. He loved his craft. It gave him a sense of peace and purpose. Holding his hands up to the light he looked at the thick blue veins throbbing under his weathered skin and wondered what was in the space between his hands and what he touched. He wondered how to push through the thin veil that separated these worlds and if he could push through maybe he would be able to reconnect with his love. He was all at once in awe, joyous and unbearably sad. This cocktail of emotions was one he found hard to come to grips with. 'Ah ya big dope, get ya head out ya bum,' he commanded himself and with that he shook himself down. Not one to dwell too long on the inner workings of the human soul he took himself off to the shower to get ready for the journey home.

Arriving home was bitter sweet. They were all relived to be back in the security and safety of Brownie's little house but there was an air of anxiety. Everyone knew there was more to be done but what it entailed was a mystery. Whenever Willow's thoughts rambled she would mentally swipe left as if she was swiping her tablet. She used this technique whenever a thought would enter her mind that made her sad, or unhappy. She found it really useful to allow negative thoughts to leave her brain. She was doing a lot of mental swiping that day.

Duke was handling it with an air of detached amusement. He knew it was all centred on him. This fact both delighted and frightened him. If he was given the choice would he choose this? If he was honest it was pretty cool, and certainly gave his ego a major boost. Then again, how dangerous was this thing going to get. It was all well and good lording it over his sister, being the epicentre of all the action, but in reality, he was rather petrified. Brownie sent his thoughts to Pam and asked her to send them a sign. He felt confident that the Universe with the help Pammy would show them the way. They just had to have patience. Walking straight past the mail on the hall floor Brownie set his bag down and got the kids a bite of lunch.

'Okeydokey folks! Reckon we all need to regroup here for a bit, eh. Relax, take a nap, go explore the area if yooz like. I'm gonna head out to me shed and get a bit of carving done. It helps get me head straight.'

'Brownie, you carve? Like what do you carve? Duke got the question out just before his sister.

'Oh, I like to do a bit of wood turning, eh. Come have a squizz if ya like,' he said gesturing to the back garden. The kids jumped at the chance for a welcome distraction.

Walking into his garden shed was like entering a labyrinth of the fairies. He had a huge table covered in wood, half-finished carvings, tools of all sorts, knives, gouges, chisels. Willow was awe struck and couldn't believe how beautiful some of the pieces were and recognised the now familiar traditional Maori designs of swirls, fish hooks and ferns.

'Wow Brownie, how long have you been into carving?' She questioned.

'Oh, a long time, eh,' he answered.

'These are amazing,' she said picking up a small sculpture the size of her palm. It was a small kiwi bird. Turning it around she marvelled at the detail and beauty of it.

'Some people reckon I'm a bit of pro ya know,' Brownie offered smiling.

'I'm not surprised' answered Duke who was walking down to the end of his packed workroom. He ran his fingers over the copious amounts of timber, small wooden blocks, and larger unfinished pieces. The air smelled of turpentine and must. The light filtered through the window and Duke could see tiny specks of dust in the ray beaming down on the bench at the end of the shed.

Brownie lovingly rubbed a large unfinished piece in the centre of the room. 'I been wrestling with this fella for a while now.' There was a man's head emerging out of the wood. Duke couldn't decide if he was coming out of the wood or being swallowed by it. His face was fierce and strong and he had a long coarse beard. Duke stopped to examine it closer. The hairs of the beard were extremely realistic and the face was covered in the traditional Maori designs. This guy had two lines radiating out from the centre of his nose across his forehead to his temples. His nose was regal and his nostrils were flared. There was the beginning of a Maori carving around his neck. Duke

stared into his bulging eyes and got the chills. It reminded him of a kids cartoon where the portraits on the walls
would watch you as you walked. Duke moved around
the sculpture and felt the eyes follow him.

The back of his head was still untouched, and it sent a
chill down Dukes spine to see it. It looked rather spooky
as if he was emerging from the mists of time, from some
other realm, coming into this world via the knowledge
and skill of Brownies hands. 'No idea who this bloke is,
sort of making him up as I go along, eh, but reckon he's
a bit special?' he said rather proudly.

'Yeah man, I wouldn't go messing with him that's for
sure.' Duke added.

Willow was taking in her surroundings. There were
benches with intricately carved backs in swirling patterns
of spirals, fish hooks and ferns. There were busts of heads
with tattooed faces and tongues sticking out. There were
large posts that Brownie explained were for the wharenui
or meeting house and other smaller pieces which were
for the waka or canoe.

'What kind of wood do you use?' asked Duke.

Willow was surprised her brother would think to ask.

'Well depends on what I'm tryin' to do eh but mainly Kauri, Totara, Rewarewa and Rimu. Cos they are all
native trees, eh,' Brownie was proud to be sharing this
information with his niece and nephew.

Duke was noticing all the shades from pale yellows,
chestnut, reddish browns to purples and almost black,
'Wowsers man, this is totes awesome.' Duke was impressed. They lingered in his work shed a while longer,

absorbing the atmosphere and learning something about their uncle at the same time.

'Brownie, these are really amazing. They're so beautiful and I can't believe how skilled you are,' Willow said without realising what she might be implying about her uncle.

'Ah yeah, don't sound so surprised eh?' Brownie replied pretending to be a little offended.

'Oh, I'm sorry; I really didn't mean that how it sounded. I mean I just had no idea that you were such an accomplished artist, that's all,' Willow hadn't got the joke.

'Ah it's alright Willow, I'm only pulling ya leg. How would ya know, eh? Yeah, I have been chipping away at this for a long time now. I did leave it for a while after Pam, well, ya know, I hadn't the heart for much of anything but lately I seem to be called back to it. I guess it's my happy place as you kids would say, eh. It helps me brain relax. Ya can't think of anything much 'cept the piece of timber in front of you. I guess it like my kind of meditation; come in here and lose all track of time. The world just floats on by. That's when Pammy would appear at the door there, holdin' a cuppa. She'd always tell me not to work too late and come give me a good night kiss,' Brownie was reminiscing now; both Willow and Duke felt the loss of his beloved wife.

Shaking himself out of his reverie Brownie suggested they all go out for some food in one of the local restaurants in the town. There was a pub called 'The Takapuna Tavern' that apparently did a wicked surf 'n' turf. Suddenly hungry and curious to see some of the locality they agreed with Duke chiming in, 'Yeps, sounds good to me, let's hit the town uncle Brownie and see what this place has to offer.'

Giggling at his lovable nephew Brownie locked up his shed and as they walked through the house, he noticed some mail on the hall floor. It must have been there since they were gone and he hadn't bothered to check it. Absentmindedly he bent down to leaf through what he expected to be nothing but junk mail and noticed an unusual envelope. It was addressed to Mr Edwin Brown C/o of Koru Carvings and designs. It had been a while since he had any correspondence for his official business and he opened it gingerly, fearing subconsciously a tax bill or some other unwanted document.

Things don't just randomly happen and certainly not like this. Just as soon as they were wondering what was going to happen next, he opened the invite to join in an artist collective of native Japanese wood turners and sculptors. Part of the exhibition was the theme of Japanese and New Zealand similarities in art and he was a guest speaker. The wheels of mystery were turning.

Willow and Duke tumbled into the hallway pulling on their jackets and stopped as they looked at their uncle holding a piece of paper in his hand, mouth open, speechless. 'Sup Uncks,' Duke was getting more creative with his home boy slang.

Brownies mouth opened and closed, words failing to exit. 'Brownie, is everything okay? You're starting to scare me a bit, what is it?' Willow was growing alarmed.

'Bloody hell, go get your bags packed, reckon we just figured out what our next step is gonna be kids, you're never going to believe this. Come on, fill ya in as we drive.' And with that the intrepid trio headed off into the balmy Auckland evening...

LAND OF THE RISING SUN

Touching down at Japan's Narita Airport, Duke still couldn't believe he was here. He looked over at a disgruntled Brownie. His bulk seemed to spill out over the arm rests into the aisle, and when he stood, he dwarfed the native Japanese man next to him. Duke was grateful to be sitting with Willow; she was slight, lean and thanks to her daily yoga practice, flexible and fit. She was able to curl up in any position during the flight and slept most of the way. Unfurling her legs from under her, she turned to Duke and with look of wonder said, 'Well Star Child, I wonder what adventures awaits us here, huh?'

'Man, oh man, Willow can you actually believe were here? I mean, Mam letting us go like that, no arguments, just a 'That's marvellous, go have fun!' Seriously, you don't think she has met a man or wants us out of the picture, do you? Like, she didn't even put up a fight,' Duke said still getting to grips with the chain of events that led them here.

'Oh God Duke, don't second guess it. She is genuinely happy for us to come with Brownie and see him in action. He is actually very well respected in his profession you know, and giving a talk on his craft, and doing some workshops is quite impressive. They don't just invite anyone to be guest speakers or whatever they're called at these art gatherings and I for one am very proud of him. He is a major figure in the wood carving world in New Zealand and his pieces are sold all around the world. He looks like a scruffy, cuddly Santa reject but he is in fact a bit of a big deal. The fact that we get to come with him is a bonus. I mean come on, we're in Japan, for crying out loud! We left for a family visit to New Zealand and now we're here,' Willow's little lecture to her brother was also a way of wrapping her own mind around the facts too. Neither of them wanted to push the train of thought any further; crystal skulls, monsters, ghouls and ghosts were being buried under the practicalities of exiting the plane and navigating the bustling airport.

Tokyo is one of the biggest metropolises on Earth and Duke felt as if every one of the 30, or more, million inhabitants were in this airport. He decided to close stick to his sister, uncle and crystal guides. He loved the hustle and bustle around him, but he was also aware that he was out of his depth and if he got himself lost, well, he just didn't want to go there. But Brownie seemed to know what he was doing and with Willow acting as second in command, they found themselves leaving the arrival terminal to be greeted by a slight, smiling, Japanese man, holding a sign that read *Mr Edwin Brown, Koru Carvings*.

Mr Masoto Hiroaki was to be their interpreter and

guide whilst in Tokyo. He was a friendly man with short black hair and small, round John Lennon glasses. His goatee beard was neatly trimmed matching his conservative navy cords, black sweater and check shirt peeking out at the neck. Mr Hiroaki explained that he would drive them to their hotel where they could rest and freshen up before going out for a traditional Japanese meal.

The gang all trundled along obligingly, the flight having beaten them into submission, going along with all instructions, both Willow and Duke fell into their own day dreams as they made their way to the hotel. The lights, bustle and noise of the Tokyo landscape rushed past them in a neon haze as they gazed out the rain drizzled windows of the car. They were both very happy to leave all small talk to Brownie and only when they were settled into the hotel did they begin opening up about the trip and what they felt it meant to each of them.

'Brownie, do you think we can hang out with you the whole time?' Willow enquired, 'I am super excited to see some of the younger Japanese artists. There is this one girl, I read about in the in-flight magazine and she's not much older than me, and she draws these amazing anime figures, and they're really beautiful, I think her name is Chi... Chiho Aoshima, yeah that's it, and then there is this really famous older lady, she's in her eighties now, her name is Yayoi Kusama, and she has been painting and doing installations since she moved to New York in the fifties. There's this one installation where the room is all white and the audience puts dots on everything and it's really amazing. That one is touring the States at the minute I think, but I'm sure we can see some of her other stuff. I think she's really cool. She lives in a mental institution and every morning she goes to her studio and works from nine 'til six then goes back to the home or hospital or whatever it is.' Willow was in full swing now.

'Oh yeah Willow girl, I hope we can take a look at some of the Japanese art eh, I'm sure we can sneak some time for a nosy around the town,' said Brownie in his understated way. 'I told ya mum it was gonna be a really ace sort of cultural travel experience eh, so I betta stick to that?' he said nudging Duke in the ribs.

'Ah man, do we really have to trawl through galleries, serio, I'd rather eat a bucket of raw fish,' Duke was not impressed.

'Choice, be careful what you wish for. Mr Hiroaki is taking us all out tonight for some native grub and I can tell yooz that raw fish is very popular here,' Brownie responded with a chuckle.

Duke sat back on the bed in a huff. He was jet lagged, grumpy and the prospect of boring art talk at dinner was getting him down. He didn't want to admit it either to himself or to anyone else in the room, but he was also trying not to think about the other unsaid agenda that they may have to deal with here; the issue of spooky skulls and other such scary matters.

'Look, Duke, pull yourself together. Everything's going to be all right. Now we're off out in one of the most exciting cities in the world. Get your head in the game, get out of your funk and let's go,' Willow demanded in her very natural bossy manner.

Duke looked at her then sighed, 'Your right sis, soz. I'm cream-crackered after the flight. Now, I am going to have a word with my buddy Ted here and soak up some of his natural good vibes.' Duke gave Ted a dig in the furry ribs at which point Ted turned around, smiled enigmatically and simply said, 'Meow'. Duke fell about laughing; this seemed to hit the humour spot. 'There you go boy,' said Brownie, 'Now let's get your happy pants on and get out there.' Brownie was all too aware that the other agenda was stewing in the background.

Willow turned to Fro'Ro who was zipping up her luminous pink hoody, fixing her aviators in preparation for the balmy Tokyo evening and asked, 'Eh, do you think anything is going to happen tonight?'

'Mmm-hmm, yes siree, ah sure do think we are gonna have one mighty fine evening my Tokyo turtleneck,' was Fro'Ro's bizarre answer, continuing, 'What say we get ourselves out into that wonderful city and have some fun, raw fish or no raw fish.' And with that she opened the door of the hotel room and led the motley crew out into the frenetic ball of energy that was Tokyo.

Thousands of miles to the West, Wayne Johnson returned to his office a changed man. He had crossed a line and there was no going back. Spooked from his experiences at the cabin, and uncertain of what was happening, he wondered who that boy was? He didn't know him, but there was something about him that felt very familiar. What was his next step?

Mrs Winters noticed his pallor, 'Senator I hope you don't mind my saying but you don't look well, a little tired perhaps? You've been working very hard lately what with the oil pipeline project, the protestors...' She let the sentence trail off, and looking at his face, wondered if his weight loss was due to worry.

'Yes, Mrs Winters, I do appreciate your concerns, but I assure you I am perfectly fine, just burning the candle at both ends,' he managed a smile.

'Yes Senator, oh by the way that journalist girl was on again this morning... She wants another interview,' his trusted employee added, almost reluctantly.

Wayne sighed. He was usually so adept at dealing with this sort of thing but today he was feeling heavy, weighed down by the demands of his position. He felt weary trying to duck and dive, keep all the plates spinning, and not get caught with anything shady. He really wasn't in the mood for some do-gooder, hungry young journo to come in here asking all the wrong questions. He didn't have the mental agility to swerve when needed or volley back her concerns. Looking up at his trusted secretary, he gave in, 'You know what Mrs Winters? You may be right. Maybe it's time I take a holiday. I think I will take your advice.'

He sat back in his large plush swivel chair, crossing his fingers with his arms resting on his stomach, and took a deep breath in, 'Yes. That is exactly what I need, a holiday. Mrs Winters, yet again, you are spot on. What would I do without you? Could you please get my travel agent on the line?'

'Of course, Senator,' and with that she turned to walk back to her desk, a happy smile spreading across her face.

Wayne rose from his desk and walked into his private bathroom. He splashed water on his face, staring at his pale complexion in the mirror. His mind was racing. He was all in now. This thing was really happening, and he had to see it through to the end. But where was he going to go? He needed a sign. Throwing down the towel, he sat back at his desk, 'Mrs Winters, hold all my calls please.'

'Yes, Senator,' she replied, pleased her boss was taking it easy. Wayne went over to the door, locked it from the inside, and turned down the lights. He needed peace and quiet and time to think. Meditation was not something new to him although he hadn't practiced in a while. But he knew the benefits of it. If he could just clear his mind he may be able to get an inclination, a thought or a feeling of what to do next.

Sitting upright, spine straight and breathing deeply, he began. In, out, in, out. Silence. Thoughts ran across his mind. He brushed them aside. In, out, in, focussing on his breath, he was sure it would work. His ego was in full swing now. Surely someone like him, as powerful, as knowledgeable as him could get this thing going. In, out, again, nothing. Persevering he sat still, feet on the ground, hands holding the arms of the chair, focussing on his breath. 'Aaargh,' exasperated he punched the desk. This wasn't working. He stood up, walked to the door, unlocked it and turned up the lights. The phone light was blinking. Opening his door, he informed his secretary he was available again.

'Oh Senator, just a moment, Jack Canshaw, from the

pipeline company phoned while you were unavailable, he wants to know if you are free for lunch tomorrow, Sushi at the new Japanese restaurant down the block?' her question was innocent enough, but it was just what Wayne had been waiting for. He froze; a shiver travelling through his body from head to toe. Slowly he closed the door and leaned against the wall. So that's where you are, he thought to himself. It was beginning to make sense, Newgrange in Ireland was the North, New Zealand was the South and now Japan, the skull of the East......

Back in Tokyo the gang explored the city and all its delights. Mr Hiroaki proved to be an excellent tour guide and showed them around the hot spots. Heading to a cafe in the Shibuya Wards fashionable Harajuku district, Duke nearly lost his mind when he encountered the pop cultural phenomena of Kawaii. It sprang up in response to the very austere post war masculine culture and now was a full-blown modern youth movement of cartoon characters, colour and costume.

'Now this is what I call a café,' Duke remarked, eyes on stalks mouth open. The waitress was dressed in a neon pink top with a puff ball skirt; her bright red bob had tiny flowers sprinkled through it. Her lips glistened with sparkly paint and she was smiling and giggling the whole time. The cafe itself was an explosion of colour and the decor was what Duke imagined the mad hatter's tea party to be like. Giant plastic teacups and saucers, unicorns, bunnies and merry go rounds in the middle. They were submerged in a world of garish luminosity and Duke was in awe. Mr Hiroaki explained that he had planned on going to a more traditional restaurant but when he saw that Brownie had two teenagers with him, he decided that this would be much more fun. 'Far out!' was all Duke could manage. He prided himself on being a bit of an aficionado on cool; listening to bands like Warpaint, Grimes, the XX, Savages, and for his hip hop fix, Kendrick Lamar, Drake and Childish Gambino. He thrived on youth culture and was always ahead of the latest trends, although he never put any effort into this, it just came naturally to him. His radar was tuned to youth, primed for the piquancy of pop, and this place was off the hook. He loved every minute of it. Ordering food, he glanced over at Fro'Ro who was sitting on the back of their neon green booth, leaning up against the wall, hands in her pockets, squinting over her shades.

'Man, oh man, this place sure does tickle my fancy,' she said to no one in particular. Ted on the other hand, was sitting stiffly beside Willow, who Duke now noticed, was looking rather uncomfortable.

'Willow, dude, chillax will ya. You look like you have a rod up your butt. What's up sis?' he asked.

She sighed, 'Look, this Japanese techno pop is literally melting my brain but don't let on. Mr Hiroaki brought us here thinking we would love it. I don't want to offend him.'

'But Wills,' as he affectionately calls her sometimes, 'I do love it. You are far too old for your age. Tell your inner hippy to piddle off back to Woodstock and get in touch with your inner Kawaii.' Willow rolled her eyes at her brother. Sometimes he could be insufferable. Duke turned to Mr Hiroaki and shouted loudly, 'KAWAII!' nodding profusely and smiling from ear to ear, holding up a tumbler full of radioactive pink sweetness. Mr Hiroaki responded in much the same manner back and not wanting to be rude Willow complied with the grinning and nodding, wishing she were anywhere else but here.

Turning to Brownie she asked quietly, 'Brownie this is great and all but the jet lag is really hitting me hard. Do you think we could wrap this up and head back to the hotel? I'm bushed.'

'Ah yeah Willow girl, don't you worry. The noise is knackering my head too, eh. I'll tell Mr Hiroaki that we need to get a bit of kip now, eh,' Brownie obliged his niece.

'Cheers Brownie,' and with that relief washed over her. She needed her iPod, some Kate Bush and a lie down. God, she thought, how old am I?

Walking through the bustling streets of Tokyo Duke couldn't help but giggle at the sight of his two crystal buddies striding ahead of him. Mahpee and Mala-Kai looked every bit the part, slipping right in with the colourful costumed madness of the young people. Ever vigilant, ever guarding, their crystal energies never stopping, the rock people were scouting the area, sensing danger, and shielding their wards from the low vibrations that were lurking in the ether.

Mr Hiroaki had planned a rather hectic day, but sensing their exhaustion, he veered towards a less adventurous itinerary and suggested they visit an area rich in craft and art. Willow picked up at this suggestion and having had his fill of fun Duke agreeable went along with the idea.

Exiting the Hibiya Line subway station at Naka-Okachimachi in Taito Ward, the gang headed south alongside the elevated Japan Rail (JR) tracks. They browsed the small outlet stores, choc-a-block with cheap trinkets and discount diamond outlets.

Duke was still in awe of the differences between here, Ireland and New Zealand. He was only fourteen but thought he had a worldly sensibility having travelled to England with his mum and a school trip to Germany, not forgetting the summer holidays on the Isle of Man. Yes, Duke was a man of the world.

However, this whole scene in Tokyo was blowing his mind. The strange Japanese writing everywhere, the people for goodness sake, were a different race. He was still chuckling at how many of them wore masks over their mouths, as if they were about to perform surgery. Every city had its own unique smell, like every person, and this one was no exception. Incense wafting from the homes in the morning. As he walked, he inhaled the steam rising from the ground carrying the not so fragrant hints of garbage mixed with smells of soy sauce and yakitori floating in the air. Turning down a side street he was hit with wafts of fish coming from Yoshiike, a large sea food market harking back to the 1920's. Feeling in the moment, ever present and alive Duke rambled behind the others, soaking up every second. He didn't want this experience to end. He loved the suspense of not knowing what was coming around the corner and he fed off the energy of the big city.

They headed southwards and entered an artisan complex known as Aki-Oka 2K540. Mr Hiroaki explains that the name means between Akihabara and Okachimachi, and 2K540 is the exact distance, 2 Kilometres and 540 metres from the marker in the central Nihonbashi district from which the distances are calculated in Japan.

Brownie was particularly interested in a store featuring kibori (wood carvings), kasuri karume (Japanese ikat style woven fabrics) and other wooden carvings. It was here that he now took note of the ubiquitous image of Mt Fuji in the background of Hokusai's, The Great Wave. This print is everywhere, famous throughout the world and he hadn't really paid attention to it before now but as the sun shone through the window, lighting up the print on the wall, something in him shifted and he knew where they had to go.

Fujisan, Mt Fuji, it was there, the skull was calling him, he was a conduit, a guide, a protector of his nephew. He understood his role now. It was through him and his work here in Tokyo that led Duke to this place. Brownie took a deep breath. He had forgotten momentarily about their other agenda, getting wrapped up in his work, and the lecture he was to give the next day. However, just as his brain wandered off the true path, life nudged him back on it. The print on the wall may as well have had a neon sign blinking for only him to see, with whoop-whoop sounds and a few fairies dancing around it for good measure.

Brownie stood stock still. Looking slowly over at

his nephew, his heart skipped a beat. Duke was giggling with his big sis over something that they were reading, who knew what it was but it tickled them both. Then a wave of sadness and sorrow flooded Brownie's heart. Why was this happening to Duke, why him? He is just a kid. Brownie wished with all his might that he could take this chalice from his nephew and carry it for him, but he knew all too well, that's not how it goes. Life doesn't work like that. What's for you won't go by you. Well, just this once he wished it would just keep on walking, nothing to see here folks, move along.

Brownie took a deep breath in, looked at Mr Hiroaki's mouth move, words were being spoken to him and he smiled politely but all he could hear was the thumping of his heart and deafening silence.

'Yo, yo, yo Uncks,' Duke appeared slapping him on the back and pulling him back to the shop, 'sup man, you look like you were in outer space?'

'Ah yeah, just the jet leg, eh. What say we get our hot bots back to the hotel. I need to prep my talk,' Brownie replied.

Willow and Duke looked at each other and cracked up. 'Did he just say, 'hot bots'? I swear that man is a scream,' said Willow as they followed Mr Hiroaki out into the Tokyo afternoon.

Much closer now, Senator Wayne Johnson touched down in Tokyo ready for action. His timing was impeccable. He sorted his affairs and booked his ticket all within a half a day of deciding where to go. He hired a car and sped through the Tokyo suburbs. This was a nice little jaunt at the expense of the taxpayer, he thought. He was on a business trip, checking out new opportunities, and whatever other nonsense he could make up. He loved being able to do this all in the name of work.

Arriving at the Hotel Kozanteiubuya near Mt Fuji he headed straight for his room. He entered, noting the white linen covered futon, the beautiful wooden floor and the enormous T.V. He opened the rice papered covered double doors to the terrace outside and smiled appreciatively at the 'onsen' - a Japanese hot tub. This will do nicely, he thought. Wayne knew he needed to tap into the energies of the kids but first things first, lying down on the rather hard bed, he fell into a deep but troubled sleep.

In his dreams, Wayne was wrestling with a demon. He could see large red eyes, and the smell of earth and bog was almost suffocating. He was lost in a forest. Wayne writhed in the sheets and when he woke he was covered in sweat. Unsettled he gathered his thoughts and swung his feet to the wicker mat. He felt groggy and needed coffee. Sitting for a moment to take in the quiet of the room he reflected on why he was here. Truth be told he still wasn't completely sure but there was a draw, a pull that was undeniable. He walked out to the terrace where the stone garden had been raked and the onsen was bubbling away.

He would avail of this pleasure later, but first there was work to do. Feeling more like himself, he took a large breath in of the fresh crisp air, smelling the dewy mist as he did so. Wayne liked to push himself and today was no exception. He did his morning ritual of push ups, squats and a spot of deep breathing. So what if he was here to stop some kids doing good in the world? He may be here for foul purpose but that was no reason to let standards slip. A shower ended his serious bout of preening, pruning and appreciating his looks. He dressed and headed off to the elegant restaurant for his much-anticipated breakfast; he was starving and felt like he could eat a bull.

Wayne was always amazed at the formality and politeness of the Japanese people. He cut a dashing figure among them with his buff swarthy tall frame gliding through the dining room. His ego was being fluffed, aware of the ladies' eyes as he drifted past. Hmmm, you still got it dude, he thought vainly to himself.Sitting at a window table, he was able to look out over Lake Kawaguchiko to Mt Fuji in the distance. This was rather a rare sight as the mist normally covered it, hence its nickname 'the shy mountain'. This place was revered in Japanese culture. He knew this was where the action was going to take place, it was the obvious choice, but something was telling him this was not where he needed to go.

Distracted by the mountain he glanced over the menu of miso soup, pickled turnip and cucumbers, blanched spinach, grilled seafood, and natto - a type of fermented soybean. He opted, with a lurching stomach for an omelette and a large pot of coffee which he was delighted to find out this hotel did. Previous experience told him not all restaurants served coffee here, tea being the beverage of choice.

He needed a plan. It was all well and good coming here, but he really didn't have the first notion of what he was going to do. The mountain was calling to him, but it was also striking fear into his heart. He wasn't used to being scared and he didn't like it. It was as if this place was not on his side. Abstractedly he leafed through some tourist information material he had gathered along the way, and there it was, looming large as day, almost calling his name, The Aokigahara Forest, or Sea of Trees. He had never heard of it but something about it beckoned to him. Wiping his mouth, and throwing down his serviette, he stood abruptly and left the restaurant, a man with a mission.

Asking for information from the receptionist about the forest, he was greeted with a rather quizzical look. It was usual for tourists to want to know information about how to get to Mt. Fuji but the Aokigahara Forest? Well, that was not so much in demand. The Japanese believed it was haunted. It had become an outlet for those wanting to commit suicide, and in this place of haunting natural beauty, they were left to do so. This very fact rendered it cursed. Wayne gravitated to it all the more. He wasn't sure if it was a test of his courage or was there a spirit calling him. Either way, he was going to go and nothing would stop him.

The receptionist gave him directions with a plea to think again. She studied him closely. Many a businessman had gone there to end their lives and she worried silently that this was his plan also. However, he looked robust, bright and it was not her job after all to judge anyone, simply to be of assistance.

Wayne drove to the northwest corner of Mt Fuji where the fourteen square miles of haunted forest was located at the base of the mountain and parked the car. He had sensibly dressed in khaki chinos, hiking boots, a warm cashmere sweater and a navy puffa jacket. Always one for a bit of style, he slung his man bag over his shoulder with water and some snacks and began his mission.

He was greeted with a large sign from the Japanese Government pleading with people to get help if they were depressed or thinking of suicide and a statement about how life was a precious gift from your parents. Normally he was not one to think about other people and after his experience in the cabin wielding his dark magic on the Taniwha, his soul had turned a shade darker. However, his humanity was not completely gone, and he did stop for a moment and think about all the people, over a 1000 apparently since 1998 that had come here to die. A wave of sadness swept over him and he was consumed momentarily by the sorrow of those people and their families.

Shaking himself out of his funk, he reminded himself of why he was here. Somehow, even before he set foot in the forest it was having an effect on him. What were these feelings that swam inside his body? Bracing himself, he entered the sea of trees and walked along a small trail that beckoned him to go further. The hands of the branches waved him down an unmarked trail.

The air was thick and heavy. The way underfoot seemed to want to pull him down, like a hidden mine of holes. There was moss over everything and one tree began to look like the next. Wayne looked at the compass on his phone, but there was no signal. He would have to follow his instinct here. However, he did need to get back out. He stopped for a moment and looking up at the tree in front of him, a chill ran down his spine. There, hanging down from the branch overhead, was a lifeless rope, falling over the tree branch like a stillborn limb.

Jumping back, Wayne took a moment, as his nerves began to waver. He untied the rope from the branch, not wanting to think why it would be there, and tied it around the tree, in a large bow shape, like he was gifting the tree as a present to someone, thinking this would be a marker for him to recognise the way out. He continued deeper into the forest past large gaping holes in the side of the hills that appeared from nowhere and looked like large toothless mouths, grinning, waiting to eat him alive.

Still the eerie feeling didn't leave him but intensified with every step. Wayne thought he was being watched. He stopped and turned around calling out, but no answer came. He noticed how there was no echo to his voice, a fact that left him feeling even more uneasy. The silence was now oppressive, and the air weighed heavy on his shoulders. The crunch of twigs underfoot took on a sinister tone. He felt the presence of every soul who passed through here. Their pain and sorrow now tangible, their thoughts audible.

Wayne slapped his head as he found his thoughts

getting ever darker. No time for that now. He knew those kids were near that mountain or at least on their way. They needed to be stopped. He was unaware at the time of the first skull activation, he failed to stop the second, but this time he was going to thwart them no matter what.

Looking back, he realised that he had no clue where he was. He thought he had traced his steps well, but it was as if this place scrambled itself and where he thought he was going, he looked back and had just come from. Just then the trees knitted together overhead to form a roof of leaves and brambles, their branches inter weaving to make a network of arms, locking him inside their wooden embrace.

Moss covered everything, making it look like the forest floor was climbing up the tree trunks. The air was dank and moist, with an after note of death and despair. Nothing nice or pleasant was allowed to exist here. Wayne took a breath and sat down beside a small cave in the side of a hill. This ain't no Disneyland, he mused to himself. The trees bent over the hole of the cave as if to shield the contents from prying eyes, hiding its treasure. Wayne was overwhelmed by an urge to know exactly what was hidden inside.Pulling out a few trinkets from his bag that he figured would come in handy, he approached the mouth of the cave. Blackness greeted him. He decided to sprinkle salt on his back, in homage to ancient wisdom of protecting oneself from demonic attachment, and thought he saw a figure out of the corner of his eye. Pull yourself together, man, you're the one with the power here, he reprimanded himself. It was time to get to business.

Wayne cleared a patch of ground and sat down, pulling a round quartz crystal ball the size of his palm out of his pocket. His trusted mirror was not here, he was unable to remove it from its resting place in the lake by the cabin; this was the next best thing; his portable oracle, a reliable friend. He lit a fire and drew a circle of protection around his body. The fire threw strange shapes up against the wall of the cave and they did nothing to ease his anxiety.

Setting the crystal ball down in the middle he began to breathe slowly and deliberately. He needed to be grounded and centred to see clearly. If he wasn't, the crystal would not connect with him and its appearance would stay cloudy. He began to feel an urge to lay down, to feel the leaves, moss, twigs, insects, the belly of the forest floor under his body. He needed to connect with its beating heart, the pulse of the ground throbbed in his head.

So, stepping outside the cave he lay on the wet uneven ground. He could hear the trees talking to each other, under him, the channels of communication open, like electricity flowing from root to root. His body began to submerge into the soil, his clothing the perfect camouflage to hide in. The forest was testing him, checking him out and his acceptance was palpable. This was no ordinary place. There were thoughts, feelings, energies and spirits in the air that he had never encountered in his life and he had to admit to himself, he was afraid.

With a start, Wayne became aware of a small, fox-like animal, sniffing around him. Turning his head sideways he came face-to-face with a tanuki. He knew what it was from previous visits to Tokyo. These little guys were part of folklore and urban myth; gifted shapeshifters. Standing in front of his nose, only centimetres away from him, this fury creature slowly and perceptibly changed into a raven. Wayne wasn't fazed; he knew this was a messenger for him. It reminded him of the day under the tree before all this began. Was it the same raven? What was its message now? The dew in the air collected on the bird's feathers and made it shimmer. It let out a shrill ear-piercing sound, turned to stare at him straight in the eyes. He thought for a brief moment it was going to attack him, but it didn't. Then without warning it took flight; the sound of its wings flapping in the air like a slow hand clap. Wayne sat up, shook himself down and retreated back into the cave.

He walked slowly over to the circle and gingerly stepped over the makeshift dust barrier. His nerves calmed once inside his protective enclosure. He threw some more kindling on the fire and immediately the shadow figures on the wall danced higher and quicker inviting him to join in, beckoning him to enter the fray. He stood looking at them for a moment convinced they would send him a message. Nothing.

Wayne sat down, calmed his breath and with glazed eyes stared into the crystal. Again, nothing. His frustration was mounting; he needed a sign. Magic might get this show on the road. Rubbing his hands over his face then over his head he sat back and thought for a moment. It was then he noticed the fire. It was growing low, but the shadows were getting higher. He looked more closely. He could make out the shape of a tiger, then the moon, a sun, a wizard, the images were coming clear and fast now. He could see the outline of Mt Fuji, its symmetrical cone shape distinct and easily recognisable. He could see the outline of a bird in flight. Then terror struck into his heart. The images all merged into the unmistakable shape of a dragon.

Thinking fast Wayne stared into the crystal ball for confirmation. There in front of him, clear as day, he could see Ted and Fro'Ro. He knew these were guides and if he could get rid of them he would strike a blow to the boy. He looked outside the cave. Circling overhead, he saw a murder of crows, their caws growing louder as they swarmed over the upper canopy of trees. They reminded Wayne of a witch's cloak. They were his allies and they knew what to do. Flying off abruptly, their goal to find the crystals closest to the boy, Ted and Fro'Ro.

Brownie spent the next day fulfilling his obligations; giving master classes in wood carving, how it's done in New Zealand and his talk on the common threads between his native Maori and Japanese art went down exceedingly well. Willow was with him the whole time. Duke jangled his crystals in his pocket as he wandered around the exhibit and took great delight in watching the people as they felt the invisible presence of his rock buddies walk among them. One small demure Japanese lady was struggling over a decision to buy a wood block print of the Tokyo skyline from an emerging young artist or a pendant made from layers of pigment tinted lacquer dried for over a year.

Fro'Ro leaned in closer to her and as Duke strolled by, he could just hear the lady say, 'You know, I think I deserve both.'

He smiled to himself as Fro'Ro straightened her shoulders, wafted past him and simply said, 'Cos that's how I roll.'

Duke surprised himself and actually had a really good day. He sat outside in the concourse and mulling over the sights and sounds of the day with Ted, concluded that this art malarkey wasn't half bad.

The gang reconvened at the hotel later that evening. Ted and Mala-Kai ever the pragmatists gently nudged Brownie to broach the subject of Mt Fuji. Mahpee sat beside him and channelled his energy to his throat chakra as he was finding it tough to get the words out, 'Look, little bro, I need to have a bit of a chat with ya.' 'Oh, this doesn't sound good,' replied Duke good naturedly.'Well, ya see it's like this right, see I think we're supposed to have a trip up old Mt Fuji here and check out 'the vibe' as yooz would say.'

Duke fell silent. They were sitting around the table eating miso soup and noodles. He gently put his chopsticks down and looked at his uncle, 'You know what Uncks, that's tots A-Okay with me. I mean, like, we all knew were here for another reason. It's been fun checking out the sights and sounds of Tokyo, but you know I'm okay with it. Don't get me wrong, I'm literally pooping my pants with nerves, and if I eat any more of that sushi stuff I think I will literally pooh my pants.'

'Euuuu, T.M.I. Duke,' said Willow but didn't pursue the slagging, she was only too aware of what was ahead of her brother and she was in no mood to add to his load.

'But I am also aware that there is a rather pressing matter that we must attend to,' Duke said rather grandly, 'and I intend to fulfil my part of the…bargain? Well I don't remember making any bargain, so let say my destiny, shall we. Yes, it's all good Uncks, I know you have my back and I'm kinda relieved we have my pretty awesome crystal buddies here too, so I'm in very good hands.' 'That's the spirit, good lad. Now don't worry 'bout a thing. We got our crystals to keep us safe. You got me on your side and who wouldn't be afraid of me, eh?' Brownie said this flexing his huge bicep and they all laughed, relieving some of the tension that had been building up. 'I'll chat to Mr Hiroaki and see if we can take a trip to Fujisan, as it's called in these here parts. Not sure what we will do exactly but it will be sweet. Now tuck into this choice grub and enjoy tonight, eh!' Brownie smiled and got stuck into his food. And the gang did just as he suggested, taking selfies and generally chatting with the extremely friendly staff whose command of the English language surprised everyone. Duke laughed as he pulled Ted into the frame only to be surprised by his total lack of presence in the photo.

'Eh Duke they're like pure energy. You can't take their photo, you donkey. Pure energy doesn't photograph. Well unless you are doing Kirlian photography. Then I think you can see peoples' aura, but like that's something else. And anyway, you would need special equipment for that and...' As Willow spoke, Duke held up both his hands and made a 'W' with his fingers, mouthing the word 'whateves' to his sister in a gesture that immediately let her know he had zero interest in her lecture on energy photography or anything else for that matter.

Mr Hiroaki joined them after dinner and Brownie arranged their trip to Mt Fuji the next day after his lectures. Mr Hiroaki explained climbing the mountain was off limits, wrong time of year, but they could visit the area and see Mt Fuji from the base. The men then got into an intense conversation about the famous artist Katsushika Hokusai who did the thirty-six views of Mt Fuji, and the one image that was a firm favourite of Brownies called 'The Great Wave off Kanagawa'. Mr Hiroaki referenced one of his last works which was of a dragon disappearing into the smoke on top of the mountain. Brownie felt the hairs on the back of his neck rise. Somehow this reference meant something. The image stayed with him as they paid the bill and headed off to bed.

Wayne beat a hasty retreat back to his hotel. The receptionist took a second look at him as he looked like he had been dragged through a hedge backwards and quite literally he pretty much had. Taking off his mud stained, damp clothing he eased himself into the bubbling onsen and let out a huge sigh. Propping himself on the edge with his arms out, his torso all but submerged, he contemplated the events of the day.

The skull was in that mountain, he was certain of

it and the kids were near. He needed to get a better understanding of what they were going to do so he could strategize. The steam rose around him and he drifted off into his own world. The sky grew dark and he could see the almost full moon directly overhead.

As the streams of steam glided up into the night time air he began to see shapes, again a dragon, a skull, a sword, then they unfurled themselves like dancing girls beckoning him to his doom. He shook his head and stepped out of the hot bath. Wrapping himself in a towel he retreated to his bedroom. He decided to get an early night although he feared sleep would elude him and get an early start in the morning. Walking over to close the window he noticed something glint in the moonlight, just outside on the ground. He hurried out, bent down and there in front of him were two large glistening, round crystals, one an opaque pink the other a striated brown and gold.

He smiled to himself realising he had managed to control the crows and get them to do his bidding. So now I have you my little rock stars, he said to himself, let's see how they get on without their trusted allies, hmmm, tomorrow just got a whole lot more interesting. He threw the two crystals up in the air and caught them with a loud raucous laugh. Flinging them into the bottom of his bag he jumped into bed eager for the next day.

SACRED MOUNTAINS AND SACRIFICE

Arriving down for breakfast the next morning Duke was astonished to see a Wizard, a sun God and a very floaty white lady drift by. He turned to Willow with a quizzical look in his eyes. She shrugged her shoulders and they both turned to their uncle together and simply pointed. Brownie obliged, 'Ah yes well, maybe I forgot to mention, I called for a bit of backup last night ya see. We need a bit of help on this one. Duke, Willow, meet Merlin, our labradorite crystal.'

Duke took in this rather marvellous looking wizard, complete with pointed hat and staff. He wore a long dark cloak that shimmered with a rainbow of brilliant hues when caught in the light. His stick was a normal piece of pale wood, driftwood it looked like, nothing special. Duke panned around the lobby of the hotel, with travellers checking in and out, lights, background music, hustle and bustle. Even if other 'normal' folk could see these marvellous rock people, he decided that they would not blink an eye; everyone was too wrapped up in their own business to care what happened to the person next to them. Their blinkers were on and their heads were down getting on with the events of the day in their own world.

Willow stepped forward and introduced herself, 'Hello, my name is Willow and I am very pleased to meet you,' she declared rather formally.

Duke took a different approach, 'Far out man, like, you are one serious looking dude.'

'Why thank you, young man, I assume that is a compliment,' the wizard replied, 'and my name is Merlin, you may have heard of me, I have become rather a legendary figure, but you may call me Merle if you wish. No need to stand on ceremony now is there. I mean we are on the same team and all that.'

'Sure, yes, and I am very glad of it,' Duke replied.

The old wizard smiled benignly at the boy and seemed to look past him, or rather through him as if he were reading him on some other, deeper level. It gave Duke the chills. It was only now he noticed how long Merle's beard was, literally down past his knees and it appeared to creep around his body and meet up with his hair at the back giving him a rather fluffy aura. His emerald eyes, deep set in his craggy face, shone with the wisdom of the ages and suddenly Duke was thrown back to the night in Newgrange when he had an encounter with another weird and wonderful wizard. 'Now I called on ol' Merle here to give us a hand, with him being a bit of a sorcerer and all that. He's pretty good at dippin' into the other realms and movin' between the worlds if yooz know what I mean, eh,' Brownie remarked. Willow and Duke did not but refrained from saying anything and simply nodded.

'He also has a pretty good relationship with them fairies ya know and could be sweet if it looks like we might get stuffed,' Brownie continued. Again, the bemused siblings nodded their understanding. Just then Mala-Kai and Mahpee appeared beside the wizard and they embraced each other like old friends.

'Like do all crystals know each other automatically?' Duke whispered to Willow.

She simply shrugged her shoulders saying, 'Your guess is as good as mine.'

The lady appeared now from behind Merle. She was draped in white silk flowing from her nine-foot body which mingled with her silver hair, creating wave after wave of shimmering luminosity. Her ice blue eyes shone bright in a face of alabaster, not unlike Willow's as she spoke, 'Let me introduce myself, my name is Luna and I am the high priestess of the moon, the moonstone to you. This is my brother Sonny, we work closely with our Uncle Merlin and we are the Feldspars.' Her brother Sonny bowed his hello.

'Sonny, what kind of crystal are you?' enquired a pragmatic Duke, noting his huge frame, gold cuffs and roman style skirt similar to Mala-Kai's. They must have gone to the same tailor, Duke thought to himself. Sonny was literally shining down on all present. His mane of golden hair hung down his back like cascading fire and his body sparkled with flecks of burning light. He looked like a golden Adonis. A disc hung from a thick gold rope around his neck. Duke noticed an engraving of the figure eight and wondered what it meant. 'I am Sunstone at your service,' he said.

'Ah, hence the name, I get it, that's pretty cool,' admitted Duke. 'Well we do try to make it as easy as possible for you. I mean my full title is Admenenon Thesuaphie Rhonnian Malchizadek Sonnandulam, but we think that's a bit of a mouthful, so you may call me Sonny for short,' the radiating orange crystal beamed his eyes on Duke as he spoke.

Duke swallowed his discomfort. 'Nice tan dude,' was all he could muster and with that Willow gave him a dig in the ribs. Duke looked at Luna with a glint in his eye, 'Eh, I won't ask what your full name is Luna 'cos I'm pretty sure I will not remember any of it.' The lady in white giggled and Duke turned again to his sister and said, 'See, rocks have a sense of humour, it's not just Ted and Fro'Ro.'

'Speaking of which, where are those guys?' Willow asked. It was only now, that Willow noticed they hadn't appeared yet. She felt in her pocket and noticed the crystal was missing. She immediately felt her throat where she wore a rose quartz pendant. It too was gone. Duke, on noticing Willow's dismay, felt for his own guardian rock in his pocket and it was also nowhere to be found. His heart began to race. Panic was seeping in. It felt like ground was creeping up over his body, he could feel vines around his limbs and he pulled at his throat as if he couldn't breathe. There was a pungent earthy smell in the air and he looked around to see where it was coming from.

Willow noticed his discomfort and began rubbing his back, saying, 'Duke, calm down, you need to take a few deep breaths. They will show up, they must be around here somewhere. Let's go back to the room and check there. Maybe the crystals fell out of our pockets at dinner. Brownie you go check the restaurant and ask if anyone found them.'

'Will do, girlie,' Brownie replied, but he knew crystals did have a habit of disappearing if their work was done or the person didn't need them anymore. Although this did seem an unlikely scenario as they were about to face their biggest challenge yet and for Ted or Fro'Ro not to be there, well the old man didn't want to think about that just yet.

Willow and Duke hurried back to their room accompanied by their new crystal allies. Mahpee turned to look at Duke and laid his hands on him. He had an uncanny ability to pour soothing energy over a troubled soul. He calmed Dukes nerves and by the time Brownie returned from checking around the hotel Duke was sitting comfortably.

'Now big man, I think we have to go ahead without them. They'll turn up, but for now we need to get going, eh. Mr Hiroaki has told me how to get there and I have booked us into a traditional ryokan, so we got a base there. What do ya say, feelin' a bit better?' Brownie tried to encourage his nephew. Duke was actually feeling a lot better. He suspected it was Mahpee's influence and as he gathered himself, the gang assembled and set off for the five lakes region around Mt Fuji.

Brownie, Willow and Duke took the JR Line from Shinjuku to Otsuki Station which took them an hour and from there, the Fujikyu train to Kawaguchiko station in the five lakes region. Duke thought it hilarious that the hei-tiki sat on Brownies head the whole way and wondered if Brownie noticed at all. Mala-Kai and Mahpee were found on the roof of the bus and the Feldspars disappeared and reappeared on arrival at the ryokan.Locating it was easy enough and the hostess was incredibly friendly. They put their bags down in the small room, sparsely decorated by western standards. There was a futon in the corner, a small table in the other. The floor was covered with the traditional tatami mat, made from rice straw and wood chips and the wooden windows were framed with latticed rice paper shutters. This was to be Willow's room for the night with a similar one for Brownie and Duke.

Willow loved it. When she was out of this 'adventure' she decided she would do as much travelling as she could. She was really enjoying the cultural differences between here and home and knew this was just the beginning. What other fabulous mishaps, treasures and people awaited her out there in the world. For a brief moment she forgot about their 'mission' and simply felt like she was on holiday or a regular backpacker and she was excited.

The afternoon light filtered through the window. It was soft and cast light shadows in the small room. After the noisy city Brownie was pleased to be in nature. The simple peacefulness of the lake soothed his soul.

They departed to the communal dining room for some refreshments. It had two long low tables with patterned cushions dotted along it, to sit on. They ate takoyaki, an octopus dumpling, udon noodles, tonkatsu, which were breaded deep fried pork cutlet, shabu shabu, a type of beef hotpot, and miso soup. Brownie loved his food and had a little bit of everything. Willow stuck to the tempura vegetables and tofu. The hostess was warm and welcoming, and the food went a long way to allay their fears of what was to come.

'Now folks, and you lovely rock people, I been doin' my research and my guts are tellin' me to head up one of the Sengen Shrines, eh. There are heaps of them all around Mt Fuji. Our lovely hostess reckons we should go to the one near here, where they used to start the climb up Mt Fuji in the olden days. It's only 'bout half hour trek. What ya reckon? We go there, see what pops out at us, eh?' Brownie asked enthusiastically looking around at them. 'Brownie, why do you think one of these what do you call it, senge shrines...' Willow started.

'Sengen, Willow. Well 'cos we can't climb up the mountain, I reckon we just go to the start. The Sengen Shrine near here is the Fujiyoshida Shrine. Most folk begin the climb half way up the mountain, but my guts are pullin' me there,' Brownie replied.

'Sounds good to me Uncks,' said Duke, and with that they prepared themselves for the weather and the hike.

While the gang were making their plans, Wayne hit the deserted streets and made his way to the strange forest to make camp and put his plan into action. He knew the kids would be there and it was going to be full moon later that night. It would happen then.Parking his car and entering the dark forest, a cold shiver ran through his body. The eeriness of the place hitting him full force again. Yesterday's cave was proving elusive to find but several others presented themselves as he wandered deeper into the belly of the forest. He began to hear voices and felt troubled and depressed. Checking himself he realised quickly that the thoughts and feelings swirling through him were not his. It was a kind of morphic resonance of all that had gone before him. It was their thoughts and emotions that he was picking up on. He was after all gifted in this area.

The heavy dark energies, the desperation and loneliness of those poor souls who had been here before were now circling his aura. They needed to attach on to a life form and his was as good as any. He needed to protect himself and quickly or there was danger of him acting not from his own agenda but someone else's. He peppered the ground with handfuls of the oceans finest and lay down in it, soaking in its briny goodness. There that should hold off any unwanted 'klingons' for now.

Wayne chose a rocky outcrop just under a large copse of matted trees, good a spot as any, he thought to himself and it provided some shelter against the light rain that now fell. Wayne rubbed the moisture from his gleaming face. Making camp against the forest wall he assembled a small one-man tent and began to make a fire. Again, he felt the eyes of onlookers. This place was filled with presence, although it was barren of life. However, Wayne's ego had had a boost after his success with the crows and he wasn't going to scare easily today.

Right on cue, the tanuki appeared again. Wayne looked deeply into his eyes, threw out an energetic cord and felt his spirit body attach to the creature. It darted off and Wayne retreated to the tent to sit in silence and follow it telepathically. Inhabiting the creatures' body, he could feel it running at speed through the dense undergrowth; the air burning in his nostrils, his canine breath panting, all four legs flying over the damp slippery ground. The animal stopped. Wayne kept his breath steady, his focus sharp, one wrong move and he would be ejected from the body of the tanuki and then he would be lost in the ether. Again, on the move, he was able to now see through the eyes of the creature. It looked up, there were bodies looming overhead, human and not human and he sensed his prey nearby. The tanuki was to be his eyes and ears on the ground. Wayne, now at one with the animal, lay in wait for them to make a move.

Walking into the wind, the gang had their heads bent in supplication to the forces of nature. Willow was sorry she couldn't climb the mountain this time. She knew that there were bigger fish to fry and so she asked her uncle what his plan was once they got to the shrine. 'Well Willow doll, I reckon we haven't really got a clue, eh,' he answered rubbing his chin.

'Well that's rather peachy Uncks, what with Fabio and his crew along for the ride and all,' Duke piped in nodding over at Merle, Luna and Sonny. Mala-Kai and

Mahpee were deep in conversation and Brownie noticed his hei-tiki jumping and gesticulating madly. 'I reckon it's just a bit further,' Brownie declared, stopping by a deserted patch of land tucked in from the main drag. The bushes waved invitingly in the breeze and a small tanuki appeared in front of them. Brownie signalled them to stop and put his finger up to his mouth in a gesture of silence. Willow and Duke dutifully did as requested. Duke looked around and noticed they were suddenly all alone. The rain seemed to get harder and Duke zipped up his rain jacket.

'See here...the tanuki,' Brownie pointed over at the little racoon dog creature popping its head out from behind a tree, '...this little fella is supposed to be a shapeshifter. It may not be this cute creature at all, eh. Mind how you go here folks, 'cos I'm not sure what he's trying to tell us.' And with that the tanuki disappeared as quickly as it had come.

Everybody carried on through the interwoven network of brambles, branches and bushes. Duke looked up from his business of pulling foliage out of his way to find Mala-Kai beside him with his shield up protecting him from some unseen danger. 'Willow I have to tell you, I'm a tad bit nervous here dude,' said Duke a little nervously.

'Shhh Duke, keep your ears open and just follow Brownie,' ordered his big sister, in all seriousness.

'Mala-Kai come on big fella, tell me what's the story here, do we have trouble ahead?' Duke asked, for some reassurance.

'Duke it is advisable to maintain a vigilant silence,'

came the foreboding reply.

'Easy for you to say, I gibber when I'm nervous man, I can't help it,' Duke replied.

They all pushed on through dense forest, hacking back the leaves. Suddenly Brownie raised his hand in a gesture to halt. Pulling back a low-lying branch they emerged into a long approach leading up to the Shrines red painted buildings at the top. The walkway was lined with impressive stone lanterns backed by tall cedars and the whole scene was straight out of another century. The sun sparkled through the tops of the trees and the air was a little warmer here.

They walked in silence except for the crunch of gravel underfoot, looking up and around as they went. Duke could feel the hopes and dreams of all the people who came here, praying for safe passage up the mountain. As they neared the shrine Brownie pointed to the tanuki which appeared again at the back of the building. He nodded for them to follow, with Mala-Kai and Mahpee already ahead. It led them to a wooden torii gate at the back of the shrine grounds. Duke looked around nervously. He wasn't sure what was going to happen, but he was certain it was going to involve him and this time he didn't have Ted at his side. Forlorn at this thought he turned to Willow, 'I sure wish Ted was here dude, I could really use his backup right about now.' 'Listen Duke you know they would be here if they could. They got lost somewhere, but I know they will find their way back to us. You just have to have faith that you will be okay, yeah. Brownie is here, and we have all the coolest rock peeps on our side. Listen bro, we're in this together,' and with that she held up her fist for him to pump.

Duke just looked her dead in the eye and laughed, 'Willow stop trying to be cool man, you know you are so not. I'm the king of cool around here, yo.'

'Muppet,' she retorted.

'Lame-o,' came his pithy reply.

Brownie now looked over at Merle who had stopped in the middle of the torii gate. There were no other tourists around. He stood dead centre and turned slowly to look them in the eye. 'The portal is opening and the entrance is here,' Merle proclaimed matter-of-factly.

'So, like, what does that mean?' Duke was curious.

'Come now my boy, no time to waste. Mala-Kai and Mahpee, I need you to be vigilant now. The shapeshifter has come. He is among us. The danger is present,' Merle said.

The tanuki appeared and began running circles around Duke. Brownie stood stock still. Merle gestured over to Luna and Sonny and they stood to one side of the gate awaiting further instruction. The wizard spun, around and around. The dust blew up and the air was filled with the broken twigs and dead leaves. He began to transform. Twirling, his dark cloak was now shimmering in the dappled light of the sun, throwing out a rainbow of colours on a mesmerized Brownie and Willow. They were hypnotised for a moment and couldn't move.

Willow was the first to break the spell and she looked around she cried out, 'Duke! Duke!' then turned to her uncle, 'Brownie, where is he?'

'Shhh girley, ol' Merle here knows his stuff' Brownie replied. The tanuki stopped moving, stared right at Brownie and then sprinted off, up the trail for the mountain. Brownie looked up after it. The mountain stood like a sentinel, guarding its secrets. Luna and Sonny entered the torii gate, and a mist seemed to float up the mountain after the tanuki. Merle had vaporised into thin air leaving both Brownie and Willow reeling in shock.

All the while, Duke felt his body lift up and float towards the wooden torii gate in front of him. He wasn't afraid. He felt the comforting presence of the wizard beside him. Entering through the T-shaped structure a zing of electricity zapped through his body. He seemed to drift up the volcanic mountain and as he did he could look down on the trail below. He was being carried on the breeze and it felt good. His body was as light as a cloud.

Looking over his shoulder he saw Merle by his side, floating effortlessly, beard and hair flying behind him, staff at his side. Duke looked below him as he passed the Subaru line 5th station. It was deserted but he could also see what it was like in the height of summer; crowds bustling about, getting ready for their climb, a Japanese natural Disneyland; both situations playing out in front of him at the same time. It was as if he could see all timelines, past and present, and all scenarios were happening simultaneously. He even saw the vending machines, packed full with all kinds of treats. It was all very pleasant, rather like the few moments in the morning when sleep still roams through your consciousness and the brain is not fully awake. He arrived at the summit and thought to himself that that was all rather easy.

Suddenly he felt nauseous and wanted to throw up but he was disorientated and dizzy. He didn't know what was happening and his nerves kicked in. The air grew cold and he shivered. He felt himself land on the top of an ice-cold mountain, all alone and not sure what was going to happen. Fear seized him. There was a rumble in the distance. He thought it may be thunder. Cold, hard reality slapped him hard in the face.

Merle appeared beside him and spoke, 'My boy I needed to float your spirit up the mountain. Usually we would not attempt this so quickly, that is why you are feeling ill now but we have no time to waste. There is imminent danger. The guardian of the mountain must be appeased. Sit down, arms crossed hands on your knees. This will balance both hemispheres of your brain.' Duke dutifully complied and put his right hand on his left knee and vice versa, and calm descended. But then, without warning, a ferocious dragon appeared over the rim of the crater at the top of the peak. Its eyes were bulging, and it was breathing fire. The scales on its back were rippling green and brown and they shimmered as they caught the waning suns afterglow.

'Guardian of the Mountain,' Merle began, 'we come in peace, we bring you gifts.' And with that he stamped his staff on the rocky ground and four crystals lay before Duke, their beauty inviting the mountain guardian to take them. The dragon rose up even higher, smoke swirling out of its palpitating nostrils, eyes wide and red, with veins of lava running through them. 'What are they?' Duke asked feebly and then he took a closer look; a green striped stone, a turquoise, a cloudy white stone and an orange flecked one. He gasped, 'Merle, no!' he screamed.Before him he saw Luna bow her head, hair flowing like the light from a candle, the colour indescribable, her gown mingling with her hair to form a river of opalescent light illuminated by the moon. Merle spoke, 'Oh, protector of this sacred site, I lay before you the moonstone, gem of the High Priestess, keeper of the feminine mysteries. This stone will keep the rhythm of the mountain in balance, as she ebbs and flows with the cycles of our lunar Goddess.'

Luna clasped the hand of her brother. Sonny stood up, tall and proud, a flame from the torch of hope as Merle continued, 'Here is the sunstone, the stone of the Solar Light. He will shine his benevolence, warmth and strength down on you and the mountain. He carries the energy of the Sun God Ra and with it the ability to use his knowledge and wisdom for the good of all.'Now Mahpee entered the circle, his muscular turquoise body rippling with energy as Merle made his next offering, 'Behold turquoise, a stone of wholeness and truth, balance and serenity. This crystal teaches the wisdom of compassion and forgiveness. It combines all the elements of air, water, fire and earth, therefore has the power and unity of the storm.'

Merle now turned to Mala-Kai, 'Lastly, we have malachite, the stone of the enlightened leader and gate keeper of the heart of the mountain'. Mala-Kai joined the circle, gripping the hand of Mahpee on one side and Sonny on the other. His green cloak blowing behind him at right angles as a fierce gale began to blow. The massive full round moon was hanging heavy above their heads, bigger than Duke had ever seen. The crystals moved toward the dragon who let out a deafening roar.

Just then hundreds of crows appeared, swooping down on the crystal offerings. Mala-kai threw his cloak over Luna as he threw his shield over Duke. Mahpee pulled his bow and arrow from his back and began shooting. Merle began an incantation and banged his staff on the ground three times. As the birds gathered overhead, the crystals ran for cover, the guardian dragon flung his tail in the air. The birds now covered the entire sky with their ashen blackness, becoming a unified cloak of mal intent.

Merlin picked up the volcanic soil from the edge of the crater as he muttered. Stamping his staff on the ground again it magically turned into a samurai sword. He swiped at the attacking birds. The sky cracked open with the sound of thunder and all four crystals made a dash for the edge of the crater just as the cloak of crows turned into one giant evil bird, swooping down to stop them. Too late. It dived down but the crystals had already jumped into the open mouth of the crater.

The mountain began to rumble. Duke thought it was going to erupt. Merlin was still at the edge, the giant evil crow made one last swoop to attack him with its beak but to no avail. Mt Fuji and its guardian let a blast of lava high up in the air and swallowed it up whole. At the same time the belly of the mountain began to roar, the skull had been activated. Duke knew it was happening. He felt himself floating, with Mala-Kai's shield in his hand.

Merlin began another incantation this time to Metatron, 'Oh Metatron, bring forth your cube of protection. Protector of children, guard this chosen one. Allow him to enter the sacred cube and dispel the forces of negativity.' A mauve haze appeared over the horizon and moved closer. Merlin appeared beside Duke with a golden helmet and placed it on his head. There was a purple amethyst in the centre of it protecting his third eye. The boy didn't fight or struggle. He trusted his crystal wizard guardian implicitly. Duke began to spin clockwise and as he did a violet light began to spill from him, with centrifugal force, throwing out the protective rays towards the approaching danger. Everything felt like it was spinning now, faster and faster. The mountain allowed its sacred contents to emerge from its volcanic depths. The crystal skull erupted from the bowels of the earth, through the centre of the mountain, up and out over the top of the crater.

This time it was the same violet purple as on his helmet. Mt Fuji was giving birth to her sacred charge. It appeared in front of Duke and Merlin like a beacon of crystalline hope, energy like lightning sparking from it, striking light high up in the sky. The air was electrified. The skull was connecting with the others through the crystalline grid. The sky was lit up like fireworks on the fourth of July. The Newgrange quartz skull spun on its axis throwing out its light connecting with the Jade of the New Zealand skull; these both tuning into the energies of the amethyst of Mt Fuji.

All three skulls began rotating in unison, igniting the crystalline grid around Mother Earth. Electricity filled the sky and the mountain hummed a low vibrational sound. The earth pulsated with new life, and the mountain was pleased.

Duke looked at Merlin. He knew he needed to get back into his physical body quickly or he wouldn't be able to go back at all. Merle threw volcanic ash on him and he felt himself sink rapidly back to earth. He threw his head back then sat up immediately, turned to his side and threw up.

'Duke, Duke what happened, are you all right?' Willow was frantic. She had witnessed the darkening of the sky, and heard the shrill cries of the birds, their caws almost deafening her and Brownie. The sky was calming now. Brownie and Willow hadn't seen any of the events on the top of the mountain. They did however, see the storms, solar flares, and lightening. They witnessed the electrified swords of energy shoot out off the top of the crater.

'Willow, Mahpee and Mala-Kai…they're gone', Duke was inconsolable.

'Now, now, don't be sad, eh. Once you connect with the Crystal Kingdom and make friends with any one of them, they will be your friend forever. Trust me kiddo, I know,' Brownie said enigmatically.

Merle appeared beside an exhausted Duke, 'Well

done my boy you did well. The skull is charged and running. It has made its connection with the others, but we must not fail in our mission to find the last one. I know magic and there was some pretty strong energy at work up there and whoever is behind it is getting stronger. It takes years to master the manipulation of the elements and creatures like that, I know, I invented it.'Brownie felt the hairs on the back of his neck stand up and turning swiftly he just caught the last glimpse of the tanuki, sprinting off in the distance. He walked over to where it had been, sitting, listening. Bending down to examine the footprints, he noticed something white jutting out from beneath a rock. He brushed away the dust and there shining in the moonlight was a white feather, the feather from their friend, Mahpee.

Shock, exhaustion and bewilderment were the overriding emotions in the aftermath of Mt Fuji. Brownie called on the special talents of his hei-tiki and Merlin to get them safely back to the ryokan. Duke was completely overwhelmed. Settling into their rooms Brownie instructed Willow to keep an eye on him and he went walking around the lake. This thing was getting even bigger than he had anticipated and now with the loss of most of their beloved crystal allies he had no idea what to do next. What or who were they fighting against?

The wind whipped up against his back and he felt a chill. Looking out over the rippling water he focused on the mountain in the background. Why had it demanded the sacrifice of the crystals? Her dark silhouette jutting into the skyline, breaking through the wisps of grey cloud, like steel piercing cream; she had secrets that were to remain hidden a while longer. The protectors of this mountain were vigilant and protected their sacred treasure very well indeed.

His hei-tiki walked along beside him, channelling a calm energy. Brownie knew he had to get Duke home before any more 'adventures' came up. Duke was fragile at this point and needed time to recover, gather his strength and most importantly spend time with his mum.

Back at the ryokan Brownie found Willow and Duke eating in the dining room. He squatted down, with a huff and a puff, on the floor cushions to join them. Their mood was sombre and quiet. 'Well, what's the story as you guys like to say, or 'what's the crack, eh?' Brownie was trying to inject brevity into the situation.

Duke looked up, 'Uncks, I don't mean to be rude but...'

'Ah yeah I know sonny, ya don't have to tell me. You're all bent outta shape on account of the loss of our buddies, eh? Me too,' Brownie replied.

'Me three,' piped in Willow asking, '…really Brownie, do you think they are gone for good? I mean, I know they were not like, real, or anything…'

'Dude, don't you dare say that, Willow how could you? They were as real as you and me, and I loved them.' Duke burst out.'Ah Duke I'm sorry, I didn't mean anything by it. I mean I know they are real, like real energy, just it's not like losing a human person or anything,' Willow replied. Brownie looked in her direction and his eyes said it all, 'not another word' was strongly implied.

212

He turned his attention to Duke and said, 'Look laddie, grief is grief is grief and it makes no difference if it's a person, a cat or a crystal, eh. It hurts. But that hurt will get better, and I'll tell yooz something for nothin', I don't think we've seen the last of our crystal buddies. I reckon they'll turn up when we least expect it. They'll always be family. You'll recognise in each and every one, a trusted friend. That'll never go away.'

They finished their meal in contemplative silence, each trying to get to grips with the events of the last couple of days. Brownie knew there was one more mission. He sat in his room rolling his hei-tiki in his hands. It communicated to him; they had been to Newgrange in the North, in winter, activating the quartz crystal skull, then summer had them activate the jade crystal skull in the South, New Zealand. Dividing up the globe into its four quadrants, the East has just been done, with Japan being the location of the third event, and the amethyst crystal coming alive and it was spring there that meant nothing would happen till autumn and it would have to be in the West.

Brownie thought about this and breathed in a sigh of relief. These kids needed a break and so did he. Happily, he thought about his lovely little house in the suburbs of Auckland and he longed for his own bed and a solid sound night's sleep. He decided to get them all home as soon as possible.

WHERE THE HEART IS

There were tears and fond farewells at the airport. Brownie had organised they fly home to Ireland on the same day he was to return to New Zealand. His work with the carvings and lectures was done and their other agenda had been put to bed for now. 'Now, you look after ya sis for me like a good boy, eh?' Brownie issued instruction to Duke, needlessly as he knew these two would forever take care of each other.

'Ah Uncks, I'm really going to miss you, ya big galah,' Duke said laughing.

'Ah yeah, this an Aussie accent you're tryin' to do, and badly at that, eh,' Brownie replied.

'Ouch, burn,' retorted Duke jokingly.

'Ah Uncle Brownie, I can't thank you enough for all you have done for us. I mean, I have no idea what would have happened if you didn't, I mean, what I am trying to say, is that I will really miss you and thank you for everything, blurted Willow, her emotions getting the better of her.

'No thanks necessary girlie, I loved every minute of it, and getting to know you two lunatics has been the highlight of me year, eh? Now tell ya lovely mum, I send my love, 'said Brownie.And with that they departed with the promise to Skype as soon as they could. Brownie boarded his flight as theirs took off into the air. Their destinations were on the opposite sides of the world, but little did any of them know how soon they would be reunited, and this time the stakes would be even higher…

Duke and Willow ran into the arms of their mum, Grainne. Duke immediately felt all his worries float away as she slathered kisses all over his face. Normally this would be a major source of intense embarrassment but today, after everything it was the best feeling in the world. It was as if she hugged him from the inside out and he felt safe for the first time in ages. He didn't realise how much he had missed her until he was hugging her as close as he could. His internal compass, with the arrow pointing to his heart had been spinning wildly and now it settled, due north and home, right here with his mum. The snow globe of emotions that had been swirling through his whole being fell calm and his internal rivers were at once flowing serenely and quiet.

'Oh, my baby, my gorgeous, gorgeous boy, I have missed you so much, you have no idea. Willow, my darling come here and let me give you a big squidge.' she said. Their mum was fond of making up words, squidge meaning hug, could also be replaced with the words snodge, lovadge, mush, mulchy squee, and lovells.'Oh, my goodness, I think you have grown. How did you get on? I know you told me over the phone but tell me everything again. How's Brownie, isn't he just lovely. I was always very fond of him and Pam; she was such a nice lady. Now, Duke have you been eating properly? Willow how was New Zealand? Did you do loads of sightseeing? You must be exhausted and Japan, tell me everything. Let's get you to the car and get home. I have all your favs in. Traffic won't be too bad getting out of Dublin,' Grainne couldn't contain herself.

Duke zoned out while his mum blabbered on to Willow. Exhaustion from the journey hit him but at least he was getting used to it and knew what to expect. He did think it funny how the Irish accents in the airport hit his ear like a salve to a burn. He was properly home and very thankful of it too.

They arrived home and got busy with all the usual tasks of a returning traveller; unpacking, loading up the laundry, raiding the fridge for familiar foods, tastes of home and hearth. Duke looked around his little bedroom, very little now as he felt he had not just grown in height, but he had really grown, spiritually and emotionally too. He searched for the familiar crystal friends, but he knew it was hopeless.

He walked down the stairs to hear his mum and Willow still talking; his mum was animated and excited. Sauntering over to the kettle and not noticing his sister, he absentmindedly grabbed the milk carton from the fridge and took a swig. Turning to join in on the chat, it was only then he noticed the look on Willow's face. She was ashen, he looked at his mum and said, 'Okay what's going on, spill,' his milk moustache a symbol of the man he had become. Grainne turned to Duke and hit him with her news.

The reason she had been keen on the two of them travelling to Brownie was she was working two jobs to save for the three of them to go to their cousins wedding in Chicago. Their cousin Olivia was getting married in the autumn and had sent an invite a few months ago. She was the daughter of their Dads other brother, Joe. Joe had immigrated to Chicago in the seventies about the same time as Pam had gone to New Zealand. Grainne didn't see how she could afford for them all to go but when the offer from Brownie came, to take the kids away, she decided to make it work and took on a second job.

With the kids gone she could concentrate on saving and really put her head down and managed to get quite a bit put by. The added bonus of them going to Japan had given her a bit more time so she broke the news to Willow that afternoon. The timing was a little off in that Duke would be going back to school, but she squared it away with the principal. They consider all travel an education of sorts and as it's a family event it was deemed okay to miss a couple of weeks at the beginning of term. Willow's college would not start back till October, so it was all sorted.This news of course had other implications in Willow's head, which were immediately transferred to Duke by the look in her eye. 'Oh yeah?', Duke managed nonchalantly. 'That's cool' was all he said and sauntered out the door.

Willow stayed in the kitchen a while longer talking with her mum about weddings, dresses, how they would manage it all and after a while declaring jet lag had hit, dragged herself to her room. She wasn't sure if she should bother her brother yet or let the news sink in first. She thought better of disturbing him and in a sudden wave of exhaustion, eased herself into her bed, fully clothed except for a hefty effort of kicking off her boots and immediately fell into the blackest sleep of her life.

Duke lay on his bed and simply took a deep breath in. He knew this trip wasn't simply a lovely jaunt to his cousins wedding. This was it, the big one, the big kahuna. He really needed to talk to Ted. His energy would calm him down. He swung his feet over the side of his bed and sat up. His mind was racing. He thought about confiding in his mum, but then decided against it. She had enough to worry about and anyway how would anyone explain this series of events. He imagined the conversation with his mum. 'So, Mum, it appears that I am somewhat of a 'chosen child'. Oh yes, your lovely son. Seems that I am a conduit for all this mega powerful energy to flow through me and activate these crystal skulls that are buried beneath the earth.

Hmm, what's that you say? Oh, how do I know this? Well, we actually had some hairy experiences on top of Mt Fuji, and also in New Zealand, when you thought we were simply sightseeing. And, oh yes, last winter, we snuck out of the house in the middle of the night, drove to Newgrange with these very large crystal people, met a wizard, and activated a skull there too. And if I'm not mistaken, there is some sort of evil entity trying to stop me. Why you ask? Oh well it's something to do with saving the world, or helping the people raise their vibration, so that evil gets vanquished. Now, fancy a cuppa?'

No, not happening, she would have him committed for teenage psychosis. Besides, they had their designated adult. Brownie had become the closest adult to him and with his Dad having passed; he also served as a Father figure for the troubled boy. Duke mused on the events and as always, looked for a silver lining and meeting Brownie and their growing relationship was one he would treasure forever.

Okay, he thought, this is happening and there is nothing I can do to stop it, so what are my choices? Fall down dead? Worry about it all summer and fret myself into a ball of anxiety? Or I can face this thing head on and deal with whatever it throws at me. Yes, that's exactly what I can do… Duke jumped off the bed and ran down to the kitchen. 'Mum, who else is invited to this shin dig, like all the family? Like Brownie too?'

'Oh, I really don't know, I'm sure he is, he is family after all, why don't you Skype him now and find out.' And with that Duke began the process of preparing for the biggest event of his life so far.

The summer passed without incident. Duke, Willow and Grainne touched down in O'Hare international airport early September. They were to be picked up in the airport by Uncle Joe, who was waiting all eager welcomes and smiles as they left arrivals. 'Grainne' a voice shouted, 'over here,' Joe called out waiving like a lunatic. He was a small, rotund, bald man with a jolly face and easy demeanour. He had a trolley ready and was eager to get them home and settled. He had done well for himself since arriving in America. He started working as a barman and worked and saved until he eventually owned his own bar in downtown Chicago. 'Finnegan's Wake' was to be the epicentre of all things wedding for the foreseeable future. It was a large establishment and had a number of rooms which would host all visiting family for the wedding of his only daughter.

Willow and Duke remembered meeting Olivia when they were small but had no idea what she was like as a soon-to-be-married woman of the world. Willow was secretly excited to see her wedding dress, what the bridesmaids were going to wear, where the venue was and basically anything and everything bridal was on her radar; although she would never admit this out loud, for fear of ruining her street cred and image of cool detachment.

Duke couldn't give a stuff about anything wedding-like however, he was thrilled to be here and super excited to see what a major American city was like. He was now, in his humble opinion, a well-travelled man of the world and after the excitement of Japan and New Zealand, he was ready for the sights and sounds of Chicago, Illinois.

The weather was mild, and the leaves were turning colour. The light snuck through the cracks in the tree tops with hues of umber and burnt sienna. The weather was still clement, and the fizz of change was in the air, where people were closing the door on summer and preparing for the colder seasons to roll in. Joe's establishment was not just any old pub. It was on a tree lined avenue in a swanky part of town. Duke was impressed when they eventually got there. There was a large wooden bar along the back wall, with plush red velvet high chairs running alongside. 'Cead mile Failte' and 'craic agus ceoil' were hand painted along one wall and a book shelf, with titles by Oscar Wilde, James Joyce, and Samuel Beckett dotted throughout. This was an Irish bar all right, but it was no spit and sawdust pub. There was a blazing fire in the corner with the lunchtime crowd tucking into Irish stew, organic smoked salmon, Dublin Bay prawns and homemade soda bread.

The feeling was of understated luxury with a large dollop of welcoming familiarity. Duke felt immediately at home although Joe did say his presence in the actual bar would have to be restricted due to his age. Willow flashed a smug smile in his direction only to have it removed pretty quickly when Joe informed her of the same rules. Drinking age was 21 in the States so they would both have to have limited access to the bar. However, he assured them this would not ruin any enjoyment as he has a fun filled few days planned for them. As soon as Brownie arrived he would usher them all off on a sightseeing trip of a lifetime.

Duke and Willow had been in regular contact over the summer with Brownie and were keen to meet up with their much-loved uncle, who was due in the following day. In the meantime, they got busy settling in, acquainting themselves with the immediate locality and getting to know their American relations.

Joe had offered to collect Brownie from the airport but he insisted on making his own way to Finnegan's.

He knew his brother-in-law would be busy with wedding preparations and didn't want to inconvenience him. Brownie appeared at the bar, small brown weather-beaten leather travel bag in hand and immediately ordered a Guinness from the barman.

'Crickey dick that's choice bro,' he announced as Duke appeared down from upstairs.

'Brownie!' he shouted and gave the old man the biggest bear hug he could.

'Duke, how yooz doin', eh? Geez it's good to see ya, I can tell ya that for nothin', and with that the uncle and nephew caught up like two old friends, chatting about school, Brownies carvings, life, the universe and everything in between and with Grainne and Willow arriving back from a shopping trip, they all enjoyed an afternoon of reminiscing and reacquainting.

The next evening was the wedding rehearsal dinner in the function room at the back of the bar. Olivia was as lovely as she was pretty, with long auburn hair, hazel eyes and a smile that would power a generator. Willow and Duke didn't chat much to her fiancé but did get an introduction to her best friend and bridesmaid, 'Willow, Duke, this is my chief bridesmaid and BFF, Abigail, Abigail these are my two lovely cousins from Ireland.' Willow was pretty smitten both with Olivia and Abigail. They seemed so worldly wise and sophisticated. She felt awkward and childish in their company and in an effort to converse she enquired after Abigail's work. She and Olivia had met in Journalism College and Abigail went on to pursue a career chasing news and doing right in the world. Olivia was working for her Dad, still undecided what direction her career would go in.

As Abigail began recounting the story of the protestors in South Dakota, and the injustices that were being propagated there, Brownies ears began to prick up. Anywhere where Native Americans are gathering and holding sacred ceremony would be something of interest to him anyway but with their other agenda looming front and centre in his mind, alarm bells began to go off. 'Tell me more 'bout this story of yours Abigail,' he joined in the conversation and the hairs on Willow's neck prickled. This was now familiar territory to her. She knew it was coming but was still not prepared. She turned to Brownie and his look said it all. 'Tell me Abigail, are you planning on visiting this camp any time soon?' Brownie asked.

'Well, as a matter of fact I'm leaving day after tomorrow. I have been following this story for a few months and I need to check on the goings on first hand. I've been coming and going all year and need to do an updated piece. The protestors are getting ready for the winter. Many of the politicians think they will cave and leave but I don't think so. This is more than just a cause. Protecting the water and the environment is their life. Why do you ask? and jokingly she added, 'You wanna come with?' 'Well now, as a matter-of-fact, I do,' he replied. And with that the plans were put under way for them to go with Abigail. It was sold to Grainne as a cultural and educational trip. It was sold to the bride as a quick visit out of state with the promise that the chief bridesmaid and a bunch of relatives would not miss the wedding. It didn't need to be sold to Willow or Duke, they knew they had no choice.

POWER ANIMALS AND EARTH
MEDICINE

Abigail, Brownie, Duke and Willow flew into Bismarck, North Dakota and drove to the reservation of Standing Rock. Abigail was initially sceptical about the Irish cousins and the Kiwi uncle joining her but after a bit of persuading she acquiesced. She realised they were serious, and really wanted to know what was going on there, and also get to know a little more about the Native American culture. Wasting no time, Abigail set to work writing a preparatory piece for her editor at the newspaper. She would follow this up with an eye witness report from the reservation the next day. Brownie and the kids took a look around the area and stopped in at a local diner for some food.

As they walked into the diner, Willow took note of an official looking gentlemen; tall, bald and very imposing, who passed her on his way out. He held the door for her and their eyes locked for a nanosecond. There was a flash of light, it momentarily blinded her, and she stopped in the entrance to hold her head in her hands. 'Yo sis you okay?' a concerned Duke asked.

'Wow, I suddenly felt very weird,' Willow answered, 'must be a bit of travel sickness or something. I'm okay, don't worry. I think I just need to get some food. Come on, let's sit and check out the delights of this wonderful establishment.'

As Wayne Johnson passed Willow, he knew immediately who she was. The girl had seen him, but the boy and the older man hadn't. Wayne threw up a psychic cloak, bent his head and disappeared down a side street. He had let the events of the protest unfold over the summer, deciding to make an appearance and check out the scene for himself. He'd searched in vain over the last few months to find Duke. His trusted mirror was showing him nothing but his own reflection. He started to think that it was all over; no omens from the mirror, no sign of the boy and no activations of skulls, crystal or otherwise.

Now stealthily sliding his hand into his pocket, his fingers felt for his crystals; the crystals he manipulated the blackbird into stealing that night in Japan. He understood the power of the crystal kingdom, but he couldn't understand why he never felt any vibration from them and why they were so cold. His piece of amber was there but the pink and brown ones were gone. It didn't matter; so long as the kid didn't have them…

Brownie, Duke and Willow were instructed to head over to a corner booth and the waitress would bring over some menus. They moved through the restaurant absentmindedly. Duke suddenly felt a shiver run down his spine. Willow got to the booth first and stood stock still, frozen, there was a silent moment then squealing with delight, she jumped on top of a waiting Fro'Ro and Ted, nonchalantly sitting there. Ted was perched on the edge of the table, bolt upright as if convening a board meeting. Fro'Ro was hanging out at the back, long lean legs draped down the length of the booth, peering over her trademark aviators, and casually met them with an understated, 'Well hey y'all, 'bout time.'

It took Duke and Brownie a moment to see why Willow had lost her marbles and suddenly the motley crew was reunited. There were tears, and hugs and more tears. Tidal waves of relief and love flooded Duke. He couldn't contain his delight and let the tears fall.

'Man, oh man, that dude sure is a piece of work,' Fro'Ro began to explain. She told them how they were kidnapped or 'crystal napped' from the ryokan and there was nothing they could do to get back. But Ted also knew that if they kept close to him they would eventually be reunited with the kids. The crystals filled them in on who Wayne was, what he was like, not good, and what he wanted - Duke stopped.

'Wait I'm confused, you mean that guy was here, is here? Now? Like, is that how come you guys are here?' Duke began to piece things together. His eyes scanned around the diner frantically, not knowing exactly who or what he was actually looking for.

'Ya, this rather unsavoury man was here, he did have us in his pocket, and yes, we did evade him,' Ted replied.

Duke had missed Ted's clipped South African accent. 'Ah dude, you have no idea how much I missed you,' Duke blubbered. 'I am sure I do,' Ted replied, smiling.

'Now listen here you lovely folks, I hate to break up the party and all that, but we got some planning to do. This just got really real, eh. We gotta figure out where the next activation is gonna be, and fast eh, cos this fella is hot on our tails,' Brownie reminded everyone.

'My dear man, ah think ah can help with this. There is a sacred mountain near here, Thunderhead it's called. It's sacred to the local Native American people and they believe it to be the heart of the world. I believe it to be a place of interest to us too. There was a very good reason you all came to this place. Once again, I repeat, everything happens for a reason,' Ted said raising his impressive brows.

Brownies Hei-Tiki appeared and began to dance around the table. 'Looks like ya may be on to something Ted,' Brownie said, 'tell us more, eh.'

And with that Ted began to inform them about Thunderhead Mountain in the Black Hills of South Dakota, one of the most sacred sites for Native Americans.

'Wait, isn't that the one with the giant unfinished carving of Crazy Horse?' Willow knew a bit about history.

Duke looked at her amazed. 'Dude, like, how do you know this stuff?' he was really impressed.

Looking him straight in the eye, she curtly replied, 'I read.' Willow continued, 'There was a sculpture commissioned of Crazy Horse on horseback pointing southeast over the lands where many of his people lie buried. It's in response to Mount Rushmore, which was considered an affront to the Lakota people.'

'Like again, dude, did you swallow an encyclopaedia or what?' Duke interrupted.

'Duke, I happened to read up on a thing or two about the area, and Chicago, and everywhere else we've been. I'm curious and I like to be informed,' Willow retorted.

'So, what else do you know about this sacred mountain, like, has it got special powers, or this dude, Crazy Horse, what about him?' Duke was actually really interested now, having a vested interest in all things 'Western' from an early age and on account of him being named after the famous cowboy actor 'John Wayne' aka 'Duke'.

'Well I don't know much more except his famous last words were 'Today is a good day to die', I think,' replied Willow.

Duke gulped and simply responded with 'You could have kept that bit to yourself.'

Wayne watched the events unfold in the diner from across the street. He had not expected this and was momentarily thrown. He could see the little gang huddled in a corner booth and sensed their scheming and plotting. Bile began to rise in his throat. The day had seen high temperatures but as night crept in, it was getting much colder. A storm was forecast but he paid no heed. The rain began to smack the concrete violently and he pulled his light jacket up high around his neck. Watching and waiting he sprang into action when they left the diner. He followed at a close pace but knew he wouldn't get caught; cockiness was on his side. He even ran up to within inches of Duke at one point, the rain and wind sheltering him from view.

With bent heads against the bad weather, Willow, Duke and Brownie headed back to their motel to action their hastily made plan. And having argued about including Abigail, they realised they had no choice as they needed her knowledge of the area, Native American culture and basic all-round travel guide experience to help them. And she was more than happy to oblige. 'Well,' Abigail said sitting back on the bed in Willow's room, 'you guys sure tell a mighty good story. If what you say is true then it's a total no brainer for me, I'm coming with, end of.'

'We were kind of hoping you would say that,' Willow said.'It's about a five-hour drive from here. If we leave early we can be back late tomorrow night. Wrap up well, the days can be hot, but temperatures can drop like crazy at night.' Abigail added.

'Now there is one more thing,' Willow began carefully. Abigail had not as yet seen Fro'Ro or Ted and Willow wasn't sure she would be able to even if they were standing in front of her; not everyone can see the crystal energy.

Without waiting on an invitation Fro'Ro rocked into the room announcing, 'Well, y'all like organised and ready for action here.' Ted trailed in behind. Abigail's mouth fell open and with that Willow's questions had been answered.

Duke piped up, 'Yo Abs, looks like you are one of us. It appears you have eyes on our crystal buddies here, yes? Let me introduce you.' And with that they all got that bit better acquainted. Fortified by the return of their crystal friends, they decided to leave early the next day and make the drive south to Thunderhead Mountain.

The next morning saw them all pack up and head in off Abigail's car. Wayne had bribed the receptionist to let him know where and when they were leaving and was outside lying in wait. Shocked and stunned to see Abigail with them, he couldn't figure out what her role was in all this and how they knew each other but he had no time to figure that out now. He had to move. Jumping into his SUV he waited until they were on the road then pulled out, keeping a safe distance behind them.

The gang travelled in silence with Duke feeling unexpectedly comfortable, like he was familiar with this area, it had a homely vibe to it and he was not as nervous as he thought he might be. Abigail on the other hand, chatted all the way, filling them in on the protest, and her personal mission to report the events and get the word out to the world of the injustices being done in the name of progress.

Taking a right turn out of Mt Rushmore National Memorial and heading west on south Dakota 244, a two-lane route took them through the winding Black Hills, past oceans of pines, slopes and jutting boulders. Eventually they reached U.S. 16, and turning south towards the town of Custer they caught sight of his nemesis, Crazy Horse. 'It says here that Crazy horse was the Sioux Warrior who prevailed over Custer at Little Big Horn in 1876. Also, he was among the last Sioux who never signed a treaty, never left the Plains, never learned English and never lived on a reservation,' Willow was reading from the guide book.

Brownie knew this place was a tourist hot-spot, not unlike Newgrange with busses going back and forth, restaurants, craft shops and the like. Suddenly he got a feeling, 'Pull over.' Abigail looked at him before obeying. Swerving to the side of the road, along a tree covered dust pathway, Brownie declared that they need not go any further. His hei-tiki was jumping up and down on the bonnet of the car and Brownie stepped out, sensing something was up. He stretched his back and wandered down the trail. It was then he noticed something sparkle in the distance, approaching, at speed, shimmering, not unfamiliar but hard to make out through the trees.

Suddenly it was as if a mirage of Mahpee stood in front of him, not quite real but then, Brownie thought to himself, what is 'real' at this point. He looked closer. It was Mahpee all right, sky blue, moccasin wearing, piercing eyes, bow and arrow on his back. 'Duke, Willow come here and check this out!' Brownie yelled. Then appearing beside the vision was Mala-Kai all glowing green, cloak flowing and shield by his side.

'Greetings beloved humans,' Mahpee began, Duke getting out of the car slowly and sleepily thought for a moment that he was dreaming. Then taking in the sight of the two guardians he was suddenly overwhelmed with emotion and stood stock still, tears running down his face. Abigail was speechless.

Willow, channelling her brother turned to the feisty reporter and said, 'What's the matter Abs, haven't you ever seen the ghost of a nine-foot-tall crystal personified before your very eyes before?' Willow was grow-ing in confidence and felt very solid and centred. She didn't know why but wasn't questioning her new-found strength and ran over to the two shimmering shadows and tried in vain to hug an empty space.

'My dear girl, we are here simply in spirit. We have travelled on the wind of the crystal grid that is activat-ed over Mother Earth. It is not fully alive yet, but it is enough for us to beam here to you. We have flown from the last activation. We are connecting Mt Fuji in the east with this location, here in the West. We sent Merlin, Luna and Sonny along the grid from North to South and when this last Skull rises out of the belly of the earth to join the others, we will see the dawn of a new day in the history of mankind. The earth on which you stand is made of pure crystal. Our brothers and sisters are wait-ing, holding the knowledge of the centuries, ready to come alive and aid man in his Ascension. It is fitting that it is here, in a place where so much pain and suffering has happened. We must help make amends and heal these old wounds.' Mahpee spoke more than they had ever heard him speak before. 'These are my people and I must aid in their struggle,' Mahpee explained.

Duke supposed he was referring to Standing Rock. The gang just stood and listened in silence. Abigail won-dered if she had fallen into a sci-fi movie and kept look-ing around to check if anyone else was there. Perhaps this is all one big elaborate joke. Her cameraman loved to prank her. Her logical mind was in overdrive, but her heart was telling her that this was real. Inexplicable but real none the less.

Next Mala-Kai spoke in some other weird foreign language and a wolf appeared beside Duke. 'Duke, this is your spirit guide, sent to protect and serve as you embark on this next mission,' Mala-Kai said.

'Cheers Dr Doolittle,' quipped the flippant boy.

Looking up to the sky, Brownie noticed an eagle fly overhead. Mala-Kai turned to him and commented that he already had the eagle's feather in his possession and this spirit guide had been with him since Japan. Brownie remembered the feather he found on the ground on Mt Fuji. Mala-Kai clarified, 'This is a symbol of your leadership and guidance. The eagle can walk between worlds, and you Brownie have this ability also. You were born with second sight. You must use these gifts now.'

Willow heard a rustling in the trees, at which point she came face to face with a massive grizzly bear. 'Willow, do not be alarmed. Your spirit animal is here, the bear represents motherhood, strength and courage. He is your friend,' Mala-Kai reassured her.

Abigail was too stunned to think straight but her talents as a reporter were not going unused and she was lapping up every word. Feeling her heart throb in her chest, she stared at the crystal vision in front of her as she was all that was left. Was she going to be the recipient of an animal guide too?

Mahpee took over, 'We must go quickly into the woods.'

Abigail guessed she was not going to be on the receiving end of animal guides, just as Mala-Kai looked her straight in the eye with what she thought was a smirk on his ghostly green face. She looked down and there at her feet was a sniffling, grunting pig. 'Ah, come on,' she finally spoke, 'These guys get eagles, and bears and wolves and I get a pig!'

Mala-Kai turned to her as the others followed Mahpee into the woods. 'Do not scoff at that which you do not understand. The pig is revered in many cultures for its tenacity and intelligence. It is a symbol of abundance and self-awareness and is known for its clear and distinctive voice.' Abigail was taken aback and looked with new eyes on her little pink and chubby friend.

'Okay, I can live with that,' she said and followed the others. Ted, Fro'Ro and Mahpee were busy moving twigs, rocks, crystals, leaves into a circle.

'So, what's the story here folks?' Duke asked.

Mahpee answered, 'We are building a medicine wheel.' 'Oh, I see, of course you are, how silly of me I should have guessed,' Duke remarked as Willow gave him 'the look.'

'Willow, dude, don't be giving me the evils, come on, you don't think this is all just a bit mental?' Duke was flinging his arms about as if to emphasize his point.

'Yes, my darling little brother, as a matter of fact I do think this is all just a tad to the right of complete insanity but what do you want to do about it now, huh?' her voice was rising.

'Willow, dude, chillax, I didn't mean to get you all hot and bothered. Look, we've got this mega cool spirit ghostly vibey animal gang along with us now so that's pretty sweet, yeah?' he tried to calm his sister.

She looked at him then over into the trees where her bear was staring back at her as if to say, eh, sorry, I think I got the wrong human. I'm supposed to represent bravery and courage and all that malarkey, and I seem to have been landed with a whiney teenager. Refund please, or at least swopsies. I'll take the other girl she looks like she's got her act together, hello, anyone there? Willow snapped out of her funk and shook herself down. Her bear was still staring at her, having now moved and she managed to say, 'Okay soz, just got a bit freaked there for a mo, I'm alright, let's get this show on the road.' And with that they got to work following Mahpee's instructions to build the medicine wheel.

It wasn't long before everyone stood back and examined the fruits of their labour. They had placed white bird feathers in the north of the circle, for the white man, yellow flowers in the east, for the oriental people, the south held red leaves for the Native Americans and black people were represented by black stones in the West. A sacred fire burned in the centre, the source of all life. Mahpee informed them that the medicine wheel was a place for vision questing, and a place for offering healing prayers for all people and Mother Earth. The circle representing the circle of life. They were tired from their efforts but elated at their creation. 'Guys, like we have built a pretty cool wheel thingy here, even if I do say so myself,' Duke said, rather pleased with his efforts. 'We must be vigilant. Our air friends are calling and beckon us to listen. The wind carries the smell of evil. We must make haste,' said Mahpee, paying little attention to Duke's words. 'Crikey that moment didn't last long,' Duke responded.

'Duke shut up and listen to what we have to do will you,' Willow reprimanded him.

'We must walk, one by one, around the circle. We must still our minds and listen not with our ears but with our hearts for any messages, thoughts or feelings that may come to us,' Mahpee continued, then looking intently at Abigail he said, 'Abigail, please, watch and wait.' Happy at the unofficial role of observer, she stood back and nearly tripped over her snuffling pig

'Brownie you must enter,' Mahpee commanded. Brownie obligingly entered the stone circle and began his walk. He was careful to stay grounded within his body and he held his hei-tiki necklace in his hand. The air became still and heavy with expectation. He gently placed one foot in front of the other and every snap of twig seemed to reverberate off the surrounding trees. Carefully he made his way around, momentarily looking up to see his eagle circling overhead. He became disorientated and then dizzy. The large oak tree in front of him took on another shape, the knotted lumps of bark blended together, and he began to see a door. He thought he caught sight of a large green figure, in the corner of his eye, with what looked like horns coiling from his head, but he didn't feel threatened by him. This being was of this place, the guardian and protector.

Each circle Brownie completed brought the visions more clearly into view. The horned creature was fairy like and seemed to be made of leaves and wood and moss. Then the door became fully visible, large, looming and opening. He reached the centre and looked out to the edge. He couldn't see anyone else now. Where had they gone? Again, the eagle cried. Brownie suddenly felt compelled to kneel down, exhaustion overwhelmed him, and he couldn't move. Head bent he looked up to see a vague outline of a boy enter the wheel behind him. Fog rolled in and he blacked out.

Meanwhile the crystal sentinels stood vigilantly at the periphery of the wheel. The wind started to blow hard and flung the dry dusty ground in the air recklessly. It was carnival day for nature and she was celebrating. Duke gulped, Willow's heart pumped, and neither of them could see their uncle. The wolf beside Duke howled and he knew that it was his time to enter. He wasn't scared as he took great strength from the protective energy of his companion.

'Duke you will be safe here. You are from this land and you are with your own people. It does not matter the story, just know the spirits of the ancestors are with you now, as way-showers,' said Mahpee.

Duke looked at Willow and offered a flippant, 'Well that's one mystery solved. Now at least we know why I look the way I do.' 'Duke we'll discuss that later, right now I think you better do your walk around the wheel,' Willow replied.

Duke followed his uncle into the wheel, his wolf by his side. He stood at the edge of nothingness, just gazing into the abyss. Wind, leaves, and broken branches, all spinning in front of him, to a thunderous drone: one step and suddenly his life would change forever. He braced himself as he entered the murky blackness…

Wayne Johnson had tailed the group very carefully and watched intently as they built their magic altar, and now he sat silently bemused in the bushes as they began to enter the sacred space one at a time. He actually had no idea what was going on but every bone in his body was screaming at him to stop them. It didn't matter exactly what was happening just that it wasn't going to be a good outcome for him. He saw the old man go first, then the boy. This was the epicentre of all the magic. The weather had turned from a light breeze to a serious storm within minutes. They were not going to have it all to themselves. What if this circle bestowed them with some special powers? Or gifted them treasures? His mind was racing. In the distance he heard a coyote howl. The storm was now a raging whirlwind the centre of which held all the answers.

Willow was on the outside looking in on a whirlpool of chaos. She couldn't see either her brother or Brownie. Panic was overtaking her, and she looked at Fro'Ro who ran to her side. Grabbing her by the shoulders she screamed at her directly in the face, 'Girl, you will know what to do, trust yourself!'

Willow soaked up the courage from her crystal, behind her she heard her bear roar, the energy charging her to run, and run she did, just as out of the corner of her eye she saw, with horror a man, the man, the bald guy, charge at the wheel, at the exact same time she did.

They both flung themselves at the mercy of the elements. There was no going back now and in that instant something inside her clicked and once the decision was made to jump, she knew nothing would ever be the same again.

Within the whirlpool silence and emptiness embraced Duke. He felt light, as if he was being carried on the wings of a cloud. Two faces loomed in front of him, Native American and familiar. He smiled and said, 'Sitting Bull, Crazy Horse, I knew you would come. I have been waiting.'

'Be still child, you are at war now between you and you. Inside of you there are two dogs. One is mean and evil and the other is good and they fight all the time. When asked which one wins, I answer, the one I feed the most. Which one will you feed?' said Sitting Bull. His long shiny black hair was plaited down his back and he wore a simple suede brown tunic. His face bore the creases of a thousand canyons.

Duke looked on in a dazed confusion. He had no idea what he was talking about. He floated higher. Now Crazy Horse spoke, 'I see a time of seven generations when all the colours of man will gather under the sacred tree of life and the Earth will become one circle again.'

Duke raised his eyes to look into his face, bigger than a mountain in front of him. What were they talking about? He looked down, the land passed by under him, rivers, hills, valleys. Then he came to a halt in front of what he knew instinctively was Mount Shasta. What the...

'You have come to join the soul of your ancestors, for you are one of us. You have returned to walk the land of your forefathers. You have come to cleanse the soil upon which much blood has been spilt. You are now the channel for all that was to merge with all that will be. Here, now, in this place where the departed souls fly westward around the world, before they ascend into the sky along the Milky way to the heart of the cosmos. The sacred turquoise jewel is buried and now will be activated. Your presence here in spirit is the key to the future, our future, your future,' Crazy Horse said.

Wayne was being engulfed by the suffocating speeding air within the whirlpool. He couldn't catch his breath and terror shot through his body. He flung his arm out and it was instantly grabbed. He roared but the sound was smacked from his lips unheard. He strained to see what had his arm, and the shock of seeing the girl on the other end of his hand nearly threw his mind over the edge.Madness descended as his back was breaking. His legs flew out behind him and it was instinct only that kept him gripping her arm. The girl became a beacon in the middle of this horror and he held on for dear life. Her body spun, a mass of flame and heat. Survival meant he had to get to her, and he grabbed her arm with every ounce of strength in his body.

Willow's head was thrown back by the force of the vortex. She was immediately shunted to the centre of the circle and became a fulcrum, a spinning spine for the wheel. She could now sense her brother was near, but it was all going so fast. She threw out her other arm to catch him, as she did she was turning faster and faster. This was too much; nausea was sure to overtake her. Both her arms were grabbed, by two hands. The shock of it startled her to open her eyes wider. She strained to see who had each hand. Twisting her head against the g-force she made out the outline of Duke on her right hand. An injection of terror now flooded her, who had her other hand? Instinctively she knew. Her head fought against the pull but she twisted it enough to see the bald head and arm outstretched of Wayne Johnson.

All three formed a pyramid that now became its own entity. They were connected, Willow the epicentre and both boy and man hung on for dear life. The sound inside this vortex was now at a deafening roar, and her cries were swallowed up greedily.

As they all spun around, nothing made sense, Willow's body was breaking under the strain of the other two people clinging to her, their life literally in her hands. She tasted the bitterness of the dirt in her mouth and the flying debris lacerated her arms and face. The flames of her hair burned up the centre of the circle, she had become the fire. Wayne lifted his head to look at her, his screams thrown behind him, unheard. It was in that moment that she saw his eyes. Two deep brown balls of horror shone out their awful truth. She turned to see those same eyes beam at her from the other side. Suddenly she knew all at once, this was the same person, this was her brother. Her head now properly swam, and she threw up violently as she still held both bodies. Now she couldn't let go. In desperation Wayne tried to pull his bulk up Willow's arm against the spinning funnel, clouds covering his view. He thought he was going to die and as he strained to see her face something in the background came into view. The boy, the boy was on her other arm. Wayne's head was going to explode. He couldn't make sense of anything and he knew nothing now except to survive. Looking up, he gave one last pull on the girl's arm, and as his head looked for her face, the face of the boy came into view through the swirling debris of leaves, sticks and dirt.

In that moment everything he thought he knew blew out his mind. He instantly connected with the boy, those eyes, those big round beacons of goodness and purity blinded him with their truth. They held the knowledge of a thousand ages and his soul reverberated with the knowledge that those eyes were his eyes. He was staring straight at himself. His oracle mirror shone back at him daily these very brown eyes. It had been giving him the answer the whole time, he just couldn't see it.

Something began pulling at Willow's feet, she looked down and Brownie had both hands around her ankles. He seemed to be stopping them all flying up higher. The earth was breaking. The hands grabbed at her tighter and faster now and climbed up her body. Their arms were eating her alive, and all her limbs were about to be ripped from their sockets.

Wayne's heart lunged, and everything became clear. He knew he was being given this one chance, this one last opportunity to save himself, to save this boy, this innocent. The tornado screamed, a dragon's roar, he saw the girl's face, she was about to break in two, he had a moment of clarity and for the first time in many years, he felt light and happy and with a heart full of joy, he released his grip. Letting go of Willow's hand he was immediately and violently flung out of the vortex. His body thrown up in the air like a rag doll. The sudden force of Wayne letting go threw them off balance and they hit the ground.

Willow raised her head to see dust and mist. She looked around for her brother and uncle but there was nothing but silence. Her shoulder sockets screamed in pain. Sitting up she held her hand to her throbbing head and tried to make sense of what was happening. What was going on? Where was everyone? Why was she on her own? Was it not supposed to be Duke who was the special one? The tom-tom beat of her brain fell into rhythm with the pulse of her heart. Her body was singing its own song of fear and wonder.

She sat and out of the mist appeared a vision, or a real human she wasn't sure. A Native American wise woman came into focus, sitting cross legged at the other side of the circle. She was wearing glowing white buckskins. On her back the skins were elaborately decorated with sacred designs and geometric shapes. A torrent of jet black hair swam down her mixed with the porcupine quills covering her arms. Her fingers sparkled with the purest blue, the turquoise of her rings reminded Willow of beloved Mahpee. Willow looked closer and could see a white calf appear behind her. She felt something lick her hand and jumped at the sight of a wolf. 'Do not be afraid my child for there is no danger here,' the lady spoke, 'Behold the wolf guardian; she is here to protect you and all you love.' Willow immediately felt comforted and safe. 'The eagle feather is for you to hold,' the lady said gesturing to a spot on the ground beside Willow. Willow looked down and there was a white feather by her leg. She gingerly held it to her face and began to cry, soft sorrowful tears. She didn't know why and had no idea where this feeling had sprung from. 'Allow yourself to weep dear one for you are not your emotions. They are merely clouds that flow through you. Give them their life and then bid them farewell. You have been through a lot, allow yourself to mourn, for the girl you once were and the lady you now are,' revealed the wise woman.

Willow was feeling overwrought and at the same time fantastic. The woman in front of her appeared as an old lady but now she seemed to get younger, she was shape shifting as she spoke, 'Dear Willow, I am White Buffalo Calf Woman and I am here to tell you it is time for you to step into your power. You have come of age; the rise of the Divine Feminine is at hand. You will now operate from your higher heart and you will guide others to so the same. You are now a teacher and a guide. The world needs to know now how to live a new life and welcome in a new dawn.' Willow was a cocktail of exhaustion and exuberance. How she could be all these mixed emotions at the same time, she didn't know but she was just rolling with whatever was coming her way, unafraid and ready.

'You will be a beacon now for other young women to

follow. You will show them it is okay to be who they are, to feel their power and their strength. It is time for you to shine from the heart. There will be no more conflict and strife among the sexes for that is for the Old World Order. When you wake from this vision you will learn of an earthquake that has happened. It is the activation of the last crystal skull.'

Willow looked up and simply said, 'But Duke?'

'Do not worry, for Duke is safe now. There was a dimensional tear and he met his future self, a self that he didn't like. Duke was a lucky boy, not many people get to see into the future like he did. The aspect of himself that he met was merely one of many that can be out there. By letting go of your arm his future self has rewritten the past. His choices have affected everything along that timeline and now the future is altered. This is something anyone can do if they wish but many do not. People are too fixated on linear time and the realm of the visible.'

Willow remembered a line from Shakespeare in school and said aloud, 'There are more things in heaven and earth, Horatio than are dreamt of in your philosophy.' Then she immediately felt silly. 'Yes dear, you speak the truth.' She felt not so silly now. At this point Willow accepted that she was having a psychotic episode, a hallucination or a very lucid dream. She was cool with it though and still in a state of great comfort and security, with wolfy by her side and in the distance, she heard her bear roar.

Willow lay down and let the ground support her. She was at once connected with the energy of the earth.

It was alive and conscious, and she was connecting with it in a way she never did before. This pulsating ball of rock and crystal was talking to her like a mother to her child. Willow knew she was communicating with the entity known as Gaia. The veins of flowing rivers, the sighing breath of the ocean, nature called to her and she answered. She knew what she was being taught and hoped that she was not the only one to learn this knowledge. Prostrate on her back, she let her feet fall to the side and her arms flop open, palms face up, and allowed the sweet ground to embrace her, a sweet savasana. It was a hug like no other she had ever felt. Mother Earth was engulfing her child in its protective embrace of love. All Willows' worries dissolved into the soil and she thanked her mother for transmuting them. At the same time, she accepted the positive energy now flowing up through the rock and dirt into her body feeding her spirit and energising her with its life force. She wanted to stay here forever. And with this thought she drifted off to sleep.

Duke knew he wasn't in his body; his spirit wolf faithfully by his side. There was a rumble from deep within the dormant volcano; the earth's generator switching on, gearing up for the explosion of a lifetime. The skull twisted and turned in its cold crystal cocoon. Thunder ripped the sky wide open and the galaxies screamed for the birth of a new day. Pulsating from deep within the belly of the earth the skull began to rise. All timelines, all knowledge, all life converged on this one moment and as the crystal skull broke free, exploding into the starry crimson air, the sky electrified into life. The missing piece in the grid of life around the earth had joined its brothers and sisters and all had become one. There was no more separation only connection. All had become balanced and the universe sang a sweet song of surrender. The rock people glistened like never before. They could shine their light freely and their wisdom would be heard. They had succeeded. Duke felt his heart beat in his ears, his mouth was dry, his body gone. He thought of his beloved uncle and felt his presence bid him farewell. Then suddenly all was black…

A NEW WAY

John Neway awoke early. He really loved spending time at his quaint little beach house in the west of Ireland. It had to be said that the weather was temperamental, but it made for great surf. He pulled back the old floral curtains, wedged open the paint sealed wooden window and inhaled a deep, soul-reviving breath of the crisp morning air.

The sun was rising over the back field, covering the dewy grass in a blanket of yellow. John's nostrils quivered with the nostalgic scent of the sea mixed with the faint aroma of geraniums. He was eager to get out there. He had learned to surf when working in California and he jumped at the chance to immerse himself in the underwater world at every opportunity.

John turned to the sound of his Labrador, Rocky, bundling into the kitchen after him. 'Hello there, big fella, and how are we doing on this fresh morning, huh? How's the old arthritis?' John said as he was fond of communicating with Rocky like a human. Rocky responded in kind, with a whimper and a sit down. 'Ah come on now buddy, a walk on the strand will do you the world of good. And we have company today,' John was scratching behind the dog's ears, which he loved, almost purring like a cat. Trundling to the small galley kitchen John absentmindedly took a mug form the shelf and put it in the coffee maker. Quaint old school lodgings he could live with, but bad coffee he could not. He stretched his arms up and inadvertently hit the ceiling. His practiced yoga body now demanding movement, he ambled outside and breathing deep he ran through a few rounds of his morning sun salutations.

John had travelled extensively as a wildlife photographer and got heavily into yoga while in India. He loved rambling around the world and felt really lucky to get to do both of his passions, travelling and photography as his job. He lived in the city but when he had some down time, he bolted down the motorway to his coastal escape. It was his oxygen and he couldn't live without the fix of sea air and solitude.

Gulping his coffee, he poured his long, lean body into his wetsuit and grabbing his board he bounded out the cottage door, devoted Rocky by his side. He winced as he hobbled bare foot across the pebbled beach and hit the icy cold water valiantly. Good surf he thought sanguinely to himself but its bitter cold, this sure ain't no Hawaii.

John swam out into the ocean's embrace and went a few rounds with the swell. He always felt right at home in the water. It was as if he could sense the teeming life under the waves, invisible to the naked eye but there, pulsating and breathing all the same. This was when he felt most alive.

John sat on his board, the water lapping playfully at his thighs and listened. He didn't know why but his heart seemed to tune into the music of the dolphins and whales. They beckoned him to go deeper and play but not today. The swell won and slightly defeated he paddled back to shore.

Two figures were walking down the beach in his direction, an adult and child. 'This must be them Rocky. Come on boy lets go and say hello,' John said excitedly as he ran over to meet the approaching duo.

A small girl pulled away from the hand of her mother and ran towards John. 'Uncle John, Uncle John,' she screamed and ran into his arms.

'Rosie, my beautiful gorgeous niece, how are you, I missed you so much.' He said as he slobbered hugs and kisses on the girl.' Rosie's mum caught up with her daughter and hugged her brother.

'Johnnie boy, you old git, how are you?'

'Lovely to see you too sis.' came his reply.

'Ah it's so good to see you really. I'm dying to hear all about your travels. Let's get back to the cottage and you can fill me in on your adventures over breakfast.'

Settling Rosie down at the kitchen table with paper and some colours the brother and sister got to cooking up a feast fit for a king. The sea air always made them hungry and as they cooked and chatted Rosie coloured happily.

'Uncle John,' she interrupted at one point as the scrambled eggs were coming off the pan to make way for the French toast, 'did you know that if I mix up the letters of your name, I get another name for you?'

'Oh yeah what's that Rosie me darling?' he questioned back. 'Well if I scramble the letters of John Neway, which you are now, you can be 'Hojn Yawen', or 'Nohj Neyaw', she tongue-twisted, smiling.

'Hmmm, not sure 'bout them, any other permutations or combinations?' he enquired absentmindedly as he slathered maple syrup on his toast.

'Well if I leave your first name as a pronounceable John, and just scramble your last, then I get 'John Wayne', I like that.'

Willow looked at her brother and joined in 'Yup, don't you remember as a boy, that's why Mum always called you Duke, after her favourite actor, John Wayne. We always played this game as kids and when Mum discovered this, she decided to call you Duke after John Wayne, who she adored.

'Ah yeah, but that name never stuck thankfully.' John replied. 'Yeah maybe it's time to resurrect it now, what do you think Rosie?' the girl squealed with delight. 'Yes, yes, I want an Uncle Duke. Uncle Duke sound's waaaaay cooler than Uncle John. And with that she ran down the hall, Rocky following, yelling 'Uncle Duke, Uncle Duke.'

John looked bemusedly at his sister, 'Wills, now look at what you've done.'

'Eh, hashtag don't care,' she giggled and punching him gently in the arm she tucked into her French toast.

ACKNOWLEDGEMENTS

This process began way before I started to write. The idea for the book came about from the time I spent with Loretto and John Collins and the work I did with them. Thank you for the guidance in all things 'ugga bugga', and your friendship and support over the years. Thank you to Isolde Norris for the introduction and opening the door to all this madness.

I have to give a shout out to the people who were there at the start, who prompted and supported me to get this book off the ground: Lucy O'Hagan and your introduction to my editor Kate Osborne, and Shane Pennell. You helped me get this from my head to the page.

Breffini Banks for your council on all things musically cool and current. Avian and Joyce McManus for your guidance and insight on Mauri Culture.

Nicola Faull, not just for your proofreading but your invaluable friendship. Jacinta and Christy Murray, I can't wait to do more crystal diving with you guys.

My sisters Margaret and Helen, thank you for your support and always being there.

And last but not least, the Allicante Madness gang, may we have many more adventures together, in this life and the next.

ABOUT THE AUTHOR

Liz Sheehan's interest in all things spiritual and esoteric led her on a personal development journey since 2014 into the mystical, culminating in this, her debut novel. She is an avid reader and is currently finishing a degree in Creative Writing and Critical Thinking to add to her science degree, thus combining her passion for understanding the reality of the world around her with her quest for knowledge into the other dimensions of reality.

Since moving from the city to the east coast of Ireland in 2014, Liz has trained as an adult yoga teacher. Furthering her studies in this area she now works as a kids and teens yoga and mindfulness teacher. Liz also trained during this time as a crystal healing practitioner and a Reiki master.

When doing a crystal healing on someone she likes to back up her practice with some scientific facts as to why these modalities work. Having seen the benefits of crystals for her own children, she wanted a book for them on crystals but couldn't find anything relevant so decided to write her own where the personalities of the 'crystal' characters would help inform the reader of the properties of the crystals; Rose Quartz for love, Tigers Eye for focus and confidence and so on.

Liz is passionate about art and paints in her spare time. She lives in Wicklow with her two children.

A LITTLE BIT ABOUT CRYSTALS

What are they?
Crystals are a special kind of solid matter where the molecules fit together in a repeating pattern. This pattern causes the material to form all kinds of unique shapes.

How were they formed?
When our earth was formed millions of years ago, gasses from deep within the earths structure mixed with seawater that was full of minerals at extremely high temperatures. As the gasses and seawater combined, the first crystals were formed. Crystals often form in nature when liquid cools, like magma which is liquid rock, and starts to harden. Certain molecules in the liquid gather together as they attempt to become stable. They do this in a uniform and repeating pattern that forms the crystal. This process is called crystallization.

Uses throughout the ages
Mayans and Native Americans used crystals to diagnose and treat diseases and to see into the future. Certain

Indians from Mexico believed that if you lived a good life then your soul went into the crystal. Then, any person who found this crystal would have good luck and good health during their lifetime. They also believed the crystal would serve as their guide throughout their lifetime.

Flint in the form of a pebble or a polished axe has been found in many Neolithic graves. According to ancient medical texts, in Iraq 5,500 years ago, Lapis Lazuli and Jasper were laid around a living person to cure their ills and Bloodstone was used for diseases of the blood. In Egypt in 1900 BCE, Lapiz Lazuli, Jasper, Carnelian and Turquoise were placed around the necks of newborn babies to protect them.

The Libyan gold Tecktite, Blood of Isis, Lapis Lazuli and Turquoise in Tutankhamun's funerary jewellery were not just for decoration: they protected and conveyed the soul to the next world.

A little bit of science

When stress is placed across a crystal, it develops an electrical potential. When an alternating electrical potential is applied across the sides of a crystal, it will vibrate at a specific frequency and this can be counted using a digital counter and thus the frequency can be used to keep accurate time. Quartz is especially suited to this as the frequency does not change much with temperature fluctuations as with other crystals. This is called the piezoelectric effect. This was discovered by Pierre Curie, Marie Curies husband in 1880. When quartz is heated it can also create an electrical potential and this is called the pyroelectric effect. Because of this quartz crystals have been used in radios, clocks and computers.

Crystals in the earth

The mineral kingdom acts as an electromagnetic distribution system for the earth. When the crystals are heated or squeezed, they release an electrical charge that runs through the earths electromagnetic field. Some minerals are magnetic like Magnetite and this helps to regulate the earths frequency. So some stones help to regulate the earths energy and some help to stimulate it.

Uses for us

When we hold a crystal, our bodies resonate with its frequency and it can help to balance our emotions, our physical health or our mental state.

We can use them in meditation. Sitting with a stone can be very calming. There are certain crystals that help us sleep. Crystals can help balance the energy in our bodies. They can help us with our emotions and help move us from sad to glad. They can keep us focused and help with our anxiety.

Cleansing the crystals

When we get our crystals it is important to cleanse them as they can pick up all sorts of energy from their journey, in the ground, travelling across the globe, to the warehouse, shop, until finally your hand.

- Run them through water
- Burn sage and let the smoke cleanse them
- Dip them in the sea
- Leave them out in sunlight or moonlight (full moon best)
- Bury them in the ground (but don't forget where you buried them)
- Reiki them

Then you can charge the crystal with your intention by holding them to your heart and sending the intention for protection/healing/love etc into the rock.

Cast of characters in Beneath The Visible

Ted: *Tigers eye* – vitality, practicality and physical action, focus, mental clarity.

Fro'Ro:*Rose Quartz* – love, compassion, generosity, kindness

Mahpee: *Turquoise* – wholeness, communication, truth

Mala-Kai: *Malachite* – enlightened leadership, creativity, confidence, protection

Amethyst Cave: *Amethyst* – protection, purification, sleep

White Beard: *Quartz* – clearing, cleansing, healing, amplification

Hei Tiki: *Greenstone* – personal power, longevity, loyalty, life force

Lord and Lady Lapis Lazuli: truth, inner vision

Sunny: *Sunstone* – leadership, benevolence, strength

Luna: *Moonstone* – self discovery, intuition, insight, dreams

Merle: *Labradorite* – magic, protection

Review

Dear Reader,

Thank you for taking the time to read this book. As an author I always appreciate feedback. It not only helps with my creative writing but also helps guide and influence others who may be thinking of reading it. I would greatly appreciate if you could take a few moments to review this book on Amazon and Goodreads.

best wishes

Elizabeth

Printed in Poland
by Amazon Fulfillment
Poland Sp. z o.o., Wrocław

61324725R00162